Demon Cursed

Book 1 of the Demon Cursed Series

SADIE HOBBES

Scottish Seoul Publishing, LLC

ALSO BY SADIE HOBBES

The Demon Cursed Series

Demon Cursed

Demon Revealed

Demon Heir

The Four Kingdoms Series

Order of the Goddess

CHAPTER 1

ADDIE

My face pressed against the rough surface. I shifted trying to get comfortable. The same rough surface scratched against my hands. Water lapped over the edge of the fingertips of my left hand.

My eyes flew open as I jolted back. "Wh-"

Ahead of me waves crashed down and then ran up the shore toward me. I scrambled back to avoid getting soaked. I stared, my mouth hanging open. It had to be the ocean I was looking at. It was too large to be a lake. And lakes didn't have waves, did they?

But I didn't recognize the beach. Where was I?

Disbelief rolled through me. What was going on?

Mind whirling my head shifted from side to side, looking for something, anything I recognized. But there was precious little light. And even that was scattered and far in the distance. The moon was full, though, allowing me to make out the outline of bleak buildings about thirty yards back. The beach itself was long, maybe fifty yards, and bracketed by a wall of rocks on either side.

There wasn't a soul in sight.

I slowly got to my feet, wiping the sand from my hands on the side of my jeans. My hand brushed against leather. I glanced down. My knife. It was still there, secured in its sheath. I grasped the handle, comforted by the familiar presence.

Right now that was the *only* thing that was familiar. Water rushed toward me again, and I backed up even more. It lapped against the edge of my worn boots. Where was I? Why didn't I recognize any of this?

I scrambled trying to remember something, anything, that would clue me in. I didn't recognize the beach, my clothes, or even know my name. I tried to scrounge up a picture of what I looked like. But there was nothing. Just a complete and total blank where my memories should be.

Panic crawled up my throat, but I shoved it away. I might not remember exactly where I was or even who I was but panicking definitely wasn't going to help.

My boots sank into the sand as I started toward the buildings slowly, keeping one hand on the hilt of my knife as I scanned the area for movement. Still nothing. It was deathly quiet, except for a small light wind.

Come on, remember something. Despite my attempts to stay calm, my heart pounded faster. I identified the beach, the ocean, the abandoned boardwalk. They weren't familiar to me, but I knew *what* they were. It was just myself I couldn't identify.

Name: nothing.

Age: nothing.

Family: nothing.

The lid I'd placed on my panic teetered. No, I couldn't give in to it. Nothing good would come of it.

The thought brought me up short. I was sure it was right. I didn't know if it was life experience that had taught me it, but it was something I *knew*. I held on to it with both hands.

The sand led to broken pavement in front of an old boardwalk, lined with abandoned storefronts. It had obviously been out of use for years. Some buildings even had scorch marks along the walls and rooftops. Empty panes with only a few shards of glass made up most of the frames.

I walked past a desolate arcade, the insides draped in shadows. Hair rose on the back of my neck. I didn't like this. Too many shadows, too much darkness, even with the moon shining bright.

Light, I needed to head to the light. There were some small areas lit up on a large hill in the distance. I was counting on those lights meaning civilization, people.

A break in the buildings appeared after about four hundred feet. I rounded the last building in a line of them and stopped still at my first full view of the hill.

From this distance, I could now make out multiple well-lit homes, although homes seemed like too small a word for these buildings. Mansions or mini castles was more accurate. But they had to be miles down the road. I followed the line of lights down the mountain and spotted a bridge outlined by bright lights as well.

On the other side were more buildings, although they were nothing like the homes higher on the hills. Smaller and irregularly shaped, I had the feeling they had been thrown together rather than carefully constructed.

I picked up my pace, careful on the swollen wood. The boardwalk had seen better days. I caught sight of my reflection as I passed an old storefront that still had its glass intact. Long dark hair, a slim but muscular build. Black tank top, sturdy jeans, and combat boots.

Nothing about the reflection was familiar. Not my eyes, my face, my clothes, nothing. I stepped closer to the glass, hoping maybe it would spark some recognition. But I could have been looking at anyone. I didn't recognize the woman who stared back at me.

But how I could I not remember?

A wind blew, stirring my hair as I stared in shock at my reflection. The girl in the glass was me, and as far as I could tell, I had never seen her before.

I took a step back, my hand going to my mouth. The strange girl in the glass did the same. Why wasn't my reflection familiar? Why couldn't I remember who I was?

The panic that I'd chased down when I'd first awoken came surging back. I didn't know where I was or who I was.

Oh God. Oh God.

The creak of a door cut through my panic. My heart raced in response. My eyes narrowed as my head jerked up. The sound came again. It was close. Two buildings down, maybe. It was the first sound I'd heard. The first sign of life. I didn't need my memory to tell me that whatever was creeping out in this darkness was probably not something good.

I pulled my knife from its sheath. Goosebumps broke out along my skin as I moved closer to the buildings. The first was a brick building, its signage long gone. The second had been a café. Its sign with a coffee cup on the end was still visible. I slipped past it, careful to avoid the cracked wood in the boardwalk and paused at the edge of the building, my nerves stretched thin as I listened.

All was silent again.

Maybe it had been the wind blowing on the door, although that seemed to have died down. Or maybe it was just a cat. I looked around with disgust, or more likely a rat.

For a moment, I debated whether to even stay. Then the scrape came again. Part of me screamed that I should run away. And yet I found my feet headed toward the sound, almost of their own free will.

I slipped around the side of the café. A former T-shirt shop was on my other side. The alley between them was ten feet wide and surprisingly free of any obstructions.

At the end of the alley was a warehouse with three immense garage doors. A faded sign read Bob's Yacht Service. A few large boats lay on their sides in the parking lot next to it. But the sound hadn't come from the parking lot—it had come from inside the building.

I wanted to know what had made that noise, but I wasn't willing to step inside that dark garage to find out.

I walked along the front of the building, careful to check for movement at each window before slipping by. By the time I'd covered the front, I had no more answers than when I began.

The town down the road beckoned. Answers seemed more likely there. Whatever was inside this place was probably not something that I wanted to—

"You need to be quiet."

"I *am* being quiet," a small voice replied.

I flattened myself against the wall as the voices drifted out through the broken windows.

"I can't see anything."

"Come on."

The voices were too low to make out gender, although they sounded young—really, really young. And definitely not a threat. For a moment, I considered walking away, but only for a moment. Something about those two small voices called to me.

I'd make sure they were safe, and then I'd see what I could find out.

It was easy to track the kids' movement. As stealthy as they were trying to be, their steps echoed. I walked along the outside of the building, parallel to their movement.

I rounded the corner. A chain-link fence blocked my way. There was a rip along the bottom that I could squeeze through. Was it even worth the effort? I hadn't heard anything but the kids. I could probably just walk around the other side and –

A heavy footfall sounded from somewhere down the alley. I craned my neck, trying to see. Maybe it was the kids' parents. They probably had someone out here looking for them. They sounded too young to be out alone.

But the hair on the back of my neck suggested otherwise.

A girl's scream filled with fear pierced through the night. "Micah run!"

Without a conscious thought, I dove for the fence. The hole at the bottom wasn't as large as I'd first thought. I pulled at the bottom of it and squirmed through. Wire slashed at my shoulders, but I didn't care.

I'd only gotten halfway through when another scream sounded. My head jerked up. Two shapes sprinted past the end of the alley. With the dim light, all I could make out were that they were small and moving fast.

Squirming, I turned on my back to wiggle my hips through. But then I went still as the person following the two kids came into view.

Or should I say, the thing.

My eyes went wide and even my breathing seemed to cut off. The creature had to be close to seven feet tall, with muscles that bulged unnaturally from its shoulders and back. But that wasn't the most disturbing part.

No, the most disturbing part were the curled horns that extended from the top of its head.

CHAPTER 2

The sight of the horned creature with pale green, marble-streaked skin momentarily paralyzed me. Images of similar creatures swarmed through my mind for a moment, almost too fast for me to catch.

"Noel!"

The boy's scream cut through my paralysis. And suddenly I couldn't move fast enough. I yanked my legs the rest of the way through the hole, ripping my jeans at the thighs on the ragged fencing. Scrambling to my feet, I sprinted to the end of the alley just in time to see the creature disappear around an enormous, crumbling brick building. I sprinted after it, my knife gripped in my hand.

A scream came from somewhere behind the building. I put on a burst of speed while simultaneously wondering what I was going to do once I caught up with the creature.

Despite my fear, my steps didn't slow. I careened around the corner and sprinted down the alley. It dead-ended in a small parking lot surrounded by wooden fencing. The two children stood facing the creature, backing away slowly.

The girl stood in front of the boy. She had long blonde hair with eyes sunken into her face. Her jeans were threadbare, and her sneakers had more holes than her shirt. She was too thin, and the top of her head only reached about halfway up the creature's chest.

Yet she stood defiantly in front of it, a rusty knife clutched in her right hand with her legs braced. The small boy peeked out from behind her. Black skin and dark eyes, he was barely four feet tall. He couldn't be any older than eight, ten at the most.

The girl waved the knife back and forth. "Get back demon," she ordered with a shaky voice.

The creature laughed, deep and full throated. "What are you going to do, little girl?" he taunted in a deep, gravelly voice.

The boy, his eyes growing even larger as he took in the demon, tugged on the back of the girl's shirt. "Noel…"

Noel gripped her knife tighter, not taking her eyes from the nightmare in front of her. "Run, Micah."

She tried to step forward, but Micah wouldn't let her go. "Not without you," he said.

Noel didn't have time to reply because the demon darted forward, reaching for her. Noel pushed Micah to the ground as she rolled out of the way. Micah darted behind her again, but they were now in the lot's corner.

The demon laughed again. "Children, you can't escape. But this game is fun." He reached for them again. The girl lashed out with her small knife. As it came in contact with the creature's skin, the tip broke off.

The girl let out a small gasp. Her mouth fell open as she stumbled back.

I bolted across the parking lot. With a leap, I plunged my knife into the demon's back, shocked when it sank into the thick skin. I yanked the blade out as the creature howled and whirled around. Its fist, which seemed to be the size of my head, struck out.

Wind blew past my face as I ducked out of the way, moving to the creature's side. "Why don't you pick on someone your own size?"

It grunted turning to face me as I backed up. The girl had called the creature a demon, and nothing about him suggested that she was exaggerating. His hands ended in sharp, dark claws. His frame was so muscled that the lower half of his pants was shredded, exposing calf muscles the size of my thighs.

"You're not my size," it growled.

With a stranglehold on my terror, I managed to speak without tripping over my words. "Nope. But I'm a lot closer than those two."

The demon smiled, showing off its full mouth of sharp teeth. "So nice of you to offer to take their place, but I think I'll just save them for dessert."

An image of a human leg disappearing into this thing's maw tripped across my mind. A shiver ran up my spine as I sized him up, looking for weaknesses. Ears, maybe, definitely the eyes.

I smiled, throwing as much cockiness into my voice as I could manage. "Then come and get me, big boy."

The demon darted forward.

It was incredibly fast for something that big. But I managed to sidestep, swiping out with my knife and catching it in the ribs. I tensed for a moment, expecting my knife to break just as the girl's had. That first hit was surely just a lucky strike.

But instead of breaking, my knife sliced cleanly into it's skin.

The demon let out a howl of outrage. "Not possible. No human can hurt me."

"The wounds in your side and back would beg to differ."

A massive claw darted toward me. I managed to slip out of the way, barely missing getting raked by them. I shot a glance at the kids. They were still in the same spot. The creature and I were blocking any exit for them.

I needed to move this thing away from them. I reached out and slashed at its forearm. The demon roared again and struck out incredibly fast, catching me on the cheek with a back fist.

Pain exploded across my face. I flew off my feet, landing in a heap against an abandoned car.

Stars danced across my vision. Laughing, the demon walked toward me, apparently not even a little bothered by the blood dripping from its back, arms, and side. "Not so strong now, are you?"

I curled my right leg under me, leaning back and faking fear.

It wasn't that hard.

The demon leaned down toward me. Before it could grab me, I dove in between its legs, slashing up as I moved. It cried out, this time a high-pitched squeal.

Wasting no time, I slashed again at the back of its legs. Blood poured from the wounds. The ground shook as it crashed to its knees.

On automatic pilot, I leaped to my feet, grabbing it by the back of the head. I plunged my knife over its shoulder and right into its heart.

Then I twisted the knife.

The demon's eyes jolted wide, complete shock blanketed its face. Its mouth gaped and its chest went still before it fell forward.

I released my hold on its head to keep from getting yanked forward myself. Breathing hard, I waited, staring at the creature, hoping it was dead. Carefully, I moved forward and rolled it over, surprised it didn't take much effort. The creature's mouth was slack, showing off its rows of pointed teeth but no breath escaped between them.

I stared at the demon waiting for it to move. It had fallen with my knife still embedded in its chest. Only about an inch of the handle was now visible.

I thought about leaving the knife there. But as far as I knew, that knife and my clothes were all that belonged to me. Besides, those kids didn't look surprised about there being demons around here and I needed something to protect myself with. So I grabbed the end of it. By the time I wiggled it free, my knife and hands were covered in blood.

"Is it dead?"

I whirled around. The girl let out a little gasp before taking a step back. The boy once again ducked behind her.

Heart pounding, I lowered my knife. "I think so. Are you two okay?"

The boy peeked out from around the girl again. "You killed it?"

"It looks like." It was once again silent all around us. It didn't seem like anyone had heard the fight. Which begged the question, "Do you guys live around here?"

Micah opened his mouth as if to answer and then quickly shut it at a shake of Noel's head. "Why do you want to know?" she asked, her eyes narrowed, her whole body tense.

Man, even saving a kid from a demon didn't win any points with this one. I respected that. "I just want to make sure you get home safe."

Micah stepped out from behind Noel. "We don't live anywhere."

I glanced around, still not recognizing a thing. "I don't think I do either."

CHAPTER 3

TWO YEARS LATER

Hushed voices in the kitchen woke me. I stared at the water spot on the ceiling above my bed. It was getting bigger. I'd have to do something about that one of these days.

"Should we wake her?" Micah asked in his attempt at a whisper. It wasn't even close, but he was trying.

"Give her a few more minutes. She had a tough night at work," Noel answered.

"She'll be late if she doesn't get up soon," Micah said.

I smiled as I listened to the two of them. Noel, Micah, and I had lived together since that night we'd met down on the beachfront. The first few days, we'd stayed down by the boardwalk in an empty former liquor store. After that, we moved from spot to spot while I looked for a job. The town of Blue Forks didn't have a lot to offer then. It still didn't.

Blue Forks, of course, wasn't the town's official name, but no one remembered what that was anymore. Its name came from an old rundown factory on the edge of town. On the roof was a giant billboard with a huge smiling blue fork. It was the first thing people saw when they came into town.

Over the last two years, I managed to pick up some cleaning jobs and a few catering jobs, even some yard work. I wasn't picky or proud. I'd take anything. After a while, I'd squirreled away enough to get the three of us this small apartment. It wasn't much, but it was an actual apartment left over from the old days, with two bedrooms, a decent-sized living room, one tiny bathroom that worked minus the hot water, and a kitchen that was slightly larger than the tiny bathroom. I gave Noel and Micah the bedrooms, and I just cornered off a portion of the living room with some blankets to make a third bedroom for myself.

They offered to share a room, but I figured they'd had precious little to call their own throughout their lives. They at least deserved their own rooms.

"We need to wake her," Micah whispered.

I pushed the blankets aside and swung my feet over the side of the bed. "I'm up," I called out.

"Breakfast is ready," Noel called back.

I smiled at her word choice. Breakfast was a rather strong term for our usual morning meal.

I ran a hand through my overlong hair. I needed to cut it soon but more critically I needed to wash it. But there was no time for either this morning. I grabbed my brush from the crate I used as a side table and ran it through my hair before quickly and efficiently pulling it into a ponytail.

I stood up and pulled my robe on over my tank top and underwear. Pushing back the blanket door, I smiled at Noel and Micah. Noel was fourteen, and Micah was twelve. Noel was tall for her age and was often mistaken for a full-fledged adult. Micah, in contrast, was short for his age and often mistaken for someone much younger.

After that night on the beach, Micah had accepted me immediately. Noel's trust had been a little harder to earn. But once I'd earned it, I knew there was nothing she wouldn't do for me, and vice versa. She was tough, smart, and way too jaded for someone her age. But she hadn't exactly had the easiest of upbringings. Orphaned at the age of nine, she'd ended up in a group home. And from the little she said about it, I knew it was a place of horrors. Micah still had nightmares about it. She'd left with Micah three years ago. They'd been on their own for a year until I came across them.

I stepped out of the bedroom and smiled at the two of them. "So what amazing creation will we be having for breakfast this morning?"

Noel smiled, holding up a plate. "Fresh apple slices with peanut butter."

"My favorite," I said as I took a seat at the table. I flicked a quick glance at the fire escape, but it was empty.

Micah sat across from me. I ran a hand over his head. "Sorry I was late last night, guys. It couldn't be helped."

"What was the party like?" Noel asked as she placed the plate in the middle of the table. From the look of it, she had sliced the apples to make sure she got every last piece of edible fruit. Thinly spread across them was peanut butter.

My stomach growled at the sight. But I only ate two slices, and small ones at that. I'd managed to eat a little at the party last night, and I knew that Noel and Micah had had little to eat. Food was a luxury these days, and we had very little money for luxuries.

I sat back, sipping a glass of water. "Oh, you should've seen it. Francesca Remiel was there, and I swear she must've been wearing her weight in diamonds. She had trouble holding her neck up, they were so heavy."

The kids' eyes shone as I told them story after story of how the rich lived. The stories from my time over the bridge were one of the few sources of entertainment we had in this world. I'd gotten pretty good at taking a boring event and making it into something fabulous."

"What about the food?" Micah asked.

"They had a chocolate fountain. Chocolate bubbled up and cascaded over the sides. People would dip cups in or little cookies."

"Wow." Micah leaned forward, his mouth hanging ajar.

I described the feast, which for a party in Sterling Peak, was just a normal night. There'd been roast rack of lamb, ham, and salmon as the main courses. And then at least twenty side dishes, plus appetizers and two ten-foot tables full of desserts. While food might be an issue in this household, and most of the households in Blue Forks, it was definitely not a problem over in Sterling Peak.

Micah sighed after I mentioned that I'd left before the Sterling Peak Seraph Force had arrived. "One day, one of them is going to look at you, and realize what you can do. Then you'll become a Ranger and we'll move over the bridge."

I smiled back at him. "Let's not get your hopes up."

"You'll see," he said.

Noel and I shared a look over the table. Rangers were the soldiers of the Seraph Force, the security force that protected people from demon attacks. They did occasionally take on a Demon Cursed as a Ranger, but it was rare.

And no one was going to invite a maid to join their ranks.

But neither Noel nor I said anything to Micah. He lived in a small fantasy world that I wasn't sure what to do about. I didn't want to take away the solace of a world that was much kinder and more hopeful than our actual reality provided him. At the same time, I knew that he needed to have his feet firmly planted on the ground. After all, life was not going to get any easier for either of them.

"How was school yesterday?" I asked, wanting to get that dreamy look off of Micah's face.

Mission accomplished. He frowned.

He and Noel exchanged a glance. "We had to duck out early. A social worker came by," Noel said.

My heart rate picked up. I struggled to keep the tremble from my hands. Even though they sat there within arm's reach, the fear of losing them jolted me. Social workers went to the schools to check and see if there were any children without homes. At least, without official homes.

And we were undeniably an unofficial home. Foster homes had to pay taxes on their kids. If we became official, I would have to choose between paying rent or paying for the kids. It was a stupid system. But the group homes got money from the government for each kid. So if you wanted to take a kid from them, you had to pay them.

It was corrupt. It was wrong. And it was how it was.

But if it came down to it, there would be no choice. I would have to pay. I was just really hoping we could avoid it for the next six years or so. "Did she see you?" I asked.

Micah took a bite of his apple slice, wiping his mouth on his sleeve. "No. Noel noticed the car before we even got into school. So we ducked down the alley by the old toy store and came back home."

"I think you should stay home today," I said.

Noel shook her head. "The social workers never come two days in a row. It'll be okay."

I waged a silent war inside my mind about whether or not to let them go. I knew they needed to go to school. Not necessarily for the education. They were both smart kids and had the basics down. And to be honest, it wasn't like lawyers and doctors were really a thing anymore, at least not for people like us.

But they needed to be around kids their own age. They needed to have a normal life, or at least as normal a life as we could manage.

"Okay, but if anything feels off—"

"Trust your instincts," they said in unison.

I raised an eyebrow. "Have I said that before?"

Noel rolled her eyes, popping another apple slice into her mouth. "Only every day."

"Well, then, my job here is done. Speaking of which …" I glanced at the clock. "I need to get moving, or I'll to lose my other job."

I hustled into the bathroom and took a super-fast ice-cold shower. Then I dashed back into my room, pulling the blanket closed. My uniform hung on a hanger on an exposed pipe, but I ignored it. Normally I left it at work, but I'd been so late yesterday that I'd worn it home. I'd had to wash it in the sink last night. It was still a little damp.

I slipped on my jeans and tank top, sitting on the edge of the bed to pull on my socks and boots. I shoved my work shoes into my backpack and then draped my clean uniform over my arm. I'd get changed when I got to work. If I wore it there, I would just get it sweaty and wrinkled. And Mrs. Uriel hated when we showed up sweaty and wrinkled.

I stepped out of the room and yelled down the hall, "Okay, I'm going."

I waited for a beat. Both doors opened. Noel and Micah hurried out. "Hugs."

I opened up my arms, and the two of them rushed me. This was our morning ritual. Everyone got hugs before they left, no matter what. The world was decidedly unstable. And I never wanted to leave the house without saying goodbye, just in case. I kissed Micah on the forehead and did the same to Noel. "I love you. And I love you."

They held me tight. They mumbled their I-love-yous into my side.

And for just a moment, everything in the world was right. The small apartment, the lousy job, the unbearable weight of just existing these days, none of it mattered right at that moment. I had them, and they had me. And *that* was all that mattered.

Too soon, Noel and Micah stepped away. I glanced back at the clock. I really was going to have to hurry to get there in time.

"Love you," I called out one last time as I flung open the door and raced down the steps.

CHAPTER 4

Hustling out onto the street, I ducked around Immanuel Sanchez, as he pushed his shopping cart filled with metal scraps from the alley that ran along the side of our apartment building. "Morning, Manny."

The Sanchezes lived on the first floor of our apartment building. It was Manny, his wife, Lisa, and their four kids, three of whom were younger than ten. Lisa worked up in Sterling Peak at one of the other houses.

Sometimes she and I walked to work together. After the birth of their baby boy, Miles, though, she'd taken on an extra cleaning job and now left hours before I did.

"Morning, Addie," he called as I ran by. Addie was short for Addison. I still didn't know what my actual name was. But the day after I met Noel and Micah, we all agreed that they needed to call me something. We passed by a store that had an old sign on the window for Addison Shoes. Next to it was a former bakery. So Addison Baker was born, a non-angelic surname. Only the Angel Blessed had angelic names.

Noel and Micah had angel last names simply because all orphans were given the same one: Rikiel. It was a label they then had to wear until they could afford a new one. Of course, the label also insured that they never did. It was like being stamped with the term Demon Cursed.

I recognized a few more people heading along the street in the same direction as me, but I didn't stop to say hello. They were more the people you saw all the time but never got to know, which was the case for most of the people in Blue Forks. They were kind, hardworking people. But we were all trying to make ends meet—during daylight hours. Because when the darkness hit, no one stepped outside unless they had to. The nights belonged to the demons now.

The Celestial Bridge, which connected Blue Forks to Sterling Peak, came into view. I smiled at the sight of it. I loved this old bridge. It was a hundred and fifty years old, made of rock and steel. I don't know why, but I thought it was absolutely beautiful.

My eyes immediately went to the highest point of the bridge. Stone-carved versions of the archangels Michael and Gabriel clad in armor with spears clutched in their right hands stood with their backs perfectly straight. Their narrowed gazes focused on a point in the distance, their backs to Sterling Peak.

Each time I saw them a tingle of warmth spread through me. Times were tough yes, but the angels looked out for us. And if the demon attacks got really bad, I and everyone else knew the angels would return to protect us, just like they had before.

Which was good, because we couldn't count on the people of Sterling Peak to come to our rescue. Twenty years ago, renovations on the bridge had been completed that allowed the first twenty feet of the bridge to retract in case of a demon attack, thus protecting all of Sterling Peak while leaving the people of Blue Forks on their own.

I tried not to focus on that whenever I saw the bridge.

"Morning, Addie," a familiar voice said.

I scanned around quickly to make sure no one was too close, and then said, "Morning, Torr."

Torr was only five feet tall. He had green mottled skin, pointy ears, and two small nubs for horns. Today he wore red shorts and a dark gray Mickey Mouse T-shirt, along with his standard black Converse sneakers.

I'd met him three months after I met Noel and Micah. One of the other demons was attacking him late one night. I intervened before I got a good look at him. And afterwards, well, it didn't seem right to kill him. He had a large gash in his ribs, and tears had welled up in his bright blue eyes. I'd never met a demon like him. He wasn't vicious. He wasn't cruel. In fact, he even seemed younger than the others.

And he could be invisible.

The first time I realized that Torr could cloak himself, I'd been terrified. It opened up a whole new avenue of fear when it came to the demons. Slowly, though, I realized that the ability was unique to Torr. He made himself invisible, but as far as he or I knew, no other demon could.

"I smelled demon blood on your blade last night. How many did you take down?" Torr asked.

I kept my head forward, talking out of the side of my mouth. "Only two. One caught up with me on the way back from the Hills last night, and the other was stalking Lisa Sanchez."

Torr shook his head. "She shouldn't stay out after dark like that."

We were getting closer to the line for the bridge, so I took out my water bottle and pretended to drink. "No choice, just like me. The Uriels had a party. It was stay or lose my job. Lisa had the same choice at her job."

Torr swore softly. "So they just sent you guys home with no protection?"

I shrugged. "You know how it is."

He didn't say anything because he knew the deal.

Sterling Peak used to be a ritzy part of Los Angeles. They didn't worry about demon attacks at night there. They had enough security to make sure that if any demon attempted to attack its citizens, it paid for that violation.

The first Seraph Force Academy had been started in Sterling Peak nearly a hundred years ago. It stood on the far side of the mountain, away from the wealthy estates, and trained the country's top defenders against the demons. There were a hundred students at any given time, give or take, plus the thirty-six full-time soldiers of the Seraph Force stationed in Sterling Peak. It was fair to say that Sterling Peak was one of the safest locations on the planet.

Downhill, though, there was nothing for the rest of us regular folks. The demons had realized pretty quickly which side of the bridge to focus their attentions on.

Not that demon attacks were new. The first demon attacks occurred over two hundred years ago. They had ramped up before the Angel War began and then all but disappeared after the war.

But they didn't go away completely. For the last hundred years, the attacks happened occasionally, once every three weeks or so. Now, it was more like once a night. Something had changed in the last few years, ramping up the attacks. Back then, when it had gotten really bad, a legion of angels descended from on high and fought back the demon hordes.

Half of the world had been destroyed as the battle raged on for fifty years. But eventually the angels were victorious. When it ended, life for humans was very different. Resources were much scarcer. Electricity had become an extreme luxury. And society had been quickly split into the haves and the have-nots.

But the haves decided they deserved a better name: the Angel Blessed. They claimed to be descendants of the archangels who had appeared to fight back the demons and then disappeared. There had been offspring of the archangels, some of whom had abilities. But from all reports, the abilities were only seen in the first generation of children, not any subsequent generations. That didn't stop the wealthy from claiming to be Angel Blessed, even decades later.

It probably helped them justify in their own minds their hoarding while other people starved and died. The name they gave the rest of us made it easier too: Demon Cursed. There was no proof that humans and demons had procreated, but that didn't stop the name from catching on. Now the Angel Blessed gathered all of their resources to themselves and gave them out only when they needed something from the Demon Cursed.

I worked for the Uriels, another one of the higher Angel Blessed families. The Angel Blessed, when they had enough resources and money, took on the names of the archangels. The richest families had the names of the archangels, while the less well-to-do had names of lower angels.

The Uriels had an enormous mansion: ten thousand square feet with ten bedrooms for a four-person family. Noel, Micah, and I could have hidden away in one wing of the house, and they probably wouldn't even realize we were there for a week. But of course, the Uriels weren't the sharing kind.

And the truth was, I was just happy to have a job, a roof over my head, and at least a little food. Plus, the cook at the Uriels often snuck me and the kids some extra food.

In my gut, I knew it was unfair. We shouldn't have to struggle so hard when those with so much didn't struggle at all. But when you were just trying to get food on the table, there wasn't a lot of extra time to fight the system.

Besides, as far as the power balance went, it was all on the side of Sterling Peak. It would be like throwing pebbles at a demon. It might feel good for a moment that you were fighting back, but it wouldn't change the outcome of the fight.

"How were the kids last night?" I asked.

Torr smiled. "Good. They came in, did their homework, and tidied up a little bit. Then they played Parcheesi until it got too dark to see. Noel read by candlelight for a short time before going to sleep."

When I worked late, Torr would sit out on the fire escape and keep an eye on Noel and Micah. He never revealed himself to them. We'd argued about it more than a few times. I thought Noel and Micah would accept Torr, especially once I explained that he'd actually been a part of our lives for almost two years now. He even slept on the couch sometimes, unbeknownst to either of them.

But Torr didn't want to risk it. And I understood that. He worried that the kids would make me choose between them and him. And although I would never let myself choose, I could see why he wouldn't want to risk that. We were his family, Noel, Micah, and I, even if two members of that family didn't even know he existed.

I gave him a smile. "Well, I appreciate it. Did you get some breakfast?"

"I did. I had some apples. Did you guys get the ones I left for you?"

"We did. Thanks."

"Do you think you'll be late today?"

The bridge was only ten feet away now. I stopped to lean down and tie my boot, dropping my voice to barely above a whisper now. "Shouldn't be. Last night Mrs. Uriel drank a lot. She'll be hung over for most of the day. To be honest, I'd be surprised if she gets out of bed before noon, and that'll only be for a quick bite to eat before she returns to bed."

"Good. I'll walk the kids home from school and wait for you."

Torr didn't wait for a response, as a group was coming up behind us. He simply walked back the way we came, skirting around the people hurrying toward the bridge. A wave of pity fell over me. I hated that he had to stay hidden. In the time I'd known him, I'd seen no evidence of aggression or violence. Other than how he looked, I'm not sure how he could even be classified as a demon.

Every time I tried to talk to him about where he came from and why he was so different from the other demons, though, he made himself invisible to me as well. It didn't take long for me to realize that that was one topic that was off-limits.

Standing up, I adjusted my bag and rearranged my uniform to remove any wrinkles before I stepped into the line. There were only ten people ahead of me. Two guards in the gray uniforms of Sterling Peak security stood at the front of the line at the bridge entrance. I groaned silently when I saw that Claude was on-duty. The guy made my skin crawl.

I didn't recognize the other guy. He must be new.

A job with Sterling Peak security was *the* dream job for anyone living down in Blue Forks: three square meals a day and an actual livable wage. Those who got tapped for the job were usually some distant cousin of a Sterling Peak's resident. Most of the guards were allowed to move into the lower levels of Sterling Peak after a year, and they wasted no time doing exactly that.

And most liked to lord that status over those who still had to commute.

I counted the people ahead, trying to figure out who I would end up with and let out a sigh of relief that it looked like I'd speak with the new guy. Anyone had to be better than Claude.

Then a guy three people up couldn't find his identification card. It took so long that instead of getting the new guy, I found myself face-to-face with Claude.

Claude was a little shorter than me, standing at maybe 5'6". He had a nearly perfectly round head and a rotund body that had only gotten larger in the last few months. Apparently he was putting all of his extra money into food. He smiled as I stepped in front of him. His gaze shifted from my face, down my entire body, and then back again. Anger rolled over me as quickly as his eyes did.

"Identification," he ordered his gaze focused on my chest.

I pulled my ID out of my back pocket and handed it over. Claude made a big show of looking at my face, back at the ID, and then back at my face again. "So how are you doing this morning, Addison?"

"Fine."

He leaned forward. I struggled not to lean back from the stench of his breath.

"You know, my offer still stands. I have a sweet little pad not far from here on the good side of the bridge. I'd be more than willing to make some room for you in exchange for some favors." His eyes drifted over me again.

"Can I have my ID back?"

Claude grinned, holding it even farther away. "I don't know. I'm not sure this is legit. I might need to take you in for extra searching."

"Claude!"

Claude winced, his shoulders practically touching his ears. He turned slowly as a woman marched across the bridge toward him. Sheila Castiel was in charge of Sterling Peak security. And by some absolute miracle, she was not a jerk like most of her staff.

The tall, muscular woman stopped next to Claude, glaring down at him, her hands on her hips, her dark hair pulled back into a no-nonsense ponytail. "Why are you holding up Miss Baker?"

Claude fumbled with my ID and quickly handed it back. "I'm not. I'm not. I was just making conversation."

She glared at him. "Do we pay you to make conversation?"

"Uh, no," he mumbled.

"That's right. We pay you to keep Sterling Peak secure and to keep the lines moving quickly. Now which is more important: making conversation or doing your job?"

"Um, the second one?"

She rolled her eyes. "Yes, the second one. Now go down and

join the river patrol. They're missing a guy and need some extra help. Perhaps it will help remind you of how lucky you are to have this position."

"Yes, ma'am. Right away, ma'am. Claude hurried off, shooting me a glare before disappearing down the path along the side of the bridge.

It was going to be one seriously smelly day for Claude. River patrol involved searching the riverbanks for any demon attack victims, and being it was the end of the month, cleaning out the nets that were used to catch the debris that floated down from Blue Forks.

Sheila rolled her eyes. "I really don't know why we have to keep that one around." She rolled her shoulders as if shaking off the encounter. Then she smiled at me. "How's it going today, Addie?"

"Good. How's Marjorie?"

Sheila's face lit up at the mention of her younger sister. Marjorie had some learning deficits, and she struggled sometimes with understanding the rules. One night when I had been coming home late, I caught sight of her walking off the bridge into Blue Forks. I didn't know she was Sheila's sister. I just knew that she shouldn't be out by herself. There was something so childlike about Marjorie, even though we were probably about the same age.

I followed her to where a man was meeting up with her. And that was when the demons attacked. Sheila had been out looking for Marjorie and arrived as I was standing between Marjorie and the last one. I'd already taken down the other one. The man had run off. Sheila jumped into the fight without hesitation, and together the two of us dispatched the remaining one. She called the security patrol to escort me home that night. I'd ridden in a car, which as far as I knew, was the first time I'd been in one.

She'd never forgotten that I'd helped her out. Occasionally she'd be waiting for me after work with some fresh baked bread or some clothes for the kids. And somewhere along the way, we'd become friends.

Sheila smiled. "She's great. She started painting. She's actually really good."

"That's wonderful. I'd love to see her painting some time."

Sheila tilted her head. "Tell you what, why don't you bring Noel and Micah over this weekend for dinner? You can stay over. There's going to be fireworks. I'm sure the kids would love it."

"Thanks. Actually, that sounds great."

Sheila smiled as she stepped out of the way so I could pass. "See you Saturday."

"See you then."

I took off across the bridge. The bridge itself was something out of a fairy tale with its stone arches and the sun shining on the water below. I loved walking across it. It felt freeing.

But today I couldn't take the time to appreciate the experience. I was running late. I broke into a jog, hurried across the bridge, and then up the hill. The Uriels were one of the wealthier families, and as a result, their home was third from the top. Walking to work was a workout every morning. Running to work was extreme exercise. But today there was no choice.

I sprinted up the hill, bypassing some other workers. I pulled into the Uriels' driveway just five minutes before nine.

Their drive was cobblestoned, so I had to slow down or risk twisting an ankle. The home was four stories high, with giant columns all along the front, which were reminiscent of a Greek temple. The gold cherubim fountain in front of the house though was more like something from old Las Vegas, at least according to the pictures I'd seen.

I quickly made my way to the side door. Before I could knock, George, who with his shaggy gray hair, eyebrows, and mustache bore an uncanny resemblance to an English sheepdog, had the door open. "You better hurry."

I squeezed past him. "I know, I know."

Ducking into the first bathroom, I quickly stripped off my jeans and tank top. After splashing cold water on my skin and toweling off, I threw on my uniform.

With a grimace, I grabbed the ballet flats out of my bag and slipped them on my feet. Mrs. Uriel didn't like to hear anybody walking around her house. She insisted we all wear these ridiculous shoes that gave zero support while standing on them all day.

But like many other things that involved the welfare of her servants, that was not Mrs. Uriel's concern.

I grabbed my brush and looked in the mirror as I pulled my hair tightly back, making sure there wasn't a single hair out of place. The uniform was the exact same shade of blue as my eyes. I pulled out one of the fresh aprons that hung in the closet and wrapped it around my waist and then placed a small little cap on my head.

Made with a very delicate material that was also durable, the uniform was surprisingly comfortable. Sad to say, it was by far the highest quality outfit in my entire wardrobe.

Stashing my backpack in the closet, I hurried into the kitchen. A quick glance at the clock showed it was 8:58.

"Cutting it close," Beth Myers, the Uriels' cook, said as she pushed the already-made-up tray toward me. I was supposed to put the tray together. But Beth no doubt knew I'd been here late the night before and would run in this morning at the last minute.

Beth had been with the Uriels since she was a teenager, and she'd been in the kitchen now for close to fifty years. She knew where all the Uriels' dirty secrets were buried, so unlike the rest of the staff, they were very courteous to her. Beth, in turn, used her sway to help make life a little easier for everyone else.

"Thanks, Beth. You're a lifesaver." I grabbed the tray and hustled down the hall. Carefully balancing the tray and trying not to slosh any of the tea, I climbed to the second floor. At the landing, I stopped for a moment to readjust the plate that had slid a little toward me. Luckily, none of the tea had spilled. I knocked on the double master doors at nine o'clock on the dot.

"Come in," came the muffled reply from the other side of the door.

Once again carefully balancing the tray with one hand, I turned the knob and slowly pushed the door open with my foot. The heavy white drapes were still drawn with just a sliver of sunlight escaping in and allowing me to see. The enormous upholstered bed, also in white, was pushed up against the wall to my right. The door leading to the bathroom was just beyond it. The shifting lump on the right side of the bed meant Mrs. Uriel was still in it.

I walked over to the side table and placed the tray silently upon it. Mrs. Uriel groaned from her position face down in the pillows. She shoved her thin pale-brown hair back. Large black circles of mascara rimmed her eyes. A quick glance at the white pillowcase showed where the lipstick, blush, and eye makeup had rubbed off during the night. "What time is it?"

"Nine o'clock."

"It's too early." She shoved herself up. The straps of her white silk negligee slipped down her shoulders.

I averted my eyes. I wasn't exactly a prude with the human body, but Mrs. Uriel thought nothing of parading around with little to nothing on. She wasn't showing off. She just really didn't think of her staff as people.

She shoved her straps back up and sat against the pillows. "My tea. Quickly."

I uncovered the tray and poured some into her cup. The scent of ginger and lemon wafted through the air. It was Beth's hangover remedy. With Mrs. Uriel, she'd had enough practice to fine-tune it.

Handing her the cup, Mrs. Uriel took it without a word and drank down its contents practically in one gulp. She shoved the cup back at me. "Come back at twelve."

Slipping her mask back over her eyes, she flopped back down, rolling over and giving me her back. I placed the cup back on the tray. As silently as I could manage, I picked it up and walked back out the door. Once again balancing the tray with one hand, I closed the door behind me and then leaned against it, taking a breath. Okay. My work day had officially begun.

CHAPTER 5

I spent the next few hours tidying up after the party last night. According to Nigel—who was the head butler, Beth's brother, and the house's most notorious gossip—the party broke up around six a.m. Mrs. Uriel had gone to bed a few hours earlier, but her children had kept the partying going. A few guests had taken up residence in the rooms on the fourth floor.

After I helped Nigel and Ingrid, the other maid, with the second and third floor, Ingrid disappeared down the stairs to help Beth in the kitchen. Nigel turned to me, watching me down his hawk-like nose. "I'm afraid you're on your own for the fourth floor. A group of Hunter's friends stayed over last night, so try to be quiet and ignore any rooms where the door's closed." He paused. "Or open and occupied."

I sighed, looking up the stairs. "How long's Hunter staying?"

Nigel looked around, lowering his voice. "Hopefully only a few days. He scared off another kitchen worker yesterday."

"Who?"

"Hilda's girl."

My mouth gaped. "She's only fifteen!"

Anger slashed across Nigel's face. "I know."

My own anger simmered just below the surface. I wasn't a fan of Estelle Uriel, but I'd take her any day over her entitled, arrogant, lecherous son. He'd assaulted me one night when he was too far into his cups, and I broke his arm. Luckily, he thought he'd fallen down the stairs while he was drunk.

Noel had wanted me to report him, but there was no point. No one would do anything about the creep. There was, however, an excellent chance I'd get in trouble for breaking his arm.

Although, he'd made certain to keep his distance from me since then. Maybe he remembered part of it. Hunter liked to give the impression that he was a tough guy. Being beat up by the house staff wouldn't exactly help that reputation.

Nigel leaned toward me, dropping his voice after glancing around to make sure no one could overhear him. "The Seven met here last night."

The Seven were the leaders of the Seraph Force. And although they were called the Seven, they currently only numbered six. Major General Rolf Remiel had left two weeks ago to help set up another academy on the east coast.

I raised my eyebrows. "Really?"

The Seraph Force was the security force in Sterling Peak. They were viewed with a hallowed air. And I had to admit, they looked intimidating. All strong, tall, muscular, male and female alike. They were all descendants of the archangels and looked it. Sheila ran basic security, but the Seraph Force trained to fend off demons. And I knew that Hunter wanted more than anything to be one of them.

Nigel nodded. "The meeting was supposed to happen at Donovan Gabriel's, but Katie came down with a stomach bug." Katie was the Gabriel's chef. "The doctor said it might be contagious, and so it was moved at the last minute. Being we were already set up for the meeting here, it seemed as good a place as any."

"Oh, it was a Council meeting last night."

Nigel nodded. "Yup."

The Council of Light was the ruling body of Sterling Peak. Six members were all from prestigious families, and the seventh member was the leader of the Seraph Force, who was also from a distinguished family.

The Uriels were very wealthy, but as descendants of Uriel, they couldn't compete with the Rafael, Gabriel, or Michael families. But they were always trying to get their foot in the door. I grunted. "I wouldn't be surprised if the Uriels drugged Katie to get the meeting moved here."

Nigel narrowed his eyes. "Me either. Well, time to get lunch ready. God forbid even in their hungover states they miss out on a meal." Nigel patted me on the shoulder and headed down the stairs.

I watched him go, noticing he'd been moving a lot slower these last few weeks. I didn't want to think of how the Uriels would treat him when they noticed. I'd need to try to see if I could cover some of his duties to lighten his load a little.

I grabbed the basket that Ingrid had emptied before heading up the stairs, my mind cataloguing Nigel's duties, trying to see where I could help. A splash of bright blue caught my eye. I grabbed the piece of silk from the top of the bannister. It was a lovely bra, trimmed in lace. Rolling my eyes, I tossed it in the basket. Hunter's parties got pretty wild. Like Mrs. Uriel, Hunter's guests didn't seem to mind public displays of nudity.

And it looked like this party had devolved, just like all his other ones. As I tidied, I found six pairs of underwear, four bras, a handful of shirts, and two pairs of pants. Apparently people just left here naked last night. There weren't enough rooms to accommodate that many.

Or they were all in one room, sleeping off a giant orgy. With Hunter, it could go either way.

The study at the top of the stairs was unoccupied, but the

remnants of the party had spilled in here as well. I grabbed the empty glasses and dirty plates, noting the fresh wine stains on the rug. I'd need to bring up the cleaning supplies later for that.

Most of the other doors were closed. I didn't try them to see if there were people inside. Tomorrow I'd do a massive cleaning. Today I just needed to get the obvious stuff.

Reaching the end of the hall, I noticed someone had left a glass tilted on its side. The contents had dribbled onto the rug. Great. I placed the basket on the table by the wall. Leaning a hand against the guest room door, I swung my arm down to grab it, balancing on one leg.

The door swung open.

With a cry, I fell to my side. Two powerful arms caught me before I could hit the ground.

Oh crap.

Mrs. Uriel hated when we interacted with guests, even if the interaction was unintentional. She wanted us to be seen and not heard. She worried our actions would be construed as us throwing ourselves at the feet of one of them.

Of course, in the current situation, I had pretty much done exactly that.

Double crap.

I wrenched myself from the man's arms, not even turning to look at him. "I'm so sorry."

A deep chuckle emitted from the man's chest. "No, not at all. My fault for opening the door."

I prepared myself to see disdain in his face, or maybe some arrogance. Instead, as I looked up, I met warmth from a pair of dark-brown, nearly black eyes. Eyes I recognized. Everyone in Sterling Peak knew those eyes.

At six foot five with the build of a Viking, Graham Michael, the Commander of the Seraph Force, smiled down at me. His mother was from China, his father from Sweden. The combination made for a widely attractive son. Until this moment, I'd only seen him from afar, but I'd heard more than one citizen of Sterling Peak comment on the fact that they'd like to do more than just look at the devastatingly handsome Seraph Force leader.

But that was not a world that I involved myself in, not even in my imagination. I liked to keep my daydreams within the realm of possibility. The baker for the Camiels? Possible. Manny Sanchez's cousin who visited last summer? Possible and better in my imagination than reality.

The Commander of the Seraph Force? I might as well daydream about living in one of these houses as well.

The Seraph Force was the national security force charged with leading the fight against the demons. As Commander, Graham Michael was also the head of the Council of Light, the ruling body for all the nation. They made the laws that influenced every aspect of life. While he wasn't a king, he presided over the meetings and determined the schedule. Each member of the Council had an equal vote and came from one of the seven ruling families: Michael, Gabriel, Rafael, Raguel, Remiel, Uriel, and Sasquael. Each family claimed a direct line to the archangels. Which made Graham Michael the most powerful and therefore the most sought after man on the continent.

I ducked my head down. "Commander Graham, I'm so sorry, really. Is there anything I could get you? Breakfast, perhaps?" Due to the fact that the same families always ran the Seraph Force, all members were addressed by their title and their first name.

"No, no, I'm fine. I grabbed breakfast back at my place. I just came to check on Donovan." He waved his hand back in the door.

Lying on the bed, shirtless with only a white sheet covering him from the waist down, was Lieutenant Commander Donovan Gabriel. He and Graham had an almost identical build and height. But whereas Graham's face was a merging of Chinese and Caucasian features, Donovan's face only held pure Persian ancestry.

Together, the two often made conversations come to an abrupt halt when they stepped into a room. Words seemed to dry up in most women's and a few men's mouths at the sight of them. Add in that Donovan was Graham's second in command of the nation's most lethal security force, and well, the two of them were the stars of more than a few individual's fantasy lives.

"I'm sorry we made so much work for you." Graham kept his focus on me as he talked. Most Angel Blessed barely acknowledged our existence. And receiving this kind of attention from Graham, well, my words seemed to dry up a little bit too.

"Um, that's fine, just fine. It's no problem."

Hanging onto the bannister, his breathing labored, Nigel appeared at the top of the stairs.. "Commander Graham ... I just learned ... you were here. What can I get you, sir?"

Graham gave Nigel an amiable smile. "Nothing, Nigel. I'm fine. Your excellent staff has already offered me breakfast, but I'm afraid I have to hurry off."

"Let me escort you down, then. Addison, if you're done, Ingrid could use your help with the buffet."

"Yes, of course." I grabbed the basket and hurried down the stairs ahead of them, listening as Nigel made small talk with Graham. I glanced over my shoulder, noting that Graham moved at Nigel's pace, even though the older man was much slower.

I shifted my gaze to Graham's face and saw he was watching me as well. Heat flared in my cheeks. I turned around, picking up my pace, but an infinitesimal part of me felt warm and not just from the sight of him. He'd taken his time walking with Nigel. It was a kind thing to do.

Huh, maybe some of these guys weren't as bad as I thought. But almost as soon as I had the thought, I banished it from my mind. Nope, I was not going down that road. Even though I could only remember the last two years of my life, I'd heard of way too many girls who'd thought one of the Angel Blessed were kinder than they'd been taught, only to learn that that kindness only lasted as long as a woman's willpower to say no.

I hurried down the stairs, wincing as I realized how unhappy Mrs. Uriel would be if she saw me going through the front foyer with a basket full of dirty dishes and clothes. Luckily, no one was around, and she was still in bed. I had another thirty minutes before I needed to wake her.

Darting down the hall, I glanced into the dining room as I passed. Inside were three guests, and fourteen-year-old Nathan, the houseboy. Nathan was George's nephew and the reason George stayed on at the estate, even though as a former member of the Seraph Force he had a retirement savings that would see him through.

I dropped the basket in the workroom and then hurried into the kitchen.

At the kitchen island, Beth blew at a piece of hair that had slipped out of her bun while she rolled dough. "The natives are getting restless. Poor Ingrid is being run off her feet going up and down the stairs delivering food and drinks."

"What do you want me to do?"

She nodded to the prep room. Through the open doorway I could see serving trays lined up on the counter inside. "Take the chafing dishes out, fill whatever needs to be filled, and then you can help out Ingrid."

I nodded and hurried over to the trays. I could easily stack them all and carry them out, but I also knew that would not go over well. Instead I stacked two and carried them out, backing out the door into the dining room.

"Oh, let me help you with that."

I looked up into the face of D'Angelo Rafael. D'Angelo was another member of the Seven and had the looks that seemed to confirm his angelic heritage. Wavy blond hair and piercing blue eyes above sharp cheekbones looked down at me with a smile.

Before I could say anything, D'Angelo had taken the top tray from me and walked toward the buffet.

I narrowed my eyes, wondering at his game. Because while D'Angelo might look like an angel, he was anything but.

A quick glance of the room showed that Amon Michael was there. Amon was a college friend of Hunter and from a Michael family in the Chicago area. Like the Michael family here in Sterling Peak, the Chicago Michaels were incredibly wealthy, with their hands in many pies. And they had a daughter who, according to the staff scuttlebutt, D'Angelo was very interested in marrying.

Not because he was in love with her. As far as anyone knew, he'd never even met her. He wanted an arranged marriage that would solidify his status as the wealthiest member of the Seraph Force. He would take the Michael last name when they married. The connection with the Michael family might be enough to solidify him as the next leader of the Seraph Force should anything happen to Commander Graham.

Amon watched D'Angelo walk over to the table and place the tray upon it. I couldn't read his expression to see if D'Angelo's chivalrous act impressed him or if he saw through the façade.

I walked toward the table, keeping my eyes down. "Thank you, Major D'Angelo."

D'Angelo laughed. "I've told you, just call me D'Angelo."

I nearly laughed out loud. D'Angelo had spoken to me half a dozen times. And each time he'd looked right through me. He preferred girls younger and blonder. I was pretty sure he did not remember me at all. And he'd definitely never told me to call him by his first name.

I gave a stiff nod and turned my attention to the trays of food. D'Angelo grabbed a biscuit and a glass of orange juice and said something to Amon before heading for the door. He left the glass on the edge of the table.

I watched him go with narrowed eyes. D'Angelo Rafael was everything that was wrong with the Angel Blessed. He was wealthy, attractive, and had way too much power for someone without compassion.

A pair of warm dark brown eyes floated through my mind, and an unfamiliar stirring erupted in my stomach. Nope, Graham Michael was just like all the others. And even *if* he was kinder, he was still completely, totally, and irrevocably off-limits.

CHAPTER 6

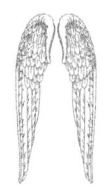

GRAHAM

The Uriels' butler was getting on in years. Graham could tell that he was having trouble managing the stairs now. He knew for a fact that the Uriels would fire him as soon as he no longer proved up to the tasks of his job.

Major Tess Uriel, a members of the Seven—and as she put it, an unfortunate relative of these Uriels—was considering buying a cottage overlooking the river. She would rarely be there and would need some help maintaining it. Perhaps he could suggest Nigel to her.

He shook the man's hand at the door. He'd known Nigel for years. He was close friends with Mary and Franklin, who ran his house. "Thank you, Nigel. I appreciate you taking care of all of us."

Nigel beamed as he held open the door. "Oh, it's a pleasure, Commander Graham. A pleasure."

Graham stepped outside, but he couldn't resist taking a quick look back into the foyer.

The maid with those incredible blue eyes had disappeared. She always did. He'd seen her on more than one occasion, usually from afar. Something about her drew his attention every time. He thought it was the confidence. Most servants walked around with their shoulders slumped, trying not to garner any attention. She did the same, but he got the impression it was an act. There was a strain of confidence that ran through her when she met your gaze. She knew what the rules were and how to follow them, but she didn't believe in them. And something about that was incredibly arresting. Of course, her looks were plenty arresting as well.

Graham shook his head as he made his way down the Uriels' steps, pushing the woman from his mind. He didn't interact with anyone else's staff. He'd had a few relationships, and they had been just that, relationships. He would not be one of those ones living down to the reputation of Angel Blessed taking whatever they wanted.

He rolled his shoulders, thinking about Donovan still asleep upstairs. Graham had left after the meeting last night, but Donovan had stayed on. Graham knew he should have stayed with him, but he couldn't handle one of Hunter's parties. The guy had the morals of a snake. And Donovan was a big boy. Plus, he'd been in a mood. It was best to just let him drink it off. But Donovan would have one hell of a headache for the rest of the day.

Graham supposed he shouldn't be surprised by Donovan's unusual bout of drinking. Donovan had mentioned that his brother and father were home. The three of them did not get along.

Or more accurately, his father and brother did not get along with Donovan.

Donovan was the firstborn which in most Angel Blessed homes made them the honored child. But not in the Gabriel home. Donovan was the only child of Sasha Gabriel's first marriage, an arranged marriage. Donovan had inherited the dark good looks of his mother. She had died during childbirth, and

Sasha had wasted no time remarrying. His younger brother was born just a year after her death.

Jayden, the younger Gabriel, was the spitting image of his father, with his blond hair, pale-brown eyes, and weak chin.

But the resemblance didn't end at their looks. The two of them strongly believed that the Angel Blessed were indeed blessed by God. And with that blessing came the entitlement to all the spoils the world offered. The Demon Cursed, in their mind, had been put on this earth to serve them, to pay for the indignity of their birth. Graham had even heard that in his younger days, Chet Gabriel had advocated for slavery for any Demon Cursed that broke the law.

Luckily, Donovan hadn't really been raised by the senior Gabriel. Chet had taken his youngest son on tours of the world, wanting to show him everything that he felt he was owed one day. Donovan had never been invited along. Instead he'd spent his time at Graham's home.

Not that Graham had a pleasant relationship with his own parents. But unlike Donovan, Graham was the second son, therefore the less important one. His older brother Brock got all the attention focused on him. He was the heir to the Seraph Force throne, a direct descendant of the archangel Michael. So it wasn't unusual for Brock to go off with his father on trips all over the world, sometimes accompanied by Sasha and Jayden Gabriel as well as D'Angelo Rafael and his father. As a result, the three spoiled boys had become incredibly close.

And incredibly dangerous.

Before his death, Brock had been the Seraph Force leader. Graham's father had been peacock proud. Their father had been unable to take on the role due to a club foot. A distant cousin, therefore, had taken on the position. Brock had taken over when he'd grown too old to continue.

Brock had only led the Seraph Force, and by extension the

Council of Light, for three years before he was killed in a demon attack. During that time, Brock had made his mark.

Graham had watched in growing horror as his brother encouraged the Seraph Force to punish any indiscretions by the Demon Cursed. He increased the penalties for even the most minor of infractions, while at the same time cutting wages and reducing food allotments sold in the markets down in Forks and across the nation.

His brother hadn't been a man of compassion. He hadn't been a man of integrity. And God help him, Graham believed the world was better off with him gone.

Graham hadn't been in Sterling Peak when Brock was killed. After two years, he could no longer stand his brother's machinations. If he'd stayed, he probably wouldn't have survived much longer. His brother had made it a point to give him the most dangerous and least respectable assignments.

And every time he came back victorious, Brock stewed a little longer in his anger. Brock held his people's allegiance by fear. Graham held the allegiance of his brothers- and sisters-in-arms through mutual respect. Brock had been determined to destroy that.

Graham had known it was only a matter of time before Brock's vindictiveness got someone killed. So rather than letting it come to that, he took an assignment to accompany an occult professor named Marcus Jeffries on his research trip for the year. They'd traipsed the globe looking for patterns in the demon attacks, trying to find any information that would help turn the tide against the attacks, which only seemed to be increasing in frequency.

It had been Graham's decision to go, but he'd been under no illusions that he would enjoy himself. So he'd been shocked to find himself fascinated with the professor's research and fascinated by the professor himself. He'd planned on extending his assignment another year when word reached him of his brother's death. He was immediately named the head of the Seraph Force.

For a moment, he'd thought about turning down the title. People had done it before. But he knew the importance of his position. As the leader of the Seraph Force and the Council of Light, he set the rules for how demons would be engaged, how society would operate.

The last time he'd gotten drunk, it was with Marcus as they discussed the pros and cons of taking the position. Marcus had pressed upon him the good that he could accomplish as leader. If he had turned it down, Graham had no doubt that D'Angelo would have petitioned for Donovan to be set aside and for D'Angelo to be named the leader of the Seraph Force. If anything, D'Angelo was worse than Brock.

Graham couldn't sit back and let that happen. If only a sliver of the policies his brother and his friends had contemplated came into play, life would get so much more difficult for the Demon Cursed.

The next morning he awoke with a pounding headache and with the realization that as much as he enjoyed the freedom of traveling with Marcus, he needed to return home.

So Graham returned with the expectation that in a few short years he would step away, having hand-picked a successor to take over. He didn't want the power that came with the position, even though Marcus thought that was exactly why he should have it.

The door opened again behind Graham. A familiar head of blonde hair emerged. For a second, Graham wondered if he broke into a run if he'd be able to avoid him.

"Graham."

He tensed, gritting his teeth as he turned to face D'Angelo. He focused on keeping his expression neutral, bordering on polite. "D'Angelo. Good morning. Late night for you as well?"

D'Angelo chuckled as he walked along the path. The sun played off his blond hair, almost making it look like he had a halo surrounding him. "The Uriels throw an excellent party. And there was a new serving girl who started. *She* is lovely."

It was difficult for Graham to hold back his anger. He clasped his hands behind his back so he didn't reach out and grab D'Angelo by the throat. Hunter also thought nothing of hitting on the young women or even girls of Forks. And neither of them, if the rumors were true, believed the word "no" was an acceptable response from any of their targets.

Yet D'Angelo was well-liked within Sterling Peak. He had that smooth veneer that never seemed to get ruffled. His good looks no doubt helped sway public opinion. So Graham knew he had to bite his tongue and bide his time. D'Angelo was well-connected with a lot of support.

Graham headed toward the fence, giving D'Angelo a nod. "If you'll excuse me, I have some work to do. It's going to be a busy day."

"Oh, yes, your professor friend is coming to town, isn't he?"

Graham eyed D'Angelo, once again marveling at the man's network of spies. Marcus's arrival was a closely held secret. Yet again though D'Angelo demonstrated an ability to see through the security Graham had put into place. He was a formidable opponent. He might not be able to take Graham on the battlefield, but in the world of politics, he could run circles around Graham, and Graham well knew it.

"Yes, he is. You should come by the house and meet him. He's a fascinating fellow."

D'Angelo grimaced. "I would love to. Although sitting down with a stodgy professor is not exactly my idea of a good time. But you never know when you're going to need a resource, right?" He slapped Graham on the back a little harder than necessary.

Graham smiled, enjoying D'Angelo's discomfort when the slap didn't move him so much as an inch. "Well, let me get to it. I'm sure you have an impressive deal to accomplish today as well with the fresh recruits coming in tomorrow. Is everything ready for them?"

Annoyance crossed D'Angelo's face before he covered it. "Of course. I have my people working on it diligently. I will review everything later today. Do not fear. All will be completed and ready for our new batch."

"I never worry when you are in charge, D'Angelo. Have a good day."

"You too, brother, you too."

D'Angelo turned for his home as Graham turned to head up the hill. He glanced back over his shoulder to watch D'Angelo. A young woman was walking up the hill. When she caught sight of D'Angelo, she quickly crossed to the other side.

Graham rolled his hands into fists. One day D'Angelo would get his. Graham would make sure of it.

CHAPTER 7

ADDIE

I had been wrong about Mrs. Uriel not keeping me late that night. She kept me for two hours after the end of my shift. Her daughter Tiffany arrived home unexpectedly from school. An impromptu formal dinner had been arranged to celebrate her return.

Of course, Nigel took me aside to share that the reason for Tiffany's return was that she'd flunked out of school. But Mrs. Uriel announced that Tiffany had returned to spend more time with her family, who she couldn't bear to be away from during these trying times.

I'd had to stay to help set up and prepare before the evening staff came in. Beth gave me a look as she darted a glance at the darkening skies. "I don't like you walking home in this. Do you want to stay at my place tonight?"

"No, I'm good."

"But there were four demon attacks last night. One of them they say went into a family's home."

I stopped still. "What?"

All the demon attacks I'd heard about had one thing in common: They occurred after dark and outside. I'd never heard of a demon entering a home. For some stupid reason, I thought they couldn't.

Beth nodded. "A young family. They killed the mother and took the husband. The child was left behind."

"Are you sure they went into the home?"

Beth shrugged. "You know how it is. That's what the rumors are saying. But that's never happened before, has it?"

"No, it hasn't." But even though I wanted to chalk it up to the rumor mill getting the details wrong, dread ran through me. If they could go into homes…

I quickly wiped down the counter. "I need to go. I can't let the kids stay alone at night."

Beth bit her lip. I knew she wanted to argue more. But there was no way to argue that Noel and Micah should be home alone. So instead, after darting another look out the window, she went back to the kitchen table and grabbed some rolls, ham, and cheese. She rolled all of it into a large napkin and handed them to me. "I'll finish up. You tell those kids I said hello. And I'll have some tarts for them tomorrow."

"Thanks, Beth."

I hurried out of the kitchen, stopping at the bathroom to change. Pulling my backpack from the closet, I tucked the food bundle inside. The kids would be thrilled. I hung my uniform up in the closet, knowing that it would be washed tonight and waiting for me tomorrow. After quickly donning my own clothes, I hurried outside.

With dread, I realized it was later than I thought. Dammit. I hated getting home this late. Lights were already on in the houses in Sterling Peak. Down the hill in Blue Forks, it was dark. No one was going to waste electricity or candles until they absolutely had to.

I hurried toward the bridge at a brisk jog. Going down the hill was much easier than my sprint up it this morning. The line at the bridge was shorter than this morning as well. There were only two people ahead of me. Both of them cast increasingly nervous looks at the darkening sky.

Once past the guards, I jogged over the bridge and then ran when I hit the edge. Four demon attacks. I didn't like the sound of that. And with them going into people's homes, well, that just wasn't good at all. I hoped the rumor mill was wrong.

And I prayed that Torr would keep watch.

By the time I reached the outskirts of my neighborhood, darkness had completely fallen. I slowed as I reached the buildings, placing my hand on the knife at my waist. I didn't run in the dark unless I knew exactly where I was going, and that there were no demons nearby. Keeping a fast pace, I made my way down the street, casting my gaze from side to side and checking behind me. Everything seemed all right.

A muffled shout reached me from an alley only two blocks from the apartment. I paused, trying to figure out if it had come from inside a house or out of it. Then it came again, followed by the clang of a trashcan.

I slid my knife from its sheath as I ducked down the alley. A man walked with his back toward me, his hands up. "No. No, please."

The demon laughed as he approached. "Where is it?"

"I don't know what you're talking about. Please just let me go."

The demon reached forward and snatched the man by the front of his shirt, holding him up in the air. "Where is it, Professor?"

"I don't know what you're talking about. I don't have the book."

The demon smiled. "Then you are of no use to me."

The demon's hand rose in the air, its claws extended. I darted forward and grabbed on to its arm, shoving it back. The demon stumbled, flinging the professor away. The man hit the wall and slid down, disappearing behind some boxes.

Shock splashed across the demon's face. "How did you do that?"

I smiled. "I've been working out."

Truth was, I didn't know where my strength came from. It was something that Noel, Micah, and I had discovered together after that first fight with the demon. I could fight them hand-to-hand. My strength matched theirs, even though my size most definitely did not.

The demon pulled a sword from behind its back. Lightning flashed along the blade. I swallowed. Well, that was new. I'd never encountered a demon with a weapon before, although I'd heard about them.

The demon must have noticed my fear. "Not so cocky now, are you little human?"

I pulled back my fear, picturing Noel and Micah. I didn't have the luxury of fear. I needed to get home. I shook my head. "It's not fear. It's excitement. Looks like I'm going to get myself a new toy."

Knife still clutched in my hand, I darted forward and then shifted to the side, cutting the demon at the waist but barely breaking the skin.

He swung at me.Ducking under his arm, I slashed out at his stomach. He let out a scream as my knife sank into his skin deeper this time, leaving a jagged six-inch cut. The demon swung wide, its hit a reaction to the pain rather than a focused move.

I darted behind him, kicked out his leg, and then plunged my knife into the side of his neck. Blood coated my hand.

He jolted forward, moving so quickly that I lost my grip on my knife, unable to yank it out before he stood up. I jumped back as he swung at me again. I backed away, my hands in front of me.

Blood dribbled from the edge of the demon's mouth. My knife still impaled in its neck, it smiled. "Looks like I have all the weapons now."

He lunged forward, his sword leading the way.

I stepped to the side and then latched on to his wrist, yanking him forward just enough to get him off balance. I wrenched his wrist to ninety degrees, facing his palm toward him before turning his hand to the ground. He let out a scream as he hit the ground, and his sword, still gripped in his hand, pointed at his own neck.

I shoved the tip into the edge of his neck and then through. I put all my weight and strength behind it and nearly decapitated him. His tongue rolled out the side of his mouth. He hissed out a breath before going silent.

I rolled my shoulders, taking a breath as the flames dimmed around the sword and then went dark. Carefully, I pulled the sword from his neck, and then ripped it from his hand.

A demon sword. A chill ran through me.

Leaning down, I used the edge of the demon's trousers to wipe the sword clean. It was a beautiful weapon. The blade was straight and unblemished. The hilt was curled with an ivory-wrapped pommel.

But I didn't have time to scrutinize it now. I stuffed it into the side of my belt. It was a little awkward, but the best I could do at the moment. I stood up and made my way to the discarded boxes.

The man was slowly getting to his feet, his eyes unfocused. I didn't recognize him. He was older, probably in his late fifties, with light-brown skin and light-brown eyes. His dark hair was scattered with gray.

"Are you all right?"

The man touched the back of his head with a wince. "I hit my head. I think blacked out for a moment."

Good, that meant he hadn't seen anything. Normally I had a black veil that covered the lower half of my face when I fought demons near other humans, but I forgot it in my rush this morning.

The professor stood up from behind me, his eyes shifting between the demon and me. "How did you do that?"

I spoke quickly. "I didn't. I was coming home and heard something. When I arrived the demon was already down. Are you all right?"

He ran his hands down his body, a confused look on his face. "I think so."

From the corner of my eye, I saw the demon dissolve into ashes. All the bodies did. For some it happened instantaneously, some took a few minutes. But all of them were reduced to ash in death. I kept my attention on the man. "You shouldn't be out here this late."

"Yes, I know. But it couldn't be helped." The man stepped away from the wall and then swayed.

Darting forward, I grabbed him before he could fall. "Give yourself a second. You've had a scare. Where do you live?"

"Not too far." He gestured vaguely toward the bridge.

Surprise ran through me. He did not look like one of the residents of Sterling Peak. His clothes had a distinctive lived-in look to them, and his pack was practically ancient.

"The bridge will be shut down by now. They won't let anyone through without special permission. Do you have that?" I asked.

The man shook his head, his eyelids dropping again.

I couldn't leave him here. And I certainly couldn't let him go wait by the bridge. They wouldn't let him cross. Already a light rain had started. He'd be huddled there in the wet until morning. That was if he even made it. In his current shape, that seemed like a long shot. At best, he'd get pneumonia.

"Okay. Why don't you come home with me? You can stay the night. It's nothing fancy, but at least it will keep you dry."

"Thank you. I would really appreciate that," he said, right before he pitched forward in a faint.

CHAPTER 8

The professor was dead weight. I checked for injuries and found nothing. Maybe he'd just passed out. Regardless of the cause, I had to get him home somehow.

I grabbed him by the arm and hauled him up, flinging his arm over my shoulder. He was surprisingly light. The jacket made him appear bulkier than he was. In fact, it felt like the guy could use a good meal. Maybe even a dozen.

Not that that made him different from anyone else around here. Of course, that did call into question whether or not he really belonged over in Sterling Peak.

I carried him along the back streets, staying in the shadows. It was blessedly quiet. I turned right at the alley that ran alongside my apartment building.

Torr sat up on the fire escape and spied us from down the street. He quickly climbed down, stopping in front of me, his hands on his hips as he studied the professor. "What happened?"

"Demon went after this guy. He passed out or something. I couldn't just leave him there."

He looped the professor's other arm over his shoulder. The weight on me immediately lifted. Torr might be short, but he was incredibly strong. He grunted. "You *could* have. You just chose not to."

I rolled my eyes. "Yeah, yeah. How are the kids?"

"I walked them home from school. One of the kids was giving Micah a hard time. That Thompson kid?"

I nodded as I pictured the boy that had been picking on Micah for the last few months. But Micah being such a sympathetic soul, he didn't have it in him to return any of the insults from the much larger Raymond Thompson.

Torr grunted. "Yeah. Unfortunately for the kid, he took a tumble down the steps of the school as he was coming out the door."

"Torr..."

Torr glared at me from the side of his eyes. "What did you expect me to do? That kid's a bully, and Micah's too nice to defend himself."

"Was the kid hurt?"

"Just his pride. I'll stick close to Micah and make sure the Thompson kid becomes awfully clumsy in his presence if he keeps it up."

I wanted to tell Torr that what he was doing wasn't right. Raymond Thompson had lost his brother to a demon attack just six months earlier. That had to be messing with his head. But I couldn't let him mess with Micah's head. "Thanks."

Between the two of us, we awkwardly carried the professor up the stairs. At the door, I dropped my voice to a whisper. "You need to stay in the apartment tonight. The rain's getting bad out there."

Torr started to shake his head. "No, I'm fine. I'll—"

"This is *not* a debate, Torr. I won't have you sitting out on the fire escape getting soaked. I'll make a bed in the corner of my room. Besides, what if this professor goes all crazy on me? I'll need the backup."

Torr snorted. "Yeah, the day you need back up against a human is the day we're all in trouble."

"You're staying inside."

Torr opened his mouth and then shut it, giving me a nod. "Thanks," he said gruffly.

I shifted, so I took all the professor's weight and then knocked on the door.

"Who is it?" Noel called, her voice meaner and deeper than was natural.

"It's me."

There was a clacking of locks as she undid all of them. Then the door swung wide. A look of relief crossed Noel's face, and I cursed Mrs. Uriel for keeping me late yet again.

The relief quickly shifted to alarm as Noel's gaze fell on the professor. "What happened?"

"He passed out as I was walking home. I couldn't just leave him in the street."

Noel met my gaze for a moment and then nodded, stepping back to give me room to maneuver the professor in.

Noel and Micah knew about my extracurricular night activities. They knew that I took down more than my fair share of demons. And we never talked about it. I figured they knew what I did, and that was enough. No need to worry them.

But one of the first things I'd done when we first met was to teach the both of them how to defend themselves. For the last two years, I'd spent hours on the weekends training them in self-defense. Over that time, the two of them had gotten pretty skilled. They didn't have my strength, but barring that, they were a match for any human at the very least. They might even be able to tag-team a demon.

A small one.

Although if I had anything to say about it, they would never have to.

Noel slipped underneath the professor's other arm as Micah came out of his bedroom, his eyes going wide. "What's going on?"

Torr slipped in quickly without touching either Micah or the door just before Micah closed it.

I quickly explained about finding the professor, briefly mentioning the demon as I maneuvered him onto the couch. The professor stirred, his face arranging into a frown. His eyelids fluttered and then flickered open before closing again. A second later, they flew open, and he tried to sit up.

I put up my hands. "Hey, hey. It's okay. You're safe."

His gaze darted around the room before it returned to Noel and Micah, who stood behind me. "What happened?"

"What do you remember?" I asked.

He stared at me, and then sank back against the pillows. "You're the one from the alley."

"Yes. You passed out, so I brought you here. I didn't want to leave you there just in case anybody else came by later."

The professor nodded his head wearily, starting to sit up. "Thank you. But I'll get out of your hair now."

"Not tonight," I said.

"But I need to get to Sterling Peak."

"Like I said before, without special permission, you're not getting across the bridge at night. They don't let anybody over there after nightfall. And it's not safe for you to just wait outside, especially in the storm."

"I don't want to put you out. I'll just go find some other place—"

"There is no other place. So I'm afraid you're stuck with us till morning." I turned and handed my backpack to Micah. "Beth sent a few things to eat."

Beth's name earned a smile. "Awesome." He grabbed the bag and headed to the kitchen.

"Can you get the professor a glass of water?" I asked Noel.

She nodded, following Micah. I glanced over at where Torr perched in the corner as he studied the professor with a look on his face I couldn't decipher.

I turned back to the professor. "You'll stay with us for the night. You can sleep here on the couch. It's not much, but it's better than being outside."

He met my gaze for the first time. "You're very kind." Then he frowned.

"What's wrong? Are you hurt?" I scanned him, wondering if I had overlooked something. It was dark when I'd first checked him.

"No, no. I'm not hurt, but… you… you fought off that demon, didn't you?"

"Like I told you, I found you afterwards."

"It was probably the Masked Avenger," Noel yelled from the kitchen.

Marcus frowned. "The who?"

Noel walked back in and handed him a glass of water. "The Masked Avenger, Blue Forks' only security force. He or she has saved dozens of Blue Forks citizens from demons over the last few years. But no one knows who they are."

"I didn't think anyone could fight a demon except the Seraph Force," Marcus said.

Noel shrugged before turning back to the kitchen. "Maybe the Masked Avenger is a member of the Seraph Force. It *is* one theory."

She provided the explanation without a hint she was lying. She was really getting too good at this.

I lowered my voice, casting a glance toward the kitchen. It wasn't very far away, but the sandwiches from Beth had caught the kids' attention. "I'd rather not talk about the demon attack in front of the kids. They know about them, of course, but I just don't want to worry them any more than I have to. You're fine, I'm fine, and that's really all that matters."

"Of course, of course. But tomorrow could you tell me how you found me?" Marcus asked.

I was saved from answering when Micah reappeared with sandwiches on a tray. "Ham and cheese. My favorite!"

Noel and I exchanged a grin. Micah said that about absolutely everything Beth sent home. The professor smiled at his exuberance, but his gaze drifted back to me. And I had the feeling that while Noel's lying had improved dramatically, mine had not. My appearance in the alley had the professor wondering. I could practically see the questions circling around in his mind.

I focused on Micah as he handed out the sandwiches, carefully cut into fourths so they'd be easier to split up.

Then I watched the professor, hoping that after a good night's sleep, all his suspicions would disappear.

And wondering what kind of trouble he could make for me if they didn't.

CHAPTER 9

The next morning, Torr slipped out before any of us woke and came back with some rolls. The kids gave me a strange look when they magically appeared in the kitchen, but I just said that they must have missed them in the bag last night. With a shrug, they accepted the explanation. They were used to food just appearing overnight.

The professor and I left for the bridge early the next morning. I wanted to give us extra time to get there given his weakened state from the night before. I was hoping it had only been because of hunger and dehydration.

As we made our way to the bridge, I could tell he was indeed in much better shape. There was more color to his cheeks, and he kept to my pace without seeming to struggle.

He also talked the entire way. Once again, he thanked me profusely for helping him and for our hospitality the night before. He spoke more about his work. He'd traveled all over the world researching demons, their attack methods, and victims, looking for patterns.

"Have you found one?" I asked when he paused for breath. "A pattern?"

"Not exactly. The demon attacks started increasing about two years ago. I'm not sure what was special about that time. But something happened that seemed to almost release a steam valve or something."

My heart rate ticked up a notch. "When exactly two years ago did the attacks begin to increase?"

"In March, as far as I can tell."

My blood seemed to freeze. March. The same month I washed up on the beach.

I forced myself to breathe normally. It was just a coincidence. Whatever was going on with the demons and the professor's research had nothing to do with me.

Even knowing nothing about my past, I was almost certain demons had nothing to do with it. It was crazy to even think about. But I couldn't help but recall that when I'd first seen that demon attacking Noel and Micah, an image of demons had flashed through my mind. In the last two years, it was the only trace of a memory I'd ever had.

In all likelihood I had been the victim of a demon attack, which was how I lost my memory. That first attack had just stirred it up. That was the only connection.

It would be nice, though, to actually know about my past. Besides that one flash, I hadn't remembered a single thing about my life before I washed up on that beach. It was almost as if I just didn't exist before that moment.

Which was insane, because I had to have existed. There must have been people who cared about me, who missed me, right? Or at the very least who knew me. Yet not once had anyone recognized me. Not a single soul in Blue Forks did a double take at my appearance. So wherever I was from, it wasn't around here.

The bridge appeared up ahead. I realized that the professor and I would go our separate ways soon. I felt a sense of loss at the idea. There was something incredibly friendly about the man. He was nice to be around, comforting in a weird sort of way.

"Do you know where you're going once you get over the bridge?"

The professor scanned the neighborhood above the bridge. "I'm looking for Graham Michael. Do you know which house he lives in?"

I pictured Graham from yesterday. Powerful arms, kind eyes. Warmth filtered through my stomach. Still not for me, I reminded myself. "Um, yeah. He's in the second house from the top. His is the white one with the columns. Do you see it?"

The professor's gaze drifted up the hill until it fell on Graham's home. "Oh my goodness."

I smiled. "It's a bit much, isn't it?"

The professor nodded, his mouth hanging open. "I mean, he mentioned his family had money, but …"

I knew what he meant. The Michaels' home was truly immense. There were four balconies, two on either side of the house on the second and third floors. Columns held up the front porch. It had a domed roof, and huge fountains dominated the yard. All the grass that surrounded it was lush and green.

"I didn't realize *how* rich they were." The professor shook his head, almost as if he were disappointed by the news.

I could understand how the professor could make the mistake. Even in my brief interaction with him yesterday, Graham really didn't give off that serious rich vibe.

"I mean, I knew he was rich but certainly not *that* kind of rich. He has the confidence of a well-to-do man but none of the arrogance you'd expect from someone with …" The professor waved his hand toward the hill.

That had also been my impression. It was nice to know it wasn't entirely my hormones directing the idea. "Well, I'm afraid I don't know him. But that *is* definitely where he lives."

We got in line at the bridge, and luckily Claude wasn't there, so we quickly made it through. Sheila, however, was there. She caught sight of us when we were halfway across. Her gaze locked on to the professor as soon as he came into view. She reached us just as we passed the archangels, their shadow cast over us. "Are you Professor Jeffries?"

The professor nodded, his voice hesitant as he took in the serious look on Sheila's face. Then she smiled, her shoulders dropping in relief. "Thank goodness. Commander Graham has been worried about you. He expected you last night."

"I ran into some trouble, but luckily I also ran into this young woman, who helped me out."

Sheila raised an eyebrow at me. "Saving people again?"

"All I need is a cape," I said lightly.

Sheila turned back to the professor. "Commander Graham will be very happy to hear you're safe. Let me give you a ride up to his home."

The professor smiled, his relief at not having to face the monstrosity of a hill obvious. "That would be lovely, thank you. But I have to insist that Ms. Baker join us. After all, she's the reason I'm here and in one piece."

Sheila nodded. "I have no problem with that."

A few minutes later, I got my second ever ride in a car. I had to admit it was nice not having to face that hill today, although watching everyone else walk by made me feel more than a little self-conscious.

When Sheila pulled into the Uriels' driveway, I quickly got out of the car, noticing George peering at us from the side door, curiosity written all over his face. "Thanks, Sheila. Good luck with your research, Professor."

The professor clambered out of the car and offered me his hand. "Thank you, Addie. You are quite literally a lifesaver."

I smiled at him and headed into the house, feeling a little lighter. The day was definitely off to a good start.

CHAPTER 10

GRAHAM

This day was not off to a good start. Graham slammed the door closed as he walked into the kitchen. Mary Elise and her husband, Franklin, looked up from their spots at the kitchen table.

"Any luck?" Franklin asked as he got up to grab Graham a plate.

Graham waved him back down. "No. What about the other search parties?"

Franklin poured coffee into a mug from the pot on the table and walked over to Graham, handing it to him. "Donovan and Mitch checked in when they stopped to get a bite to eat, and then they went back out. I haven't heard from the other two."

"Dammit," Graham growled, taking a sip of coffee. The jolt of caffeine was welcome. Marcus should have arrived last night at the latest. Graham been waiting all day for him. As darkness fell, he'd sent out search parties, first through Sterling Peak and then down into Blue Forks. But there'd been no sign of him.

Graham himself had been out since the bridge had closed.

"Any signs of more demon attacks?" Franklin asked.

Graham nodded. "I found scorch marks in Blue Forks. Someone tussled with a demon."

"And won?" Franklin said.

Graham nodded. After each attack, scorch marks stained the ground or walls where a demon died. Their bodies went up in flames and all trace of them disappeared within seconds, only the burn marks being left behind.

"Our Masked Avenger?" Mary asked with a raise of her eyebrows.

Graham inclined his head. "So it appears."

In Sterling Peak, Graham had been coordinating with Sheila since he'd been made Commander. They had succeeded in at least interrupting several attacks, but it had done nothing to stem the tide.

But someone had been doing the same on the other side of the bridge. Over the last two years, he and his fellow fighters had seen more and more evidence that someone was not only fighting the demons but winning. The victims they had come across had been nothing but effusive. Yet they hadn't been able to describe their hero.

Graham had just about lost his mind when the first one suggested it was a slight female. The individual's face had been covered with a veil that went up to her eyes so that the victims could describe no more of her than her size and the color of her eyes—a bright blue. Every victim since had been adamant that the individual who had defended them from the demon, the individual who had *defeated* the demon, had been most decidedly female.

Graham wasn't sure what to do with that information. He had investigated every blue-eyed woman in Sterling Peak. The only blue-eyed women here were either too young, too fat, or too old to possibly be the one they were talking about. So who exactly was the one-woman vigilante team?

He didn't think he'd find her in Sterling Peak, though, because that was not the area that she was trying to protect. No, she was on duty in Blue Forks. And she had proven to be much more efficient than Graham's own security detail. It required two or three Rangers working together to take down a demon. It was galling.

So last night he was unsurprised to find evidence of yet another demon being taken down. This time, though, he'd been unable to find a victim. It had been too late to knock on doors when he found the scene, but he'd asked around this morning. No one reported seeing or hearing anything. But hopefully by the end of the day he would learn who the victim was.

Of course, that wasn't getting him any closer to finding the professor.

When Graham had met him, Marcus had also been a man searching for answers. His wife had been killed in a demon attack ten years earlier. Together, Marcus and his wife had been researching demons for decades. After Helen died, Marcus had redoubled his efforts. He'd given up his home and his teaching position to search the world for answers. He and Graham had stayed in touch, and Marcus had contacted him just a month ago to say that he'd uncovered something that he thought could change everything.

So Graham had invited him to Sterling Peak. Through his travels, and as the leader of the Seraph Force, Graham had amassed a collection of occult and supernatural tomes and weapons that would surpass any universities. Whatever Marcus had found, it would be best if they staged the next move from here, where Graham had resources at his fingertips.

But Marcus had never shown up. Graham had gotten word that the ship Marcus had sailed on had arrived, and Marcus had disembarked yesterday. Marcus had elected to walk, which was not surprising. It would have taken him most of the day to get to Sterling Peak. He should've arrived by nightfall at the latest though.

But there'd been no sign of him after the docks. And there was still was no sign of him. That had Graham beyond worried. He had no idea what the organization of the demons was like. But there was a good chance they knew that Marcus was looking for a way to stop them. And if Marcus was right and he was getting close, it wasn't exactly a stretch to imagine the demons might target him.

Marcus himself had mentioned that he'd barely escaped two previous demon attacks.

And now he was afraid that his friend's luck had run out.

Graham downed coffee and placed the mug on the counter. "Okay. I'll do another sweep of Blue Forks, maybe take the road down to the old dock. It's entirely possible that—"

The doorbell chimed. Graham's head jerked up, his eyes narrowing before he hastened to the front door. Anyone in the search party would have just come around the side and let themselves in.

But Marcus wouldn't be comfortable doing that. He'd never been here before. It seemed unlikely, however, that he'd be the one standing at the front door. Nevertheless, Graham's hopes raised.

He hustled down the long hallway, cursing his family and their extravagant ways. His home was a fifteen-bedroom behemoth. There were an additional twenty bathrooms and two full kitchens. Plus a pool, tennis court, and even a bowling alley. His father had built it fifty years ago. While people were fighting and dying, his father had made sure that his family lived in the lap of luxury.

Graham curled his lip at the thought of dear old dad. They'd never seen eye to eye. Graham was the second son, the less important one. His father had given all his attention to Brock. But Graham supposed that was a blessing. Mary Elise and Franklin had basically raised him. They'd been his de facto parents. And whereas his own parents had turned Brock into a cruel, arrogant man, Mary Elise and Franklin had emphasized compassion and integrity. In many ways, Graham knew he'd been the lucky one.

When Brock died, his parents had taken it hard. But perhaps even harder for his father was the idea that one day his beloved legacy would end up in the hands of the son who hated him.

His father had taken off for a tour of Europe with his mother shortly thereafter. They returned every once in a while for a week, sometimes three, before taking off for another travel. Graham liked to think it was his presence that was driving his father away, but he knew it was the ghost of Brock.

It took Graham a full two minutes to reach the front of the house, by which time the doorbell had rung an additional two times. Obviously whoever was behind the door was unfamiliar with how long it took to reach it.

Graham pulled the door open.

Marcus whirled around, his face lighting up. "Graham! It *is* the right house. I was beginning to worry that—"

Graham pulled him close and hugged him tight. "Marcus."

Marcus patted him awkwardly on the back. "Good to see you too, son."

Graham released Marcus, emotion making his voice harsher than he intended. "Where have you been? I've been looking for you—"

For the first time, he noticed Sheila standing at the edge of the landing. "Sheila. Thank you for bringing the professor to me."

Sheila inclined her head. "I can't really take responsibility for this one. I met him at the gate of the bridge. Addison Baker is responsible for the safe return of your friend here."

Graham didn't recognize the name. That was a question for a later time. "Yes, well, thanks to her, then. I'll be sure to reach out to her."

"Have a good day, Graham. Nice to meet you, Professor." She turned and headed back down the drive.

Graham turned to the professor and raised an eyebrow. "What happened?"

The professor grinned in response. "Do I have a story to tell you."

~

Graham wanted to demand answers from Marcus immediately, but manners had been instilled in him from birth, so he showed Marcus to a guest room and gave him time to get situated. After Marcus took a shower and filled his belly, he sat at the table with Graham, Mary, Franklin, and Donovan, who'd arrived to find out what had happened.

As Marcus told his story for the second time, Graham wanted to know exactly how hard Marcus had hit his head.

"So you're saying some tiny slip of a girl took on a demon all by herself?" Donovan leaned back in his chair. He raised the dark sculpted eyebrows that drove the ladies more than a little bonkers in Sterling Peak and anywhere else he went.

Marcus nodded eagerly. "I couldn't believe it myself. She did it. The demon had his arm out. He was about to run me through, and she got in between us and stopped him."

"You said she denied it was her," Graham said.

"Yes, yes. I was confused at first after the attack. But I know what I saw. She was the one who saved me."

Graham leaned forward. "So how exactly did she stop him? A sword? A club?"

Marcus shook his head. "No. She grabbed his arm. She blocked his arm with her own."

Donovan sat back, shaking his head. "That's impossible. A grown man can't do that. *I* can't do that. And you're telling me some little tiny girl held off a demon on her own with what, a tiny little knife?"

"I know it sounds crazy. I have never seen anything like it

before. But she did. She held him off. She fought him off. And she won."

Everyone was silent. Graham didn't know what to think. He was glad to see that Marcus was home and safe, although he was beginning to doubt exactly how healthy he was. Maybe all of this focus since Helen's death had put a strain on his mind. He wouldn't be the first one to go a little nuts when demon hunting. There was one guy he'd come across in Germany who had raved about invisible demons talking to him. Before that, he'd been one of the top hunters in the nation.

"I promise I'm not crazy. She really did protect me. And then, somehow, she even got me back to her apartment."

Donovan wiggled his eyebrows. "Now you're getting somewhere."

Marcus gave him a look of reproach. "Where she lives with the two wards that she's taken on."

Donovan looked properly chastened.

Marcus continued. "Although she didn't specifically say so, I could tell that going out and taking on demons wasn't exactly news to her two wards. It did look as if it made them uncomfortable or at least worried, so she tried not to mention it."

Mary piped up. "Perhaps she's your Masked Avenger."

Graham's gaze darted toward her. He hadn't even thought of that. Despite the eyewitnesses, he'd been looking for someone like either him or Donovan—over six feet tall, lots of muscles, trained in warfare. Although whoever it was had been protecting Blue Forks, a *female* from Blue Forks hadn't even entered his mind except for Bertha down at the café. She looked like she could take on a legion of demons. Her fighting skills, however, left a great deal to be desired.

Not that he didn't know any tough female warriors. It's just that they trained for years to have that skill. And no one down in Blue Forks would have the time for that. They were too busy working to survive.

"All the victims and witnesses said that the Avenger was a small female," Franklin reminded him.

Graham nodded his head slowly, his mind struggling to accept that fact. He honestly thought that the witnesses had been mistaken. It had always been night when the attacks had occurred. He knew from experience that demon attacks happened so fast that it was hard to see what was going on. He thought perhaps the demons were just very large, making the Avenger look smaller in comparison. But if Marcus was right ... "Her eyes. What color are Addison Baker's eyes?"

"Blue," said Marcus. "The most brilliant shade of blue."

CHAPTER 11

ADDIE

I had put in a full day and was more than ready to end it when four o'clock rolled around. Thankfully, Mrs. Uriel was out and therefore couldn't hold me over again. The extra money from the last two days would be good, but I needed a break.

As I stepped outside of the Uriel property, my gaze shifted toward the Michael estate. I wondered how Marcus was getting on. But being that Graham Michael was looking for him, I was sure that he would be all right.

I really wanted to go see for myself. But a Demon Cursed did not just invite themselves over to a home in Sterling Peak. So after one last look at the Michael estate, I turned toward the bridge. As promised, Beth had packed some extra tarts for the kids as well as the leftover chicken from last night's dinner. We would eat well tonight.

I was halfway down the hill when Sheila pulled her golf cart to a stop next to me. "Want a ride?"

I grinned as I climbed in. "Two times in one day? To what do I owe the pleasure?" Then I frowned. "You're not taking back Saturday night's invitation, are you?"

Sheila laughed as she started us down the hill. "Absolutely not. Marjorie is so excited. She's working on a new masterpiece to show you."

I watched Sheila from the corner of my eye. There was something about her tone. "All right, spill it. What's going on?"

"I just thought I should give you a heads-up. I dropped Marcus off at the Michael estate."

"Is everything all right? Is he okay?" I flashed on him dropping into a faint. Maybe something had been wrong with him. I should have checked him closer.

"No, he's fine. In fact, according to Marcus, he's fine thanks to you."

I groaned. He hadn't bought my story that I'd just come across him in the dark, in the back of an alley, in the rain, right after someone else had saved his life. I can't imagine why. It was so convincing.

Sheila watched the road with one eye, me with the other. "Yup. I'm afraid the Masked Avenger has just been unmasked."

Sheila had known about my daily activities almost since they began. But she understood why I wanted to keep it a secret. I couldn't let anything endanger Noel, Micah, and my living arrangement. And being it wasn't exactly legal, I certainly didn't want anything official happening.

"What will happen now?" I asked.

Sheila glanced around before lowering her voice. "I can't say for sure. I do know that the Seraph Force has been awfully curious about you, especially Graham. I just wanted to give you a heads-up and warn you that he'll probably reach out to you, and soon."

I groaned again. "Is there any way you can stop him?"

Sheila gave a good-natured laugh. "Have you seen the size of that man? I'm not sure that anyone could stop him. And most girls would be quite happy to have his attention."

"Yeah, I don't need his attention, not any of it."

"Well, I'm afraid you have it."

I slumped down in the seat, trying to figure out if there was anything else I could have done. I suppose I could have knocked the professor out before I took out the demon. Or better yet, the demon could have knocked him out. *That* would have been helpful. I sighed. "No good deed, huh?"

"I'm sure you'll be fine. He'll probably just stop in to say thank you. After all, I doubt he even believes it."

I perked up at that statement. "That would be great."

"But I wouldn't count on it. He might not believe it right now, but he will eventually come around. And he will probably try to recruit you for the Seraph Force."

I was already shaking my head.

Sheila ignored it. "It would be a great thing for you and the kids. The guy has a lot of pull. He could make you guys an official family and then you guys could be over here in Sterling Peak."

I shook my head, even though the idea had a lot of appeal. "You guys already have enough security. The people in Blue Forks don't. Have there been any more discussions of starting patrols over there?"

Sheila frowned. "Graham mentioned it at the last Council meeting, but they tabled it. I haven't been able to speak to him directly about it since then. Sasha Gabriel still has a lot of sway on the Council, and I don't think he'll support extending security over there. But Graham is receptive to the idea. He's not like the other ones."

Sheila slowed the cart and waved for the men to move the barricades. Once they were clear, she drove onto the bridge.

I sighed. "Well, hopefully this will all blow over. I'm sure he's got too much on his mind to worry about some no-name over in Blue Forks."

Sheila pulled the cart to a stop. "I told you, Graham isn't like the other ones. He'll want to talk to you."

I climbed out of the cart, thinking of all the parties I'd seen with Graham's peers. They seemed much more concerned with getting underneath someone's skirt than with considering the weighty issues of the day. And the Seraph Force focused their attention on Sterling Peak. The only time they seemed interested in someone from Blue Forks was if they'd broken the law or if they needed to scratch an itch. And as soon as it was scratched, they disappeared.

It was tempting to imagine living on the other side of the bridge. But the decision to let me keep Noel and Micah wouldn't be up to just Graham, and I couldn't take that chance. There were too many potential downsides.

I shook my head. "No. I think he'll already have forgotten about it. I don't think I'll be hearing from Graham Michael anytime soon unless it's a request for more champagne at one of the Angel Blessed parties."

CHAPTER 12

GRAHAM

George, the guard for the Uriels' side door, still had callouses on the palm of his hands from his training back when he was a member of the Seraph Force. He'd been a decent soldier back in his day—consistent, dependable, and strong as a bear. His grip showed that while his hair may have grayed, his strength had waned little. "Thanks for talking to me, George. I really appreciate it."

George's mouth disappeared into his mustache as he smiled. "Any time, Graham. And that Addie, she really is a good person. I mean, for her sake, it would be great if she got a job on your estate. Sure would be a loss for the rest of us, though."

"Nothing is set in stone yet. But I appreciate you taking the time to talk to me."

"It's nice how you take an active interest in the hiring of your staff. Not a lot of people do."

Graham smiled. "If she's going to be working with my staff, I need to make sure she's on the up and up."

"You couldn't find anyone better than Addie. She's completely trustworthy, just an all-around good person."

"Thanks, George. I appreciate it. Have a good one."

"You too, Graham, you too."

Graham turned toward his estate with George's words echoing through his head. *Trustworthy. A good person.*

It was not the first time Graham had heard those words. Every single staff member that Graham had interviewed at the Uriel estate had said the same thing. Everyone seemed to love Addie. Not just because she was friendly, but because she was also genuinely helpful and kind.

And she'd helped out more than one individual without being asked. In fact, the story George had told him was the last in a long line of good deeds. A few months back, the granddaughter of Beth, the Uriels' chef, had been sick for two days. She needed a special medicine, but Mrs. Uriel wouldn't give Beth the time off to go one town over to get it. It was a four-hour walk one way. Addie had gone on her day off to get it for her without even being asked.

Each of the staff had some story like that. But none of them suggested that Addie was the Masked Avenger. In fact, all of them seemed to suggest that she was just sweet. That sweet image simply didn't go along with the person who Marcus had described. It worked with a woman helping a man down on his luck. It just didn't go along with her also being a demon-fighting army of one.

Graham didn't know why he was fighting this so hard. Maybe he'd just built up an image of what the Masked Avenger looked like, and the woman Marcus described simply didn't fit the bill.

Graham walked around the side of the house and let himself in through the smaller side door. He hated the front entryway. It was just too much. But his parents loved it, especially his father. He loved the look that crossed people's faces when they saw it for the first time. They were awed, jealous, and most importantly, intimidated.

Stepping into the kitchen, Graham caught sight of a familiar pair of leather boots propped up on the edge of the table. "Don't let Mary catch you with your feet on her table."

Donovan quickly swiped them off. "Don't tell her."

Graham grinned. There wasn't much that put fear into Donovan, but Mary being upset with him definitely did. Although Graham supposed it wasn't really fear, more that he didn't want to disappoint her.

None of the members of the Seraph Force did.

Mary and Franklin had been like surrogate parents to all of them. They'd never had kids of their own, but they'd been with Graham's family since before Graham had been born. Whereas Graham's parents had been cold and standoffish, Graham's childhood memories were of hugs and laughter in Mary and Franklin's kitchen. Graham might not have a lot of warm feelings toward his own parents, but he was forever grateful that they had brought Mary and Franklin into his life.

Pinching a croissant from the plate on the table, Graham took a seat across from Donovan. "So what did you find out?"

Donovan wiped his hands together, croissant crumbs falling onto the plate in front of him. "Not much. She is a woman of mystery. The first record of her only goes back about twenty months. I don't have any record of her before that."

That didn't necessarily mean anything. It wasn't unusual for Demon Cursed to slip from town to town, leaving no paper trail behind them.

"Any record of her having wards?"

Donovan shook his head. "Not legally. But that doesn't rule out the possibility that she's doing it unofficially."

People did sometimes take on wards illegally, but usually there was some familial connection, they had something to hide, or they just didn't want the Blessed in their lives.

Graham couldn't blame them for that. Abuse was rampant within the system. Taking children away from someone over money was not unheard of. And taking in wards unofficially seemed to fit the profile that the staff at the Uriel house had provided.

It wasn't her taking on two wards that he was having trouble with, or her helping Marcus and escorting him back to Sterling Peak this morning. It was the idea that somehow this slim young woman had taken on a demon in hand-to-hand combat and won. And if she was actually the Avenger, then she had done it several times. That was the issue Graham was having trouble with.

At the same time, Graham couldn't help but wonder if maybe that was just him being a sexist. He'd met more than a few female warriors in his time that he wouldn't want to go up against. But they'd had extensive training. This woman was twenty-four at best. And if she'd had extensive training, she would probably be doing something other than serving the Uriels.

"None of this makes sense." Graham stood, wiping his hands off.

Donovan was in the middle of reaching for another croissant. He raised his eyebrows. "Where are you going?"

"To talk to Addison Baker."

CHAPTER 13

"You didn't have to come, Marcus."

Graham scanned the street as he walked. Darkness had fallen about an hour ago. He'd planned on heading right to Addison's home after speaking with Donovan, but he knew he couldn't arrive empty-handed. After all, she did help out Marcus last night. So he'd asked Mary what he should bring. Once Mary learned what he was doing, she'd insisted on filling a few packs, which had taken a while. It was dark before he even stepped outside. He thought for a moment about postponing until tomorrow, but he really wanted some answers.

But Graham also didn't like being in Blue Forks after dark with Marcus. Marcus had a brilliant mind, but he was not much of a fighter.

"What are you worried about? He's got you, and more importantly, he's got me." Donovan slapped Marcus on the back. "He'll be fine."

Marcus stumbled forward a little bit with a wince.

Donovan tagged along, for which Graham was grateful. If a demon showed up, Donovan would get Marcus to safety while Graham handled the situation.

Hopefully.

Straightening, Marcus glared at Donovan. "Yes, well, I wanted to express my thanks again to Addison. Without her help... well, I would've been in a lot of trouble. And I feel the least I can do is make up for some of the food that I ate. I don't think she had much to share, and yet she didn't hesitate."

Graham felt a twinge of guilt at his words. He knew that people down in Blue Forks struggled. Yet Graham had made precious little headway in getting anyone in Sterling Peak to change the way things happened. Truth be told, Graham rarely thought about the plight of the people down in Blue Forks, except for their physical safety. Their comfort in their everyday lives wasn't one of his chief focuses.

And Marcus was making him realize that perhaps it should be.

They'd turned onto the principal street, or at least what would pass for a principal street. Half the buildings were left over from before the Angel War. The recent constructions, if possible, looked worse than the older ones. They were made from whatever scrap material people could hobble together.

He'd never really contemplated how people lived over here. Part of him had always thought they deserved to live this way. That they'd deserved this. After all, they were Demon Cursed. His entire life, all of Angel Blessed society told him either directly or indirectly, that they were paying a penance for their birth.

But his travels had shaken that belief. Mary and Franklin had shaken that belief. They were Demon Cursed too. He'd somehow come to believe that the prejudices didn't apply to them, but until he'd met Marcus, he'd never really expanded that view beyond them. Those prejudices had justified treating people as second-class citizens for no other reason than where they'd been born.

It had opened his eyes. And it was making him really uncomfortable.

Marcus paused, looking around. He pointed to a two-story brick building. "I think it's that building over there."

According to what information Donovan had found, Addison Baker rented the second floor. It was a two-bedroom apartment. There was another two-bedroom apartment on the first floor.

Marcus had moved down the street and stopped across the road. Graham and Donavan stopped next to him. The old brick building was in decent shape, at least for a building in Blue Forks. It looked like it had once been a dress shop. There was still the faded outline of a dress on the side wall. But the front door had long ago lost its paint. Part of the door jutted out, warped by water over the years, leaving him surprised it even closed. It certainly wouldn't keep anyone out.

The plumbing was no doubt wretched, and the walls were probably peeling paint. He'd been in buildings in Forks before, but usually that had been while running down someone who'd done something that made them deserving to live in such a place. This was the first time he'd be *visiting* someone who lived here.

And what a pretentious jerk that makes me.

Donovan looked at the apartment building and then back at Graham and Marcus again. "What are we waiting for? An invitation? Let's get going."

Shaking himself, Graham crossed the street. Marcus adjusted the bag he held on his back. Bottles clinked. They were full of pomegranate juice, one of Graham's favorites, and some of the last bottles in Graham's pantry. But he could always get more. And Marcus was right—Addison and her wards had helped Marcus out. The least he could do was to provide some food and drink. His own pack was weighed down with food, as was Donovan's. Mary had really gone overboard.

There was a small foyer on the first floor of the apartment complex. A door to the left led to the first-floor apartment, and the stairs straight ahead led up to the second-floor apartment.

"I'll do a quick perimeter check, and then I'll meet you upstairs." Donovan stepped back outside, shutting the door behind him.

There was peeling paint on the walls like Graham had suspected. The handrail was long gone. Holes in the walls showed where it had once been secured.

Marcus edged past Graham and hurried up the stairs. He knocked quickly on the door.

"Who is it?" a young male voice asked.

"It's Marcus. From last night?"

After a moment, the door's locks clicked and swung wide. Standing in the doorway was Addison Baker.

She was stunning. She had long chestnut-colored hair, skin so pale it looked like smooth porcelain, heart shaped lips, and the brightest blue eyes Graham had ever seen. She wore jeans and a T-shirt, which in no way took away from her beauty. In fact, it enhanced it. She was a woman comfortable in her own skin.

And she was the servant who'd fallen into his arms at the Uriels' home.

Graham stepped forward. "It's you."

She crossed her arms over her chest, looking uncomfortable. "Uh, hi. What are you doing here?"

Marcus pushed Graham aside. "You two know each other?"

"Uh, not really. I just saw Commander Graham at work the other day." Addie flicked those bright blue eyes toward him before directing her attention back to Marcus.

Marcus smiled. "I wanted to say thank you for everything you did for me last night. And so I brought you a thank-you present."

Addison's face softened as she spoke to Marcus. "That wasn't necessary. We were happy to help."

A young boy peered around her side. "There's a present?"

Marcus laughed. "Just some food and drinks. I thought I'd bring dinner, seeing as how I ate all of yours last night."

Graham could tell that Addison wasn't sure about inviting them in. But she glanced back at the boy, and then at the tall, blonde girl who now stood at the boy's shoulder, hopeful looks on both of their faces. With a sigh, she stepped aside. "Please come in."

CHAPTER 14

ADDIE

I was happy to see Marcus again and glad to know he had a place in Sterling Peak. But I wasn't sure what to make of Graham Michael being in my kitchen. Well, my kitchen, which was also my bedroom and my living room.

I mean, Graham was a large guy, but this close up, he seemed even larger. And my place seemed even smaller. In fact, if his home was anything like the Uriels, my entire apartment probably fit in their front foyer.

Internally, I chastised myself for my thoughts. I had nothing to be embarrassed about. We lived honestly. And we took care of each other. And that was all that mattered. I took the bag from Marcus, noting the weight with some surprise. "How are you feeling?"

He patted my hand. "Much, much better. I'm afraid I didn't eat or drink enough in the last few days before I set off on my long walk. And then, add in the demon fighting, and well, it was all a little too much for me."

"But you're all right now?" Micah asked.

"I'm fine. Mary, that's Graham here's cook, has been feeding me all day. In fact ..." He opened up the bag I'd placed on the table. "She loaded us up with dinner for about eighteen." He started pulling box after box and bottle after bottle out of his pack.

Graham put his pack down as well and started pulling more boxes out.

I shook my head. "This is too much. We only gave you a little bit, and—"

"Miss Baker, I really appreciate what you did for my friend. Please let us do this." Graham's dark eyes stared into mine.

Butterflies took off in my stomach as I tore my gaze away. No good came from feeling like that. *He's not an option*, I reminded myself. But my imagination was not listening to me as I stared at the bulging veins in his forearms as he placed pomegranate juice on the table.

A knock sounded at the door. Glad for the distraction but also confused, I glanced over at Torr, who sat in the room's corner perched on my bed. He didn't look at all alarmed, so I knew whoever was at the door wasn't a danger.

"That's my friend Donovan," Graham said.

Noel crossed the room. "I got it."

She pulled open the door, and what I can only describe as a Viking stepped into our living room. Donovan was the same size as Graham, and with two of them in the room, it seemed like they had halved the available space.

Noel stared at him with her jaw practically on the ground. I hid my smile at her befuddled look. I couldn't blame her. Donovan was gorgeous. He had jet-black hair long enough to tuck back behind his ears. Light-brown eyes stared from his chiseled face, and his shoulders were almost as wide as the doorway. He had to turn slightly sideways to make it through the door. "Well, it looks like the party has started."

Marcus introduced me to Donovan, who took my hand and kissed the back of it. "Ah, the heroine."

I pulled my hand back, rolling my eyes as I turned to Noel and Micah and introduced them. Donovan gave them an easy smile and shook Micah's hand before kissing the back of Noel's. Her cheeks flamed, and for the first time ever, she seemed at a loss for words.

But Micah wasn't. "Are you part of the Seraph Force?"

"I sure am. And we're always looking for new recruits. Are you applying?"

Micah tilted his head, considering the offer. "No. Noel and Addie need me. But I can fight. Noel too. Addie taught us."

"Then you must be very good," Graham said, his eyes focused on me.

I told myself to look away. And yet my gaze stayed locked with his.

"We are," Micah said, puffing out his chest.

I finally wrenched my gaze away, my heart rate racing more than during a demon attack. *Oh, Graham Michael you are dangerous to my world.*

Donovan laughed, but not at Micah. "Now that's what I like to hear. Confidence."

Donovan and Marcus kept up a constant conversation with Noel and Micah. I could see why women threw themselves at Donovan. He was beautiful, but it was more than that. There was something about him that just pulled people in, adult and child alike.

Graham, however, was carefully laying out food, pulling out plates and silverware from God knows where, some other pockets in that giant sack that he'd carried, maybe. It looked like Donovan was the social one, but Graham was the one who got things done. An interesting dynamic.

Despite the incredible beauty of both men, I kept finding my gaze going back to Graham. Donovan was gorgeous, but there was something about Graham that pulled at me in a way that Donovan didn't.

Once all the food was laid out, there was an awkward moment when we realized there weren't enough chairs for everyone. But Marcus just grabbed a plate, loaded it up, and then sat on the couch. Everyone followed suit.

I noticed Graham and Donovan took very little, no doubt wanting to leave as much for the rest of us as possible. I felt a second twinge of embarrassment. But the kids were happy, and honestly that was all that mattered. They loaded up their plates. I had to stop Micah from loading his plate so high that food would topple off. "You can always come back for more."

He looked at me in shock, as if the idea of getting second helpings was something completely foreign to him. And I realized it was. I couldn't remember the last time we did second helpings of anything. I'm not sure we ever had.

He smiled at me, a smile so filled with happiness that it made my throat catch. I wanted to see that look more often. I wanted to know that his belly was full and that his heart was light if even for a moment.

I caught Graham's gaze on me yet again. We shared a look of understanding. He knew what this meant to Micah, and he was just glad to be able to make a young boy happy.

I smiled back at him. The feeling of warmth that spread through me worried me as much as the butterflies. Butterflies were a sign of lust, desire. That was okay. I could deal with that.

But warmth. Warmth was a sign of something deeper.

I turned away, making myself a small plate. I started to pull one of the kitchen chairs into the living room.

"Let me get that," Graham said, taking the chair from me.

Our fingers touched. Electricity raced through my arm, and I even felt light-headed. "Uh, thanks," I mumbled.

He set the chair down at the edge of the couch, and after I took a seat, placed another next to it. He took a seat in that one. No one was paying us any attention. Marcus and Donovan were telling the kids a story about some fishing trip in Spain that took a turn when sharks started to circle the boat.

The kids were leaning forward, listening eagerly.

"And so I stood on the bow of the boat, vowing to save my friends," Donovan said, his hand to his chest.

"That's not how it happened," Graham murmured to me.

"So how did it happen?" I whispered.

"Donovan got raging drunk and dropped our dinner overboard. The sharks came running. Donovan then passed out after dropping the oars overboard. Marcus and I slowly made our way back to shore, a little hungry but no worse for wear."

Donovan was acting out the lashing rain and howling wind.

"And the hurricane?"

"A little drizzle."

I laughed out loud. A grin spread across Graham's face. If I thought he was hot before, it was nothing compared to that face smiling down at me. And everything else seemed to slip away. I vaguely heard the others talking but wasn't really paying attention.

Until Donovan finished his story and Marcus asked the kids a question. "So, how did you all meet?"

My attention immediately zeroed in on Marcus. Noel didn't even look at me as she answered, her tone breezy. "Oh, we've been together for years. Addie often says she can't even remember a time before we were together."

I took a bite of potatoes to hide my smile. God, I loved her.

Micah immediately piped up. "Have you ever been to Egypt?"

"I haven't," Donovan said, "but Marcus has."

"Really? What's it like?" Noel asked.

And this time I knew she wasn't pretending. History fascinated her, and Egypt was one of her favorite places to read about.

Marcus leaned back, his hand on his stomach. "Oh, it's incredible." He launched into a description of the pyramids. An hour passed, and the conversation flowed without a single break. There were lots of laughs. Torr even crept a little closer while staying well out of anyone's way. And I caught more than a few smiles on his face as he listened in.

Donovan eventually looked at his watch and nodded to Graham.

Graham stood up. "I'm sorry to break this up, but I'm afraid we need to get back."

The feeling of disappointment that flowed over me surprised me. I'd forgotten for a minute that these three men weren't our friends. I'd forgotten we barely knew them. I'd forgotten about demons, Blue Forks, Sterling Peak, and everything else that existed outside this room. It was like a contentment bubble had dropped over the room, insulating us from all the worries of the world.

But Graham's words popped that bubble, and reality crashed back in. These guys weren't our friends. Graham and Donovan were Sterling Peak elites.

"Of course," I said, getting to my feet, my voice stiff. "I'm sorry we kept you."

Donovan stretched his arms above his head, turning his back to work out a kink. "Are you kidding? This has been great." He stood up and nodded at Micah. "And I'll be back to challenge this one to chess, being he thinks he's so good."

Micah and Donovan had traded quips about their chess ability.

His awe of the man long gone, Micah grinned. "Anytime, big man."

Donovan laughed out loud at the statement.

Marcus took Noel's hand. "And I'll bring by those books I told you about. I think you'll really enjoy them."

Noel's eyes shone. If there was one thing that Noel loved in this world, it was reading. "Thank you. That would be wonderful."

The men brought their plates back into the kitchen without

being told. Grudgingly, I had to admit someone had raised them right.

Before I knew it, they were heading for the door.

Graham stopped next to me. It surprised me how far back I had to crane my neck to look up at him. "Could I speak with you privately for a moment, Miss Baker?"

"Addie. Everybody calls me Addie."

"Addie," he said softly.

And God help me, but I loved the way my name sounded on his tongue.

"I'll be outside for a bit," I told the kids with a quick glance at Torr, who gave me a nod.

We walked out into the hallway. Donovan and Marcus went down the stairs ahead of us. We stepped out into the night, and I stopped. "What is it?"

"Marcus said that you helped him in an alleyway and that you saved him from a demon."

I kept my voice even. "No. I found him after the demon attack. By the time I got there, it was only Marcus lying on the ground. He was out cold, so I brought him back here, and by the time I got him here, he woke up. It was raining, so I let him stay the night. That's all."

Graham looked down at me, as if trying to gauge if I was telling him the truth.

Struggling to keep my expression neutral and not look away from his gaze, I gave a slight laugh. "Although it would be really cool if I could take down a demon. The kids would love it."

Graham gave me another smile. "That's what I thought. Marcus must have been mistaken. I mean, demons are incredibly powerful, and it takes two, maybe three grown men to take one down. And no offense, but you're not all that big."

For the first time in my life, I was kind of insulted at being told I wasn't that big, or at least I think it was the first time in my life I was insulted by it. I took a step back, trying to rein in my annoyance. "Right, well, thank you for the food. I really appreciate it."

Graham frowned. "I think I've insulted you somehow."

I took a breath, annoyed that I was annoyed. This is what I wanted, though, for him to not connect me with the attack. "No, not at all. I just don't like leaving the demons alone at night. I mean, the kids. Be careful heading back to Sterling Peak."

I turned and fled back into the house, feeling my cheeks heat. What the heck was that? I'd never gotten so tongue-tied around anyone in my life.

It was over. It didn't matter. Graham would forget about us soon enough. Which was for the best. I didn't need to be a notch on someone's belt.

I opened the apartment door. Noel and Micah looked up from their spots on the couch. It looked like they'd started to clean up and then got waylaid by a second helping of dessert.

"There's more dessert," Micah said around a mouthful of chocolate.

Noel grinned at me. "So good."

I smiled at their happiness but also knew that it was my job to bring us back to reality. "Well, enjoy it, because this isn't going to be a regular thing. So we need to save as much as we can for later. When you're done, we'll see what we can freeze for some other nights and then kind of make our plan for the rest of the week, okay?"

They both nodded, their mouths too full to answer. Once Micah swallowed, he asked, "Do you think Donovan will really come back and play chess with me?"

My heart broke at the hopefulness in his voice. And I realized that Marcus, Graham, and Donovan were the first guests we'd ever had to the apartment. I probably needed to warn him not to get his hopes up. "I don't know. He seems pretty busy, but it seemed like he wanted to. I'm sure he'll be back, eventually."

Chicken.

Micah gave me another giant smile. He picked up his plate, licking the last of the crumbs off of it. "I'll start going through the food."

Noel came over and stood next to me. She linked her arm through mine, leaning her head on my shoulder. "I wouldn't have been able to tell him the truth either. Don't feel bad."

I let out a sigh and leaned my head into hers. Who knew? Maybe Donovan and Marcus would keep their word. And for the kids' sake, I really hoped they did.

CHAPTER 15

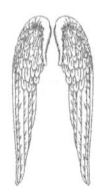

I felt unsettled after Graham, Donovan, and Marcus left. And even the kids seemed a little more subdued, coming down from their sugar and company high. The night had been enjoyable. There'd been a lightness to it we hadn't had in a long time.

Maybe not ever.

With a start, I realized that it was because we had felt safe. I don't think it was just because Graham and Donovan looked like warriors of old. It was because we felt like we weren't on our own. That we had other people, if only for a moment, we could call upon.

But that wasn't true. They had come. They had said thank you. And they had left. We couldn't expect any more from them than that. Heck, most of the residents of Sterling Peak wouldn't have even done that much.

But part of me wondered if maybe it wouldn't have been better if they had never come by at all. They'd given the kids and me a glimpse of what life could be. And it would be hard to shut away the memory of that peek.

Torr had moved to the chair next to my bed. He appeared lost in thought. Apparently the visit had affected all of us. A knock at the door caused all of us to turn.

Hope flared in my chest before I quickly squashed it. It couldn't be Graham.

Manny's voice came through the door, confirming my thoughts and extinguishing the hope completely. "Addie?"

I could hear the stress in his voice and hurried over, flinging the door wide. Manny stood in the doorway, wringing his hands. Sweat had broken out across his forehead.

"What's wrong?"

"It's Cecelia. She left."

Cecelia was Manny's sixteen-year-old daughter. She was a good kid, smart. And usually pretty levelheaded.

"What do you mean she left?"

Manny ran his hand through his dark hair and tugged on the ends. "She asked to spend some time with her friends tonight, and I said no, it wasn't safe. She went to her room and slammed the door. Lisa went to go check on her. The room was empty, the window open. She went somewhere. I've searched the streets, but I haven't seen any sign of her. Have you seen her?"

"No. I'm sorry, I haven't. But let me get my jacket, I'll help you look."

Relief flashed across Manny's face before he shook his head. "No, no. You need to stay home with the kids. The demon attacks—"

I grabbed my jacket from the hook by the door. "I'm coming with you."

Manny finally nodded. I turned back to Noel and Micah, who were watching us with big eyes. They'd obviously heard everything. "Keep the door locked and stay inside. I'll be back as soon as we find her." I glanced over at Torr, who gave me a nod.

"Wait." Noel hurried forward as Micah disappeared down the hall. "I might know where she is."

"What? Where?" Manny asked.

"I heard some kids talking about a party on the beach. Over by the old boardwalk. I don't know for sure if she went there. But I know that some kids were talking about going out there tonight."

I closed my eyes in exasperation. The beach was where I'd first woken up. It was my first memory ever. And it was also isolated and far from help. If the demons attacked, there'd be no one to help the kids.

There'd be no one to even hear them scream.

"Here." Micah hurried over with the sword I'd taken off the demon last night. I'd forgotten about it. I'd rigged up a scabbard from some scraps of leather we'd scavenged from an old chair a few weeks earlier when I'd had a vague idea about creating scabbards for Noel and Micah if I managed to get them swords or knives. I slipped it over my shoulder so I could grab it quickly.

Manny's eyes widened at the sight of it, but he didn't say anything else. After eliciting a promise that they'd keep the doors and windows locked, Manny and I hurried down the stairs, bursting out into the night.

And I prayed that we weren't too late.

CHAPTER 16

Manny and I didn't full-out sprint to the beach for two reasons. One, we wanted to keep an eye on our surroundings just in case we missed the kids and they weren't actually at the beach. And two, there was no point sprinting there and then being too winded to fight if we needed to.

It was a good three miles to the beach. The whole way there, I struggled to come up with a reason Cecelia would do something so reckless. How any of the kids could. They knew how dangerous the demon attacks were. They knew they happened at night. Why on earth would they think risking everything to spend some time on a beach was worth it?

Thank God that Noel hadn't gone with them. But maybe she was still too young. Maybe this was what I had to look forward to.

Next to me, Manny didn't say anything. But the look on his face made clear how worried he was. Manny was a wonderful father. When he wasn't working, he was always playing with the kids, laughing with them. If anything happened to Cecelia, it would absolutely break him and Lisa. Blue Forks people didn't have much in terms of material goods. One good aspect of that was that people realized they needed to focus on the important things like family.

Maybe Noel was wrong. Or maybe she was right, but Cecelia wasn't one of the kids by the beach. Ahead, I saw the old fairway where I'd first met Noel and Micah. I pictured the demon from that night. He'd been my first kill. There'd been dozens since then. But I remembered every detail from that first attack. The details from all the attacks in between had faded and blended together, though.

"Look." Manny pointed toward the beach where a glow stood out close to the water's edge.

The kids had created a bonfire. I growled. Why not just put out a "Hey, demons, here we are" sign?

Manny and I picked up our pace. If Cecelia wasn't amongst the kids, we couldn't in good conscience leave the rest of them here. We needed to get them all back home.

The sky was pitch black. Clouds had rolled in, blocking even the stars. But thanks to the flames, I counted seven kids. In the dim light, I couldn't tell if any of them was Cecelia.

Manny grabbed my arm. "She's there." He pointed to a figure at the edge of the group, her arms wrapped around herself, looking uncomfortable.

For a moment, my heart went out to her. She definitely looked like a kid who didn't belong and regretted the choice she'd made. Then my anger returned to the fact that all of these kids were now in danger.

"You see anything?" Manny asked, looking around. I knew he was asking about demons.

"No. I think we got lucky." I didn't add in the "so far". It was still a long walk back to town.

Manny hurried forward and called out. "Cecelia!"

Cecelia's head jumped up as she turned toward her father, her mouth opening in a silent *O*. She took a tentative step backward and then held her ground, realizing there was nowhere to go.

Manny marched over to her, and I knew she was in for the lecture of a lifetime. The other kids stopped to watch, guilty looks on their faces.

I walked over to the remaining kids. "Okay, we need to get you guys home."

One of the kids, a tall blonde-haired boy a little bigger than the others, with the confidence and arrogance that came with youth, smirked. "We're not going anywhere. We didn't break any rules. We're allowed to be out here."

"You're allowed to, but it's stupid. We need to get you home before you attract too much attention."

The cocky kid smiled again. "I'd like to see you make me."

I gritted my teeth. God, I hated kids like him. If he was this arrogant at his age, God help the world when he got older.

If he got older.

I opened my mouth to tell him exactly where he needed to go and how to get there when a scream cut through the night.

"Demons!"

CHAPTER 17

I whirled around, my heart beating furiously. Three hulking figures appeared out of the darkness. The smoke obscured their features as they approached.

Damn it. With the ocean at our back and the rocks lining the sides of the beach, we had no clear avenue of escape.

I pulled my sword from the scabbard. "Get back!" I yelled at the kids. They scrambled behind the bonfire while I stood in front of it.

The cocky kid swallowed hard, standing next to me. His entire body shook as he stared at the approaching demons growing larger.

I flicked a glance at him. "Go. Stay with your friends."

He did as I told him. Manny raced over to me, after pushing Cecelia toward the other kids.

I kept my gaze on the approaching threat as he reached my side. "I'll engage them. When you get a chance, you get the kids out of here and back home."

He shook his head. "I can't leave you here."

"You're not leaving me here. You're getting those kids to safety. *That* is the priority, okay?"

He gave me a small nod, pulling his machete from the holder at his waist.

The demons stepped into the light of the flames. Each of them looked as if someone had sculpted them from hard granite. The firelight highlighted the muscles in their arms and legs. The one in the middle was seven feet tall with green mottled skin. But the other two were shorter, maybe six feet, their skin more gray than green. I'd never seen them attack in a group before. But then again, I didn't know anyone stupid enough to go out in a group at night. Maybe that had attracted them.

In all the time I'd been fighting demons, I knew very little about how they tracked humans. How did they find us? Why did they choose the ones they did? I realized that could be really, really useful information right now.

And if I survived this, I would make sure I tracked down Marcus to see if he could shed any light on it.

One of the smaller demons peeled off, trying to circle around Manny and me to get to the kids.

I shifted my sword to my left hand, pulled my knife from my belt, and hurled it at him. The knife point embedded in the demon's eye. He stopped still and then went face first into the sand.

I let myself have one self-satisfied smile, but that was all I had time for. The large one roared as he sprinted forward, the smaller one close behind.

I darted forward to intercept. The large one swung its claws toward my head. I dropped below him, sliding my sword across his ribs. He screamed as fire erupted from the sword as it made contact.

Shock jolted through me as the fire remained along the blade.

The demon whirled around. "Where did you get that blade?"

I smiled back at him. "I took it off a demon I killed."

The hilt of a blade materialized above his shoulder. The demon pulled his own blade from his back. I felt lightheaded at the sight of it. I thought I had gotten lucky: I had a weapon, and he didn't. But could they all do that? Did they all have access to swords?

The demon's sword ignited, matching mine. Without another word, it lunged toward me. I parried the attack and then slid another hit along the creature's other side.

It bellowed in a rage, swinging wide. I dove low, rolling along the ground, out of his reach. From the corner of my eye, I saw a demon advance on the kids while Manny held another off. Where the hell did the fourth one come from?

"Get in the water!" I yelled at the kids as I scrambled to my feet.

Cecelia grabbed on to the arm of a girl and yanked her toward the water. The other kids followed suit, all of them diving in. With powerful strokes, they swam away from the shore. Manny struggled to fend off his demon. He wouldn't last long. The fourth demon chased the kids to the shore and then roared, not following them in.

I rolled to my feet as my demon lurched toward me. Distracted by the appearance of the fourth demon and Manny's fight, I barely avoided his next thrust. I felt the heat of the sword along my cheek.

I couldn't help anyone else if I was dead. I had to focus.

Another shape lumbered out of the darkness. What the hell? Where were they all coming from?

The demon stepped into the light. Another big one, its skin green mottled with brown spots. It raced toward me and reached out with both arms as if it would bear-hug me. I dropped to the ground, rolling between his legs and sliding my sword along its knee, cutting the tendons there. With a scream, it collapsed, its leg useless.

I jumped to my feet and dove over the demon as the other two sprinted for me. The one from the water's edge had apparently decided I was the bigger threat. I kept the fallen demon between us as I saw two more shadows hurrying toward us and down the beach.

I groaned. Seven demons? Come on…

Manny let out a scream.

"Dad!" Cecilia yelled.

I flicked a glance at him and saw the demon struck him along the shoulder. Then an arrow embedded in the demon's back. It arched its torso with a scream. Manny grabbed his machete, and with one clean swipe, took the demon's head half off.

The demons in front of me whirled around. I didn't wait to see who was coming. I thrust my sword through its back, burying it up to the hilt, then yanked it out. And as the creature dropped, I jumped onto its back, using it as a catapult. Swinging with all my might, I sliced across the throat of the largest demon. Its head tipped to the side, and then rolled from its shoulders. The demon's body dropped.

I touched down on its back, rolling off and getting back to my feet as Graham and Donovan stepped into the light.

CHAPTER 18

GRAHAM

Graham couldn't believe his eyes. He had never in all of his life seen anyone fight like that. Addie was graceful and deadly. She didn't even look winded.

Donovan stood next to him, his mouth gaping open. "You saw that, right? I'm not hallucinating?"

Graham shook his head, trying to wrap his mind around the incredible scene he'd just witnessed. "If you're hallucinating, then so am I."

Addie only met his gaze for a moment across the fire before she hurried over to the man she'd been searching with earlier.

After leaving Addie's place, Graham had decided to do a patrol of Blue Forks. It was his night off from patrol with the Seraph Force, but he was antsy. And he needed to do something. Donovan had joined him. So they'd escorted Marcus to the bridge, and after checking in with Sheila, headed back into town. They'd caught sight of Addie and a man walking and followed them.

They'd lost them for a minute. It was only the scream that had led them to the beach.

His heart had been in his throat when he saw Addie facing off against that group of demons. But then shock had turned to an even deeper shock. She moved like no one he'd ever seen. She was tiny, and yet with one slice, she'd taken off that demon's head.

And then there was her sword. It had flames coming off the blade. Where had she gotten that?

Addie turned and yelled out to the water. "It's okay. You guys can come back."

For the first time, Graham noticed people bobbing out in the water. God, he was all sorts of out of it. The group slowly made their way back to shore. They were just kids. The oldest couldn't have been older than seventeen.

Addie reached her friend and was checking out his wound.

"Donovan, check out the kids," Graham ordered, not able to tear his eyes away from Addie.

Donovan nodded and strode toward the water while Graham made his way toward Addie. He inspected her from head to toe but saw no sign of injury. He flicked a glance back at the demons that littered the beach. There were five of them. She had taken on four of them herself.

His mind still struggled to accept it. He'd never heard of that many demons attacking at once. Or maybe demons did attack in groups but no one survived to tell the tale.

So how had Addie survived?

She glanced over her shoulder at him. "He's hurt."

Blood stained the man's shirt, starting at the shoulder. Graham pulled off his shirt, ripping it into strips to wrap around the man's wound. It was an awkward location to wrap. The injury was high up on the shoulder. Graham used the remainder of his shirt to create a sling because the movement of his arm was going to disturb the injury.

"Daddy!"

A young girl soaked from head to toe hurried over to the man. Tears streamed down her cheeks as she wrapped her arms around him. "Daddy, I'm sorry. I'm so sorry."

The man patted her with his uninjured arm. "It's all right. Everything's all right now."

The fire that had been on Addie's blade had been extinguished. She touched the hilt for a second, a look of surprise across her face before she slipped it into a makeshift scabbard on her back.

"Where did you—"

She speared him with a look, a look of confidence and authority. The look of a warrior. "Now's not the time. We need to get these kids home."

He closed his mouth and nodded. She was right. The questions could wait. Getting everyone to safety needed to be the priority. Although he didn't think demons would attack again tonight after having lost so many.

Donovan had all the kids huddled together. He scanned the area, a hard edge to his face. He looked angry on the kids' behalf. He'd slipped into warrior mode as well.

"Let's get everybody back to town," Graham said.

Donovan nodded, his bow and arrow in his hands again. Donovan was the one who'd taken down the fifth demon, the one who'd attacked Addie's friend.

She walked over to the demon she'd beheaded and picked up his sword before she slid it into her scabbard as well. The bodies of the demons burst into flames seconds after she'd removed the sword. He stood next to her and watched the bodies disintegrate into ash.

The flames of the bonfire threw shadows across her face. The angle was just right. They made her blue eyes appear to glow.

Graham couldn't help but think of the paintings he'd seen in Rome of warrior goddesses. Addie deserved to be immortalized in paint exactly as she stood right now.

Beautiful wasn't a strong enough word. Fierce wasn't adequate either, although both applied. She was stunning, lethal, and a complete enigma.

Who exactly was Addie Baker?

CHAPTER 19

ADDIE

The walk back to town was unsettling. I felt Graham's gaze on me more than a few times. He didn't say anything or ask any of the questions I knew he had to have. And I couldn't tell from his expression what he was thinking. Did he think I was a freak? Was he mad? Impressed?

At the same time, I was annoyed that I was even thinking such thoughts. It didn't matter what Graham Michael thought. I had saved those kids, and that was the most important thing. That was all that mattered.

And yet I felt like electricity was traveling over my skin. Why did he make me feel like this? He was not the first guy I'd been attracted to. I'd had a few ... well, I wouldn't call them relationships, but they were fun, at least for a little while. But even without touching me, I felt every move Graham made. The air around him felt charged, and I wanted more than anything to move closer to him.

So I made sure that I stayed on the opposite end of the group from him. I needed my wits about me. I needed to be aware of my surroundings. I didn't know what was up with such a large group of demons attacking at once. But until the kids were safely home, until I was safely home, I couldn't let my guard down.

One by one, we escorted all of the kids back to their homes. All the kids were subdued, even the big blonde kid. His only words on the trip back were a quiet, "Thank you," before he hurried into his house.

Finally, it was just the five of us. Manny looked awfully pale. He'd lost a lot of blood. I glanced at Donovan, him being the safer bet of not have me talking like a tongue-tied schoolgirl. "Do you guys have a doctor that can look at him? That cut is awfully deep."

Manny's head jerked up. His eyes shifted away from both Donovan and Graham. "No, no doctor. We can't … I'll be fine."

But I knew what he meant. He couldn't afford to pay for a doctor. Another luxury that the Demon Cursed could not count on.

"I have a personal physician that I will send first thing in the morning. And don't worry about the bill, I'll take care of it," Graham said.

Manny looked like he was about to argue, his pride not wanting to accept such charity.

Tears flooded Cecelia's eyes. "Thank you. Thank you."

Seeing the relief on her face, he nodded.

I stepped forward to jog ahead to let Lisa know we were back when the apartment building door burst open. Lisa met us halfway across the street. Her eyes first took in Cecelia with relief before they widened at the sight of the makeshift bandage on her husband. "Manny."

She hurried forward, hesitating to wrap her arms around him, no doubt worrying that she would hurt him. Manny lifted up his uninjured arm. Lisa slipped under it, hugging him tight.

Cecelia curled in on her mother's other side, and the family just stood embracing each other.

Graham, Donovan, and I stopped, looking away for a moment

to give the family some privacy. Donovan finally cleared his throat. "I have a little medical training. Would it be all right if I came in and took a look at the cut?"

Lisa wiped at her eyes. "Yes. Yes, thank you very much."

With a quick glance at Graham and a wink at me, Donovan escorted the Sanchez family into their apartment.

Graham turned to face me. "Do you want to go tell your family you're all right?"

I nodded to the windows above. "They already know."

Graham looked up. Noel and Micah were framed by one of the windows, looking down. Micah waved. Graham waved back. Torr stood framed in the other window. It was too dark to make out his expression, but he definitely didn't wave.

I crossed my arms over my chest. "It's been a really long night. How about we save the questions for tomorrow?"

"Will you be at the Uriels tomorrow?"

I shook my head. "No. It's my day off."

He smiled. "Excellent, then I'll bring over breakfast."

CHAPTER 20

Although I told Graham that I didn't want to speak because it had been a long night, I was completely unable to get to sleep that night. After Graham left, I was on a bit of an endorphin high for the next hour at least. Plus, when I got back upstairs, I had to give the kids a blow-by-blow. Torr crept a little closer when I mentioned the fact that there had been multiple demons at the beach.

Finally, I was talked out and beginning to feel the drop that followed the endorphin high. I ushered the kids off to bed and took a short cold shower, trying to wipe away the memories. It didn't entirely work. There had been *five* demons. If Donovan and Graham hadn't come along, Manny would most likely be dead. And who knew, maybe I would be as well. It was only the distraction of their arrival that had allowed me to take down the two I had been fighting with.

Why did the demons show up en masse? Because there'd been a group of kids on the beach? Was it something about being out in the open?

I shut off the water, quickly drying myself and throwing on my pajamas. Normally I didn't mind the cold showers, but tonight

I could have really used a hot one. I wrapped my robe around me as I opened the bathroom door and questions swirled through my mind.

The world had been plagued by demons for 150 years. The attacks only seemed to be increasing in frequency, and yet we still knew precious little about how they attacked and why, only that they seemed to focus on those who were out alone at night.

Why they chose one person over another still remained a mystery. I mean, Marcus wasn't exactly a big guy, but I'd seen demons target strong, muscular individuals, people who would fight back. Sometimes we found the bodies of their victims, and sometimes the person just disappeared. It had gotten to the point that if someone disappeared, it was assumed that they had been the victim of a demon attack.

So what was it the demons were looking for? Was there something about the people in particular that they were targeting, or was it just some sort of random luck? Did they just go after whatever unlucky soul they came across?

As I padded out of the bathroom in my bare feet, I stopped to look in on Noel. She had a book tucked underneath her pillow like she did every night. Some kids had teddy bears; Noel always slept with a book. I closed the door, not letting the lock catch. Neither of the kids wanted their doors completely closed. A sliver of space was necessary for them to feel safe, knowing help was only one quick yell away.

Across the hall was Micah's room. He lay on his stomach, one hand touching the floor. His covers had been thrown off and lay in heap on the ground. Picking them up, I carefully tucked them back around him, smoothing them down before kissing him on the cheek. He was twelve but growing up quickly. A little too quickly as far as I was concerned. Noel too. But I suppose I didn't have any control over that either.

The only thing that made me feel better was the fact that I had prepared them the best I could for what the world might have in store for them. Or more accurately, what the demons might have in store for them.

This was not a world where you could count on someone coming to your aid. You had to be able to defend yourself and those you cared about.

And most importantly, you had to be able to run.

I stood up and walked to the door, pausing to glance back at Micah. If anything happened to either him or Noel, I didn't know what I'd do with myself. They were the only things anchoring me to this world.

I still knew nothing about my life before I woke up on that beach. I didn't know if I fell off a ship and somehow drifted onto the beach. I didn't know if I walked there just to fall unconscious on the sandy shores. I didn't know if I had a huge family teeming with siblings, cousins, and relatives or if I was completely alone in the world.

But none of that mattered. Noel and Micah were my family now. And I would do anything to protect them.

I closed Micah's door, checking in on Noel again before heading to the living room.

Torr sat on the couch. "Are they asleep?" he whispered.

I nodded. "Yes. They're both out cold."

A shimmer rippled over him. He would now be visible to anyone who looked in the room. Keeping himself invisible didn't require too much energy, but he often dropped the invisibility when it was just the two of us. I think psychologically he wanted to be seen, to be a part of this world.

"Do you want something to eat?" I asked as I headed to the kitchen. I'd boiled some water before I'd gone in for my shower. Now, it would be the perfect temperature. I poured the two of us mugs of hot water, dropping a lemon slice in each. Lemons had been in the bag of goodies that had been brought over tonight. I'd grown to like the simple taste of hot water and lemon from working at the Uriels' home.

"I wouldn't mind one of those eclairs if you have any left," Torr said with a hopeful note in his voice as he followed me.

I smiled, pulling one out of the fridge and putting it on a plate for him. As I handed it to him, his eyes lit up, not unlike Micah's had earlier.

I grabbed the mugs of lemon water for both of us, and then we made our way back to the couch.

Torr took a bite of the éclair. He smiled with a sigh, licking his lips. "That is delicious."

"Apparently the Michael's chef is something special."

"That she is." Torr shoved the rest of the éclair into his mouth and licked his fingers. I eyed him as he sat on the corner of the couch. His muscles were accentuated as they pressed against the cushions. Torr was incredibly strong but on a much smaller scale than the other demons, another factor that led me to believe that he was younger than his compatriots. I had the feeling he was probably around Noel's age, although when I asked him, he said they really didn't keep track of time like that.

"So what do you think about tonight? About the demons attacking as a group?" I asked.

"It's not unheard of. Humans tend not to gather in large groups at night anymore, at least not outdoors. Back in the olden days, it wasn't unusual for demons to band together to attack a target."

I sighed, leaning back on the couch and pulling my knees up to my chest. I wrapped my arms around them. "It was scary, Torr. If Manny and I hadn't shown up, all those kids …"

"But you did show up. And you saved them. Focus on that, and not on what could've happened. Focus on what did happen."

I groaned. "Graham and Donovan saw me fight. Graham's coming back in the morning to ask me questions. I don't know what to tell him. I don't know why I can fight the way I do. I don't know why I'm stronger than almost anybody I know. I don't even know my real name. What should I tell him?"

"Whatever you're comfortable telling him. You don't owe him answers. He can't demand something you don't know. If you think something's none of his business, tell him that."

He was right. It wasn't any of Graham's business, not really. But I had a strange feeling that I was at a turning point and that everything was about to change.

CHAPTER 21

GRAHAM

Donovan and Graham spoke long into the night while they tried to unravel the mystery of Addison Baker. Graham still couldn't come to grips with what they had seen. If someone had told him about it, he would've thought they were nuts. Even seeing it, he wondered if maybe he was nuts.

She wasn't waif thin. She was strong. But she shouldn't have been strong enough to fight the way she did. She'd leaped up, and with one sweep, managed to take off that demon's head. He'd never seen anything like it in his life. He didn't think it was even possible.

And that sword of hers had flared to life when she used it. Where had she gotten that? He groaned. "Aw, crap."

"What?"

"The sword. Addie took the sword from the demon she beheaded. I should've taken it from her so we could study it."

Donovan arched an eyebrow. "You should've *taken* it from her? I would have paid to see you try."

Graham glared at him but knew he was right. If she could take down a demon...

Donovan leaned his elbows on the table. "What do you think she is? I mean, she lives down in Forks, but she has to be one of the Angel Blessed, right? Maybe an angel came to town, met up with her mom, and whammo, bammo, little baby Addie was born?"

"I don't know. No Angel Blessed has been born with abilities in generations. And there have been zero sightings of angels in nearly a hundred years."

The Angel Blessed were supposed to be the ones who were descended from the archangels. Back in the early days of the Angel War, when an offspring of the angels had been created, there were all these tales of incredible skills, strength, even wings. But that had been a long time ago. And while an Angel Blessed's kids these days often had a slight edge in the physical realm, it was nothing compared to those early offspring and most likely due to a better diet. Angelic traits had been diluted in each successive generation, until they simply no longer existed.

"She *has* to be a direct descendant of an archangel. Maybe they interacted again with society and no one knew. Someone took a long weekend incognito," Donovan suggested again.

Was Donovan right? Was it possible that an angel had reappeared for a quick dalliance without anyone knowing about it? "It has to be. That's the only thing that makes sense."

Donovan smiled. "I still can't get the image of her swinging at that thing's head out of my mind. That was incredible."

"She didn't hesitate."

"No, she's done this before."

"Yes, that's pretty clear," Graham said dryly.

"So what are you going to do?" Donovan asked.

"I'm going to speak with her in the morning. I'll see what she knows, and then I guess we can just take it from there."

"You need someone to go in there and persuade her? Perhaps I should be the one doing the questioning." He wiggled his eyebrows.

Graham knew exactly what kind of questioning Donovan had in mind.

"You don't touch her." The words were out of Graham's mouth before he even realized he was going to say them.

Donovan's eyebrows shot up before he grinned. "So it's like that."

Graham stood up, carrying his plate over to the sink. "It's not like anything. We need information, and she might have it. I don't want anything getting in the way of that."

"If you say so." Donovan stood up and stretched. "Well, I need a good night's sleep, even though I did very little tonight to earn it. But I think I will keep that image of Addie beheading that demon in the forefront of my mind as I fall off to sleep. Hopefully it will make her the star of my dreams."

Donovan got his plate to the sink and patted Graham on the shoulder. "If it's okay with you, I'm going to bunk in the guest room tonight."

"Ah, I guess your little brother is still home?"

"Sadly, yes, and some of his simpering friends arrived today." Donovan shuddered.

"It's all yours."

"You going up?"

"In a minute. I want to make some notes for Marcus about tonight's attack. You should probably jot down your impressions as well, and we'll discuss it with the Seraph Force tomorrow."

"I will before I go to sleep." Donovan shook his head. "Five demons. I didn't think I'd ever see the day when humans would walk away from that kind of onslaught. It's a whole new world, brother."

"Yes, it is," Graham said softly as he watched Donovan head for the stairs.

He started to wash the dishes, thinking about the attack. But instead of analyzing it, he kept focusing on a mesmerizing pair of blue eyes.

CHAPTER 22

ADDIE

I tossed and turned for most of the night. I think if I was lucky I got about an hour's sleep. I was nervous, actually nervous. Facing down five demons, not a shiver. Sitting down and talking to Graham Michael? I was pretty sure I would barely be able to string a sentence together.

I slipped out of bed early and threw some cold water on my face. Torr was sleeping quietly on the couch. I was glad to see he was still around. Often he'd slip in and out like a ghost in the night as soon as I was awake. He didn't want to chance Noel or Micah coming across him. He was a good man, or I guess a good demon. He should be able to live his life out in the open, not hiding and skulking in the shadows.

The sun was just breaking along the horizon when I decided to go for a run. I needed to feel the ground underneath my feet. I needed to do something. The kids wouldn't be up for at least another hour.

I knelt down next to the couch by Torr, reaching out to touch his shoulder. His eyes opened before I made contact.

"I'm going to go for a run."

He nodded. "I'll keep an eye on everything."

I placed my hand on his shoulder and squeezed gently. "Thank you, Torr, for everything."

He gave me a brief smile before his eyes closed again.

We'd talked late into the night, and I was guessing he hadn't gotten much sleep either.

I silently let myself out of the house and quietly made my way down the stairs. The Sanchezes' apartment was quiet, for which I was grateful. I'd stop in today and see how Manny was doing. I hoped Graham remembered to send his doctor for them.

I stepped outside, arching my back, and took off at a slow pace. My mind turned with worry about the conversation ahead. Graham could make a lot of problems for me if he wanted to. He could put Micah and Noel into the system if he wanted. He had a lot of clout.

I pictured his face, and in my gut I knew he wouldn't do that. He wasn't looking to make problems for us.

He *was* looking for answers, though. But I didn't have any of them. So I needed to decide what to tell him.

Only Noel and Micah knew that I had washed up on the beach two years ago. I told everyone else that we had all moved from a town a few hours down the coast. No one had questioned the story. People moved in and out all the time.

I didn't think Graham was going to buy that story, though, at least not without a few more details.

I picked up my pace, lengthening my stride and letting my mind go blank for a while. I needed to just breathe. What would be would be.

I focused on my pace, going faster and faster. Before I knew it, I had passed out of the Blue Forks boundary. The streets beyond Forks were even less well kept than the streets within it. Nature had quickly reclaimed its due. If I didn't watch my footing, I would trip and sprain an ankle or worse. It kept me a little on edge and definitely more focused, which was what I needed.

I reached the five-mile point and then turned around and headed back, keeping my pace blistering. I needed the run this morning and the clarity it would offer. My mind cleared. It was just me and my trail. There were no demons, no Graham, no stress.

I slowed as I reached our block and then shifted down to a walk, trying to get my breathing under control. A glance at the clock above the bakery told me that with my pace, I'd managed just under six minutes a mile. That was good. It was in keeping with my normal pace.

I was hoping to get it down to five minutes flat, but that would take a little more training than what I was currently capable of, at least for a long run. I could do a four-minute mile for a single mile, but for ten miles like this morning, I was lucky if I managed a 5:45 mile.

By the time I reached the apartment building, my breathing was back to its regular rhythm. I let myself in. The Sanchezes' door opened almost immediately. Lisa stepped into the hall, closing the door behind her.

"Morning, Lisa."

"I didn't get to tell you last night how much we appreciate you going after Cecelia like that. If Manny had gone by himself..." Lisa's eyes filled with tears.

"I was happy to help. How's his shoulder this morning?"

"It's good. Graham's doctor came by about an hour ago. She put some medicine on it and gave us more medicine that we're supposed to use for the next few days. She said he should be fine by the end of the week."

Graham had sent his doctor. A warm feeling again filled my chest. He'd kept his word. "I'm glad he's okay. How's Cecelia?"

"Scared. She didn't even really like those kids. They asked her to go, and she was mad at us, and so..." Lisa's voice dwindled off again. "Luckily they're all home safe, thanks to you. And I think Cecilia's learned a pretty important lesson from all of this."

"That she has."

Lisa wrapped me in a hug, her body trembling. "Thank you, Addie. You're an angel."

She gave me a quick smile before disappearing back into her apartment. I climbed the stairs, feeling a little happier than I had earlier. She'd called me an angel.

While I might not agree with the sentiment, it was nice to know that somebody thought so.

CHAPTER 23

GRAHAM

Graham shifted the baskets from his right hand to his left. They weren't heavy, but he was feeling antsy, unsettled. Nervous.

He huffed out a breath. He rarely got nervous. When he was a kid, his father and brother had beaten and insulted that out of him. He'd learned not to show fear. But today there was no denying it—he was feeling nervous.

Graham had filled the baskets with an assortment of foods, including fruit, for Addie and her family. The second basket was for the Sanchezes on the first floor. He felt a little silly walking around carrying two baskets like he was Dorothy, but there was really no other way to get the food over to them.

He spied the apartment building down the street. There were only a few people out, and for a moment he thought maybe it was too early, that he should circle the block or something. But then he got a hold of himself.

I am Graham Michael, the Commander of the Seraph Force. I do not circle the block. He needed answers to Addie's abilities and not just to satiate his own curiosity. Her skills were incredible and could be very valuable to the Seraph Force. He also needed to see what she knew about demons.

Graham crossed the street, and after letting himself into the apartment building, he knocked quietly on the door downstairs. A sleepy-looking Cecilia opened the door, her dark hair falling into her face. She hastily pushed it back. "Commander Graham."

Dark circles were under her eyes, and there was a pale cast to her skin. It looked like it had been a bad night, probably for all of them. Graham handed over the basket. She took it by rote as she stared at it in confusion.

"Just some food and extra bandages. The doctor said it's important for your dad to eat well to regain his strength."

Tears shone in her eyes. "You've already done so much."

Guilt hit him in the chest. He hadn't done much at all. And a basket of food shouldn't reduce someone to tears. But if you've been struggling, he supposed it would. Lisa appeared and added her thanks to Cecilia's.

Graham managed to extricate himself from the profusion of thanks and escape up the stairs. Once again, Graham knocked softly, wondering if maybe it was too early. He'd told Addie that he would be over this morning, but they'd had a late night. Maybe they wanted to sleep in.

He growled at the indecision racing through his mind. What the hell was wrong with him?

And the minute the door opened, he knew. Addie stood in her bare feet, her hair still wet from a shower. She once again wore a simple T-shirt and jeans. And Graham knew for a fact he'd never seen a more beautiful woman in his life.

Donovan was right: he was in trouble.

He realized with a start that he had been simply staring at her, not saying a word. But neither had she. It was as if they were both afflicted by sudden mutism.

"Hey, Graham. How's it going?" Micah ran up behind Addie.

His eyes and smile were bright. He looked like *he'd* had a good night sleep. Maybe Addie hadn't told them all the gory details of the fight.

He tore his gaze away from Addie and smiled at Micah as he hefted the basket up. "Morning, Micah. I brought breakfast."

Noel called from further in the apartment. "Then what are you doing out there? Come on in."

Addie stepped aside. "Yes, of course. Please come in." She gave Graham a tentative smile.

And he smiled in return, finally looking forward to the morning.

CHAPTER 24

ADDIE

I stepped back into the apartment to let Graham in, and once again I felt like every cell in my body was singing. Being near him was not good for my mental health. He was all-consuming. And too off-limits.

"Let me take that," I said, reaching for the basket.

"Careful, it's—"

I took the basket, carrying it easily.

"Heavy," he mumbled.

"She's really strong. Cool, right?" Micah asked.

"Very cool," Graham said.

I placed the basket on the table and started pulling out wrapped packages. It smelled wonderful. There was fruit, jam, and croissants that were still warm. There was even some fresh squeezed orange juice. The kids were drawn to the table like moths to a flame.

"Grab plates," I said to Noel. She quickly pulled some out of the cabinet. I lathered strawberry jam on two croissants and gave one to each. "Eat them while they're warm."

The kids each took a bite, and the looks on their faces sent a bolt of pure contentment through me.

I looked up at Graham, who smiled back at me. And something kindled in the air between us.

There was a knock on the door, interrupting the moment. I frowned, flicking a glance at the fire escape. Torr wasn't there. Maybe it was one of the Sanchezes?

"I got it." Graham moved to the door, his gait predatory. And I wasn't afraid to admit, I liked watching him move. And I couldn't help but wonder how well he moved in other situations. I pictured him moving on top of me, and my breath came out in a little gasp.

"You okay, Addie?" Micah asked, jam smeared at the corners of his mouth.

I tore my gaze from Graham's back. "Yup, just anticipating a croissant."

I quickly grabbed one, keeping my eye on the door as Graham called out. "Who's there?"

"Donovan."

Shaking his head, Graham opened the door. The Viking walked into the apartment and grinned at a surprised Micah as he held up a wooden box. "I heard Graham was coming over for breakfast, and I thought I'd bring this over so that you could get a jump-start on practicing."

Micah's eyes widened as he walked over. Donovan handed him the box.

Micah opened it slowly, as if wanting to prolong the moment. The box was lined with red velvet, and nestled inside were chess pieces made of the darkest, sleekest mahogany.

"The board's underneath," Donovan said as Micah just stared at the pieces.

His hands reached for a knight, his fingers running over its smooth finish. His eyes wide, he smiled up at Donovan. "Thank you."

Donovan shrugged, but I could tell that Micah's appreciation of the gift really touched him. "No problem. And no excuses when we play and I kick your butt. Do you have time for a game now?" He raised an eyebrow.

Hope splashed across Micah's face as he looked at me.

I shook my head. "No. You have school. In fact, you two need to eat quickly or you'll be late."

Micah grumbled but walked over to the table with the mahogany chess set tucked under his arm. He laid it reverently on the table and kept one hand on it while he finished breakfast. I smiled, watching him. That was a nice thing of Donovan to do, and Micah was going to relive this moment for a while. He and Noel played chess with an old set that was missing the pawns. They substituted with a saltshaker and an old toy soldier.

"Oh, that reminds me." Graham walked over to the basket and rifled through. He pulled out two large tomes. He handed them to Noel. "Marcus thought you might like these."

Noel let out a little gasp, grasping the books. I didn't recognize the titles. One seemed to be a history of the Angel War, and the other was a biography of the archangels. She clutched them to her chest. "Thank you. Thank you so much."

She smiled at me before joining Micah at the table. She kept her books within hand's reach.

My throat tightened as I watched them. They were both over the moon with their gifts. I was glad that they appreciated getting things, but I also knew that part of that appreciation was because gifts were so rare in our life. And usually when we gave gifts to each other, it was something practical, like fresh fruit or a second-hand pair of shoes that was in better condition than our current pair.

For a moment, I felt bad about what I couldn't provide for them. Then Noel looked up at me, her eyes shining, sharing her joy with me.

In that moment, I knew that these gifts, while incredible and greatly appreciated were not the most important thing. Together, Noel, Micah, Torr—who now sat outside on the fire escape—and I had made a family. That was the most important thing.

The kids ate quickly, and each grabbed a pear to eat on the way as I ushered them out the door. Donovan elected to walk them to school. I could see that Micah was thrilled at the idea. Torr was less than thrilled, but he walked alongside them nevertheless. And for once I was glad that Torr hadn't revealed himself. I wasn't sure how Graham and Donovan would respond to his existence.

I closed the door and turned around to face Graham. I felt awkward now that it was just the two of us. The air felt charged.

Graham nodded toward the kitchen. "Do you mind if I get some more coffee? I didn't sleep well last night."

The mention of sleep caused me to yawn. "Only if you pour me a cup as well."

"Deal."

Only a few minutes later, the two of us were settled on the couch, mugs set on the table in front of us.

"So," Graham started. "You killed five demons last night. Is that an unusual number for you?"

"Actually, it was only four."

"Four, then. Is that normal for you?"

I studied his face. There was no accusation there, just open curiosity. "I've never come across a group like that before. I've occasionally faced two, but never more. I'm glad you two came along. I don't know what we would've done if you hadn't."

Graham raised an eyebrow. "Oh, I think you would have figured it out. That move where you took off that last demon's head, I've never seen anyone do that before. You must have some serious training."

I shrugged. "I don't know."

He frowned. "What you mean you don't know?"

I took a deep breath, watching him. Did I trust him with this? Was it safe to tell him about my history? At the same time, I couldn't imagine what he could do with my history that would cause me difficulty. So I released my breath and told him. "I don't remember anything before two years ago. I woke up down on the beach, and I ran into Noel and Micah. As far as I know, that's where my life began."

Graham leaned forward. "You have no memories from before that point?"

"Not a thing. It's all a complete blank. It was as if I just popped into existence at that very moment."

"But you've had flashes of memories or a sense of déjà vu when you went somewhere or did something, right?"

The image of demons slid through my mind but I banished them away as I shook my head. "Never. I have absolutely no inkling of who I was before I woke up on that beach. I could have trained for years or not trained at all. I just know that when it comes to fighting demons, I know what to do. I know how to hurt them."

Graham studied me for a long moment. "And you've been fighting demons ever since. Going around town at night and defending people."

Now there was a trace of accusation in his voice.

I speared him with a look, some of my anger rising. "Somebody has to. All of you Angel Blessed keep security over the bridge, leaving us to fend for ourselves. And how are the people down here supposed to protect themselves against demons without any help?"

Graham looked taken aback by the vehemence in my tone, but I didn't apologize. I wasn't sorry for what I'd said at all.

"We defend ourselves just as you can defend yourselves."

I snorted. "Just as we can defend ourselves? You have the latest weapons and training. Here, everybody works themselves hard from dawn to dusk and sometimes later. And then what? We're supposed to train after a full day of work being run off our feet by those in Sterling Peak?"

My anger spiraled. I knew I needed to reel it in, but I couldn't. Words poured out of my mouth before I could stop them.

"What do you do all day, Graham? Are you busy running after your master? Or do you sleep in when you've had a rough night? Do you take it easy? Do you get to spend hours thinking about strategy and how to attack a demon? We don't have that luxury down here. We work for our living. It's not just handed to us."

I slammed my mouth shut. Where had all of that come from? I stood up from the couch to put some space between myself and Graham. I don't know what about him made me so angry right now, but I realized that anger had been simmering under the surface these last two years. Sterling Peak had left all of us in Blue Forks at the mercy of the demons without even a care. He acted as if our ability to defend ourselves was equal, but our lives were anything but.

"I never really thought about it that way," Graham said.

"Of course you didn't. Angel Blessed don't think about the Demon Cursed. Demon Cursed." I scoffed. "We all know we're not Demon Cursed. It's just a convenient title to make you feel better about treating us like crap."

"Where is all this anger coming from?"

I stared at the concern on his face and knew he didn't deserve me yelling at him like this. The anger had come over me out of nowhere. I took a step back, shaking my head. "Sorry, I just … I think I need some air."

I walked over to the window and opened it, climbing out onto the fire escape. A light breeze blew, cooling some of my anger. I gripped the railing, staring down into Blue Forks. There were only two people in view. Everyone else was either sleeping, in preparation for working tonight, or already at work. What I'd said was true. The Angel Blessed had created the ridiculous notion that we were Demon Cursed to justify the imbalance of power.

Even so, Graham had been nothing but kind to me and my family. And for that, I had yelled at him and blamed him for all the ills of society. That wasn't fair either.

Metal creaked as Graham stepped out onto the fire escape behind me. "I'm sorry, Addie. I should have done more. I should've thought more about what people down here were going through."

"It's okay. I mean, it's just your life, right? We all go along just kind of accepting it without really thinking too hard about it."

"That's not an excuse. That's not acceptable. I should go. Thank you for talking to me this morning. And for helping Marcus out. If you ever need anything..."

I shook my head, feeling a catch in my throat. Why did this feel so final? How could I have messed everything up so badly? But pride wouldn't let me show him my hurt. "I'm sure we'll be fine."

I felt him staring at me, but I kept my gaze on the street below. The creak of metal was the only indication that he'd left. I turned to watch him go. I kept my gaze on his broad shoulders as they walked through my apartment for what I knew was the last time and let himself out the door.

This was for the best. Nothing good could come from the Angel Blessed being in our lives. The kids' hopes would get raised, and then when they left, they would be devastated. So this was good. This was how it should be.

And yet more than anything else, all I wanted to do was cry.

CHAPTER 25

ADDIE

I spent the rest of the day moping around the apartment. I knew I needed to kick myself out of this funk that I'd put myself in, but I wasn't sure how to do it because I'd come to a realization: I had a massive crush on Graham Michael. Even though I told myself that I wasn't one of those girls, apparently I was.

But I was also smart enough to realize that a crush on him was completely and totally pointless. He was never meant to be a part of my life. He was an Angel Blessed for God's sake, and the leader of the Seraph Force. I cleaned an Angel Blessed home for a living. There was no future for us.

And besides, there was no indication that my crush was anything but one-sided. Graham Michael had his choice of pretty much any girl. I was not going to be a choice for longer than a night.

At the same time, I had to admit, his reputation wasn't like the other Angel Blessed. I'd heard of him with a few women but it wasn't one night stands. He didn't go through women like it was his right. An image of D'Angelo's smug face wafted through my mind. Now he lived up to the Angel Blessed bad reputation.

But still I'd never heard of Graham being involved with a Demon Cursed. Angel Blessed didn't get involved with Demon Cursed, at least not emotionally. And from how much he consumed my thoughts and the way my body reacted to him, I knew just a physical relationship wouldn't be possible, at least on my side. So I'd gotten angry and shoved him away.

Besides, what I'd said about the differences between Blue Forks and Sterling Peak was completely true. The Angel Blessed had all of these resources at their disposal, and they used them to protect themselves to their fullest advantage. They'd even created a means of cutting off the bridge if a group of demons attacked.

Which meant they'd leave the demons in Blue Forks.

Meanwhile the people of Forks had to fend for themselves. And most of the time, people couldn't fend very well. Take Manny. There was no one for him to go to for help besides me, and that was based on geography. I was his neighbor. There was no law enforcement body that he could ask to help him.

Even if it had been in daylight when Cecelia had gone missing, he wouldn't have been able to go over to Sterling Peak and ask them for help, simply because they wouldn't have given it to him. We were completely and totally on our own.

But while everything I said to Graham was accurate, it also wasn't his fault. He hadn't set up society like this. The beliefs that the Demon Cursed didn't deserve any more than they currently had was ingrained in this world long before either he or I was born.

So while what I had said was true, and while my anger was justified, the target of my anger wasn't. Graham had been nothing but completely decent since we met him. He didn't have to come back with the professor and thank us for helping him. He could've simply sent a note with a basket of food and called it even. He'd taken it upon himself to come back and help.

And him and Donovan showing up at the beach had also helped. Without that distraction, Manny would be dead. And then they had escorted all of the kids home and made sure they were safe. They didn't have to do that either.

I was beginning to think that maybe my view of the members of Sterling Peak was not entirely fair. Apparently I held some deep-seated rage toward the people who lived there. Until I'd spoken with Graham, I hadn't even realized it.

But whatever I felt for Sterling Peak or Graham didn't matter. Graham Michael was officially out of our lives. Although I really hoped that Donovan wasn't, at least for Micah's sake. He was so excited about that chess set. He'd be crushed if Donovan didn't come over to play him at least once.

But in reality, it was probably better if he didn't come back. Graham, Donovan, Marcus, none of them were part of our lives. And it would be better for everyone if they just made a clean break now.

Yup, that was definitely the best plan.

I crushed the pillow from the couch to my chest and crashed onto my side. I sighed. *Yup, that's exactly what I want.*

CHAPTER 26

GRAHAM

Graham walked slowly down the stairs of Addie's building her words ringing in his ears.

Angel Blessed don't think about the Demon Cursed. She was right.

He stepped outside into the quiet and glanced toward Sterling Peak. Most of its residents would still be sleeping while their Demon Cursed staff cleaned and cooked for them. Graham shoved his hands in his pockets, finding for the first time a want to linger in Blue Forks. So instead of turning right towards Celestial Bridge, he turned left.

Graham walked around Blue Forks and looked at it with fresh eyes. The poverty was clear but for the first time he really took a deep look at what that actually meant. The homes were shabby and in disrepair. The missing glass panes of windows were often replaced with spare bits of plastic or just cloth to keep out the cold. Some didn't even have that much.

There weren't many people out. He only saw about five, each gave him a nod of respect as they passed.

Without conscious intent, he found himself walking past the

Blue Forks one and only school, the place where Noel and Micah spent most of their day. Before the Angel War, the crumbling brick building had been an elementary school housing hundreds of kids between the ages of five and nine. Now, it housed students up to grade twelve.

He knew though that by the time the twelfth grade rolled around, most kids would have already stopped going. They'd need to get jobs to help support their families.

Half of the front stone steps had been roped off to avoid anyone using them. An old handicap ramp was missing along with half of its ramp and all of its railing. Like a lot of the houses, glass panes were missing from the windows, which meant when it rained the water would get inside.

He didn't want to distract anyone by going inside because he knew the commander of the Seraph Force would cause a stir. But he wanted to see inside. His policies affected people through the nation and yet he had never been inside a school only a few miles from his home.

He walked quietly along the side of the building, realizing that across the bridge, he would never get this close to the school without being stopped by security. But there didn't appear to be any security here.

Careful to stay out of sight, he peered inside. Children a little younger than Micah sat on the floor as a teacher stood at the front of the room giving a lecture. The kids each had a small notebook and one pencil, although he saw a few of them sharing a pencil. He walked past and peered into the next classroom, which had chairs for the kids. But this time the teacher sat up at the desk resting her head on it while the students read from old tattered textbooks.

He glanced into three more classrooms and saw similar scenes: not enough equipment and definitely nothing that a child should be happy to attend each day.

And yet the kids didn't look unhappy. He saw more than a few smiling with friends, whispering quietly to one another. The school was horrible, but it gave the kids a chance to socialize.

And he realized he never heard of the kids in Blue Forks having a place to gather. There were no clubs like there were over Sterling Peak. There was no recreation area either. The kids in Blue Forks went to school and then they went home and they worked. No wonder those teenagers had taken a chance to go to the beach that night. It was one of the few places available to them where they could just hangout.

He turned and headed towards the bridge. He made it there quickly, or maybe it took a while. He wasn't really sure as his mind was lost in thought. Bypassing the line, he received a nod from the guard on duty as he slipped beyond the barrier. He stopped in at the security shed. The guard on duty jumped to his feet. "Commander Graham. It's an honor, sir."

Graham waved the man back down as he stepped inside. "I need you to contact the Seven and have them meet me at the Academy this afternoon. Tell them to be there," He paused. He had that blasted Council meeting first, "tell them to be there at three."

The man reached for the phone on his desk. "Of course sir. Is everything all right?"

Graham shook his head. "No, but it will be."

CHAPTER 27

The Council meeting had been painful, brutally painful, but at least this meeting was being held during the day. Graham naively thought maybe they'd get some work done.

But yet again the Council meetings had devolved into an excuse to drink, eat, and show off the host's latest acquisition. Today, Angelica Rafael, D'Angelo's mother, had shown off her complete mastodon skeleton that she had purchased for an exorbitant sum.

As Graham stared at it he couldn't help but wonder how many of those busted windows in Forks could have been fixed for the same amount. It made him more than a little testy.

Which is partly why the Council had not been receptive to his suggestion of extending the Seraph force protection to Blue Forks. Dion Raguel had the gall to suggest the meeting had gone on long enough and that they could discuss it next time. Then he'd gone into a long-winded diatribe about the inferior fruit he felt was being sold in the market.

It had taken everything in Graham not to flip the table over on the man.

I am not meant to a politician, he thought.

He'd known it for years. And with Brock designated the heir, he didn't need to be. And no one had bothered to teach him how, for which he was actually grateful. The last thing he needed was his father's lesson on how to get through life.

But as a soldier under Brock, he had learned how to follow orders . . . and how to follow the letter of them and not the spirit if he didn't agree with the morality behind them.

So while the Council had droned on, he'd fine-tuned his plan.

Now Graham tucked his head, leaning into the hill as he made his way quickly toward the Academy. The Academy was where all the Seraph forces in the nation trained. Sterling Peaks wasn't a large city. There were many much larger cities across the nation. Yet, this had been the headquarters for the archangels during the Angel War. As a result, it seemed only right to build the Seraph Force headquarters here.

On his way to the academy, Graham passed mansion after mansion, all of them growing grotesquely larger the higher he climbed. By the time he was a half way up the hill, most could easily fit at least half of the homes down in Blue Forks within their walls.

"Angel Blessed don't think about the Demon Cursed," Addie's voice whispered in his mind.

He knew the people of Blue Forks had a tougher road but he never really thought about it the way Addie had made him think about it.

But it wasn't just her. The truth of the matter was that he'd been thinking about protection for Blue Forks for a while. But he hadn't really made it a priority. In part because the masked avenger was protecting people of Blue Forks at night. Since the Avenger had shown up, the number of missing in Blue Forks had dropped precipitously.

Now that he knew that was Addie out there protecting the

citizens of Blue Forks, though, he felt a greater urgency to help. Because something settled uncomfortably in his gut at the thought of her being out there alone.

The gates of the Seraph Force headquarters came into view. The headquarters had been brought over brick by brick from England. But unlike the buildings down in Blue Forks, the headquarters had been well maintained over the years. The heavy gray bricks were solid and forbidding to anyone who would think of causing harm. Heavy thick doors had wide rock slabs steps leading towards it.

Graham nodded at the guard at the gate and again at the one by the door. But they didn't hold the door open for him. At the headquarters Graham wanted the Rangers to focus on their tasks. They weren't glorified doormen.

He stepped into a massive foyer with a stone staircase directly in front of him that split into two against the far wall. There were four floors, the top two were available to Rangers who had completed training and would be stationed inside Sterling Peak. Three of his Seven had also taken advantage of the offer not wanting to live with their wealthy relatives in town.

He couldn't blame them.

The second floor contained classrooms that were used to discuss battle strategy, the Angel War, demon anatomy and lore.

To the right of the front foyer was a long hallway. Old tapestries draped the walls depicting scenes from the Angel War. On the right of the hallway was a museum of artifacts from the Seraph Force history. Then to the left was a library. A copy of every known tome on the Angel War and demons was inside.

But neither of those places was Graham's destination. He turned left. His footsteps echoed off the stone tiles as he made his way to the end of the hall. There only thirty-six Rangers in residence at the moment. Another hundred would arrive within the week to begin the new semester. The students were housed in barracks out back. The time in between semesters, Graham enjoyed, when the headquarters was quiet.

He bypassed the main office and made his way to the lounge at the very end of the hall. That's where he preferred to meet with the Seven.

The Seven were the top Seraph force officers from each ruling family. They decided the priorities for Seraph Force training and the assignments for the Seraph Force nationwide. Graham was the final decider, but he listened to the other six carefully weighing their opinions. He respected their opinions. As he opened the door to lounge, he caught sight of D'Angelo on the other side of the room fixing his hair in the mirror.

Well, he respected almost all of their opinions.

All of the Seven had the rank of major. When they retired they would have the rank of Major General and take on the running of one of the other academies across the nation. Along the back wall, Major Tess Uriel took aim and released one of her knives at the dartboard against the far wall, just as Graham entered. It landed just off center.

Donovan laughed from where he stood leaning against the wall near her. "Ha. You missed."

With her dark red hair pulled back and pale brown eyes flashing, she turned around and scowled. "That's because the commander came in and distracted me."

She gave Graham a mock glare.

Graham held up his hands. "I think it's only fair she gets to throw again."

Tess grinned and pulled another knife from her belt. Without waiting for Donovan's reply, she released it. It flew straight and hit right at the center of the bull's-eye. She let out a whoop. "Pay up, Gabriel."

Donovan pushed away from the wall. "Whatever."

"Looks like we're last," Major Laura Raguel said as she walked in with Major Mitch Sasquael right behind her. Laura had once again shaved her head, leaving only a dark brown peach fuzz covering it. Coiled muscles in her arms showed why she was victorious in all push-up contests. Mitch was more slender but fast, incredibly fast, when it came to hand-to-hand.

With the exception of D'Angelo, they were all principled people. People who while from the leading families hadn't actually been tarnished by that association. Tess was wealthier than almost all of them except for Graham. Yet she lived in one of the rooms on the third floor. She didn't like the trappings of wealth.

But after last semester, Tess had been looking into getting a place for her, Laura, and Mitch. Apparently the grooming habits of some of the last batch of Rangers had been a little too much even for his battle hardened majors. Laura and Mitch had the rooms on either side of her. None of them put too much stock into the wealth they all had at their fingertips.

With the exception of course of D'Angelo, yet again. He used his wealth and connections every chance he got. But he was a talented fighter. And he followed orders. So there was nothing Graham could do about removing him from the Seven.

He waved all of them over. "Glad you guys could make it."

They all took seats on the three couches that had been set up in the middle of the room. Brock had had the Seven meet in the conference room down the hall. He also made sure that there was a full course meal for every meeting. Graham preferred a much more casual approach when possible.

Tess took a seat next to Donovan hitting him on the leg to get him to move over. "So what's going on?"

Graham looked at the faces in front of him trying to gage what their reaction would be. "I've decided to start a new pilot project. We're going to be patrolling Blue Forks in addition to Sterling Peak at night."

Laura's eyes grew wide. "The Council approved?"

Graham shook his head. "No. I decided we're going to make

the program voluntary for now. Only people who choose to be part of it will be. It will not be required of anyone."

"Why exactly are we going to be patrolling Blue Forks?" D'Angelo asked as he lounged back in his chair rather than sitting on a couch with the rest of them. The choice of seats spoke volumes about how well he belonged with the group.

"Because we have been derelict in our duty to the people of Blue Forks. They can't protect themselves. And it looks like the demon threat is increasing," Graham said.

Tess leaned forward. "Increasing how?"

Graham took a deep breath. "There was a large demon attack on the beach in Blue Forks yesterday. And people in Blue Forks are ill-prepared to protect themselves against it."

"But why should we bear that responsibility? I mean, we already give them jobs. I'm not sure why we also need to protect them," D'Angelo said.

Graham clenched his fist trying not to lash out at the man. This was what residents of Blue Forks expected of people of Sterling Peaks: derision and arrogance. "Like I said, it's voluntary. You are not required to take part D'Angelo. But we are going to patrol Blue Forks."

Tess grinned. "I'm game. And I'm off duty tonight so I'll take a shift."

Graham smiled at her. "Good. You can make a rotation so everybody knows who's on duty."

Donovan stood up. "I'll help. I'll speak with the Rangers and see who's interested in signing up."

Graham was glad Donovan volunteered. He would have asked him to gather the names anyway. Donovan had a way of being able to make people do things that they didn't actually want to do. "Good. That's good. Okay. That's everything. Let's make it happen."

Everyone stood and started to file out of the room with D'Angelo going first. Donovan held back. "So I guess this is all the result of a conversation with a certain lady with incredible blue eyes?"

"I guess you could say that."

"So how did it go this morning? Did you sweep her off her feet?"

Graham winced. "Yeah, I can most definitely say that did not happen."

CHAPTER 28

ADDIE

Torr, Noel, and Micah arrived a little after three. Torr slipped in behind them just before Noel closed the door. After all this time, he'd really learned to time it perfectly.

Micah smiled at me, his eyes bright. "Is Donovan here?"

"No, sweetie."

His smile didn't dim. "That's okay. I need to practice anyway. Noel, do you want to play?"

She nodded. "Why don't you set up in your room? I'll be there in a minute."

Micah practically ran down the hall with his bag, where he'd placed the chess set before going to school this morning.

I turned my gaze from Micah to Noel, who stood with her arms crossed, looking at me. "What's wrong?"

"What? Nothing. How was school?"

"It was good," she said, not taking her gaze from me. "Now what's wrong?"

I sighed, slumping down onto the couch, giving up the pretense. "I don't know."

Noel took a seat next to me. "It's Graham, isn't it?"

I groaned, grabbing a pillow and dropping my head into it.

Noel laughed, pulling the pillow away. "Seriously, what's wrong? He's awesome. And he obviously likes you."

"Not after this morning," I grumbled.

"What did you do?"

"Oh, I don't know, just blamed him for everything that was wrong with Blue Forks."

"I'm sure it's not as bad as that."

"Yeah, it is. I basically said that he cared nothing about the people of Blue Forks and the people of Sterling Peak were spoiled brats who kept all the resources to themselves and from any of the people who really needed them."

Noel stared at me, her jaw hanging open, before she laughed. "Oh."

I nodded. "Yeah, oh. He left about five minutes after you guys did."

"I'm sure he just had somewhere to go."

I shook my head. "Nope. He planned on asking me a bunch of questions about where I was from and all of that, and then I got really angry thinking about the differences between here and there. He didn't ask me many questions after that. In fact, he didn't ask me anything. He just hightailed it for the door."

"Well, at least you didn't have to answer a lot of uncomfortable questions."

I groaned. "God, I was awful."

"I'm sorry, Addie. But I'm sure it's not as bad as you think."

"Noel, are you coming?" Micah called from down the hall.

Noel gave me a look.

"Go on. I'm just going to sit here and stew in my funk."

She gave me another concerned look.

I waved her away. "Seriously, go. He's really excited, and I'll be okay. I'm just being ridiculous."

"Being a 'not ridiculous' person, I'm sure this will be just a stage, and then you'll be back to your normal self." She gave me a hug and then headed down the hall toward the room.

She was right. I wasn't a mopey person. In fact, I very rarely gave in to bouts of self-pity. And when I did, they lasted a few minutes, not a few hours. This wasn't me, and I wasn't going to allow it to continue.

So I got up and straightened up the apartment. Then I got dinner together and forced myself to think of anything but Graham Michael. Which wasn't so easy being all the food had been provided by him. After dinner, Noel and Micah set the chessboard up in the kitchen. Torr lay on my bed dozing, and I knew I needed to go out and go for a patrol.

And for the first time ever, I really hoped I ran into a demon.

***

Sadly, the night was quiet. I wasn't sure if it was because the demons were reeling from last night's attack or if I was just seriously unlucky.

At the same time, I knew it was wrong to wish a demon would appear just so I could take my angst out on someone who actually deserved it.

There weren't many people out. Word of last night's attack had spread. The lights were off in most homes, no one wanting to attract any attention.

But as I turned the corner at the old market, I ran into a most unexpected individual. Donovan's grin lit up his face as he caught sight of me. "Addie!"

He wrapped me in a hug, pulling me off my feet. I couldn't help but laugh, my spirits lifting. It was hard to be down around Donovan. His upbeat nature was infectious. He gently lowered me to the ground.

I grinned up at him. "Thanks again for the chess set. Micah and Noel were playing when I left the apartment."

"That was the plan. Because when I sit across the board from him, it will be no holds barred."

An auburn haired woman with a strong build standing just behind Donovan snorted. "Oh, please. Your chess strategies are about as complex as a two-year-old's who's trying to sneak a cookie." She extended her hand to me. "Hi. I'm Tess."

Strong hands, with callouses from fight training wrapped around mine. Tess was Major Tess Uriel, a member of the Seven. My guard was immediately up. "Addie. Nice to meet you."

Tess's eyebrows rose as a smile spread across her face. "So you're Addie. I've heard a lot about you. According to Donovan, you single-handedly took on a horde of demons, beheaded them with one swipe of a magic sword, and left their corpses smoldering in the ground."

I winced at the description. "I think he might've taken some creative liberties with that story."

"I did not," Donovan said indignantly. "That's exactly how I remember it."

Tess jabbed him in the ribs with her elbow. "Donovan does tend to take a few creative liberties with all of his stories. Graham gave me the real story, and I have to say that's no less impressive. You really took down three demons?"

"Actually, it was four."

Tess's eyebrows nearly disappeared into her hairline. "*Very* impressive."

"What are you guys doing out here?" I asked.

Donovan frowned. "Didn't Graham tell you? The Seraph Force will be patrolling Forks from this point forward."

My jaw dropped. "What?"

"Graham's idea. He came back this morning and created a new schedule. We'll all be doubling up on patrols until we get some new recruits."

"He-he did that?"

"I guess that short conversation you guys had this morning must have been pretty persuasive," Donovan said.

I didn't know what to say. He'd listened, and he'd made changes. And now I felt like even more of a heel. He'd done all that even though I'd yelled at him.

Tess's gaze shifted to the sword strapped along my back. "Is that the demon sword?"

I nodded.

"Any chance I can see it?" Tess asked hopefully.

I hesitated, reluctant to pull it from its scabbard. I was strangely protective of it. The second sword I'd left at home under the couch. I'd told Noel and Micah where it was, making them promise not to touch it unless it was an absolute emergency. I pulled it free.

Tess reached out a hand and then pulled it back. "Do you mind?"

I extended it to her hilt first.

She gripped the handle and took a step back, taking a few swings. The moves were practiced and easy.

"It's got a really nice balance to it." She stepped closer to one of the street torches and frowned. "What's engraved on the blade?"

I moved closer to her and peered down. She was right. There were marks there.

"I'm not an expert, but I think that's Enochian, the language of the angels," Donovan said.

"Why would Enochian be on a demon's blade?" Tess asked.

"Probably because the demons used to be angels," Donovan said.

Everyone knew the tale: The archangel Lucifer led a rebellion in the heavens with a third of the angels. When they lost, they were cast out and became demons.

"So this could be an angel blade," Donovan said.

I hadn't thought of it that way. Tess handed me back the blade, her eyes shining. "Either way, it's pretty cool."

I slid the blade back into its scabbard.

"You patrolling?" Donovan asked.

"Yeah, it's been pretty quiet."

"Mind if we tag along?" Tess asked. "You could show us Blue Forks."

"Actually, that sounds pretty good." And it did. The funk that had settled over me like a shroud since the morning started to lift.

I patrolled with Donovan and Tess for the rest of the night. And it was fun. Tess was not what I expected. The only Angel Blessed I'd come in contact with so far were the rich and spoiled. But Tess was down to earth and funny. She and I even tag-teamed giving Donovan a hard time about his many fans. Donovan then teased Tess about her apparently infamous failures in the kitchen. And they both teased me about planning to sit back with popcorn if a demon attacked and just watch the show.

When I finally made it to bed that night, I knew my ideas of some of the Angel Blessed were changing. And instead of going to sleep drowning in misery over my horrible interaction with Graham, I was smiling picturing Tess somehow managing to burn tea.

CHAPTER 29

Noel, Micah, and I spent Saturday night at Sheila's as planned. The fireworks had been spectacular. The members of Sterling Peak sat outside, watching the bursts of color against the night sky, all of the Seraph Force out on patrol.

I tried not to think of the fact that all of the people in Blue Forks were at best looking out their windows at the display. The streets were not safe enough for them to be out.

As we sat outside and people milled by, I found myself searching the crowds for Graham. But there was no sign of him

Which I told myself was a good thing really. Even without seeing him though, I felt his presence every night for the next week. Thanks to Graham, each night at least two members from the Seraph Force were on patrol over in Blue Forks.

I patrolled as well, although only for half the time each night. The Seraph Force had reinforcements who came in and took half a shift. Being I was on my own, I only did the first few hours into the night. That week, I only came across one demon, and he was easily dispatched. Tess and Jane, another member of the Seraph Force, dispatched one as well later that week. But overall, it was pretty quiet.

During that time, I didn't see Graham at all. Not on night patrol duty or when I went over to work at the Uriels.

Not that I was looking, or at least so I told myself each time I felt that small well of disappointment in the pit of my stomach when another day passed without seeing him. Or when I caught the broad shoulders of one of the male members of the Seraph Force and realized it wasn't Graham.

But in reality, it was for the best. Because if I didn't see him, then I would stop thinking about him sooner, right?

Noel didn't ask me about Graham after out little chat, but Micah wasn't quite as restrained. Luckily, Donovan showed up earlier in the week to play chess with Micah. They hadn't finished the game yet, although they'd spent hours sitting across the board from one another. It sat there waiting for them to complete their challenge.

For Micah's sake, I was glad that Donovan kept his word. He'd even brought some extra books from Marcus for Noel. In fact, both kids seemed to have come out of meeting Marcus rather well off, as they'd both made new friends. I suppose I had as well. I'd met a dozen members of the Seraph Force now, including all the members of the Seven. And I had to admit, with the exception of D' Angelo, they were all pretty decent people. But I couldn't help but wonder if I would see Graham again and how that interaction would go.

One thing incredibly strange did happen though just the night before. For the first time ever, a demon actually ran from a fight with me. I'd heard one in the back alley behind the food market, so I'd crept along, and sure enough, one was skulking about. Instead of attacking anyone though, he was peering in the window of an apartment. Then it turned and moved on to the next one.

For a moment I wondered if maybe it was like Torr. So I decided to follow it. Luckily I was downwind.

Then I saw a man step out of the back of his home down the

street, only about thirty feet from the demon. The demon growled low in its throat. I knew that sound.

"Get inside!" I yelled as I surged forward, pulling my sword. It flared to life in my hands.

The man's eyes bulged as he took in the demon. Then he sprinted for his back door.

The demon stopped still, looked at me, and then started to sprint down the alley, *away* from me. I paused, completely shocked by its behavior. Then I took off after it, scanning the alley ahead, trying to see what it had zoned in on, but there was no one in sight.

As the demon ran, its shape became more translucent, until it completely faded from view.

I stuttered to a stop as I reached the spot where it had been just a moment ago. For a second, I worried it had gone invisible. I closed my eyes, straining to hear anything. But it was gone.

I ran into Enid and Mitch of the Seraph Force a short time later and explained what had happened. They promised to pass the information on to Marcus and Graham.

Since then, I'd been unable to get it out of my mind. In all my time, I'd never seen a demon run from a fight. I'd never even heard of it.

Now I stifled a yawn as I walked along the old North District. No one was out. The demons definitely weren't out. And I was struggling to stay awake. I'd spent most of the night wondering about the demon who'd run away. And for the last three nights, Mrs. Uriel had kept me late, so it was all catching up with me.

I hadn't seen the Seraph Force yet, but Tess had told me she was on duty, so I knew they were out here somewhere. I supposed I could call it an early night.

As if I'd summoned her, I caught sight of Tess as she crossed the road up ahead with Laura.

"Hey," I called out.

Tess stopped, her hand immediately going to the scabbard at

her waist before she smiled. She and Laura changed directions, heading toward me. I met them halfway. Both grinned their hellos.

"Quiet night," Laura said.

"Quiet week," I replied. "I'm beginning to think you Seraph Force have scared off all the demons."

Laura had an olive complexion and deep-brown eyes. I was pretty sure her hair was black, but it was hard to be sure because she kept her head shaved. She flexed a rather impressive bicep. "It wouldn't be unheard of."

"I heard you ran into some trouble the other night, though," Tess said, her brow raised with concern.

"Not much. I ran into a demon down by the market. As soon as I pulled my sword, it ran off."

Laura's eyebrows rose. "That's what Mitch said, but I thought he must have gotten it wrong. I didn't think they did that."

I shrugged. "I didn't think so either. But this one did."

Tess frowned. "That's really strange."

"But good," Laura said. "If these guys are scared of that sword, then I say we all get versions of it and walk around with them in our hands like torches."

"Were you able to light it?" Tess asked.

I nodded, remembering the flash of fire across the blade. "Yeah. As soon as I pull it from the scabbard and aim it at a demon, the flames ignite."

"Have you tried to ignite it without a demon?" Laura asked.

I shrugged. "I mean, I've taken it out before. But I haven't actually tried to ignite it."

"Have you shown Marcus the engravings on the blade yet?"

"Yes, he stopped by earlier this week. He sent a note asking if I could bring the sword by so he could do a more in-depth analysis. Donovan said he was out of town for a few days, though."

Tess nodded. "That's true. He left with Graham four days ago, but they came back today."

My stomach did a little flip-flop at the mention of Graham. He'd been out of town. Maybe that was why he'd stayed away.

Ha. Sure.

"Do you think Marcus will be there tomorrow? I can bring the sword by then."

"Yes. He should be. Do you want me to take the sword to him?" Laura asked.

I was tempted, but to be honest I didn't want to let the sword out of my sight. That strange territoriality had only increased. I shook my head. "No, it's okay. I have to go to the Uriels anyway. I can drop it off with Marcus and then pick it up at the end of my shift."

Laura's eyes went wide. "I don't know how you do it. Patrol all night and then work all day. You must be exhausted."

I shrugged. I wasn't tired very often, although tonight I was feeling it a little bit. "Not really. I guess I don't really need that much sleep."

Tess sighed. "I wish I had that problem. When my head hits the pillow tonight, I will be out for hours. I may not get up till noon."

"Must be nice," I said lightly. "But being you two are out here, I think I will actually call it a night myself. Maybe get a little extra sleep tonight."

"Don't worry. We got this," Laura said.

We exchanged goodbyes, and I promised to stop by at Tess's tomorrow in Sterling Peak after work. She had a better scabbard that would work for the demon blade.

I headed down the street, wondering at the changes in my life lately. I can honestly say Tess and I were on our way to becoming good friends. And now I had company, even if only for a little bit, on my nightly patrols. Donovan had stopped by twice, and Marcus had been by at the beginning of the week again. Overall it was pretty amazing how different my life had become.

The only thing missing was Graham.

The thought slipped into my mind before I could tamp it down.

No. He was not supposed to be part of my life. I was grateful that he'd introduced the rest of them to me, but Graham was not a part of my life. I could be friends with all the rest of them because that was all I felt for them: friendship. But with Graham . . .

The rattling of metal behind the school building caused me to stop. The hairs on the back of my neck rose as I turned. It could be a cat. Blue Forks had a lot of strays.

A louder thud sounded.

I pulled my sword from the scabbard. If it was a cat, it was a really big one. Slowly, I inched alongside the brick building. All thoughts of calling it an early night vanished. I reached the edge of the building and peeked around the corner.

An immense demon stood there, hands on his hips, with a scowl. "Where are you?" he growled.

I scanned the area, trying to figure out who he was talking to. Maybe there was another one like Torr that I wasn't able to see.

That thought was terrifying.

He glanced my way. I jerked my head back, my breath coming out fast. I gripped the sword. For the second time, I was coming across a demon that wasn't attacking anyone. I seesawed between going in for the kill and following him to see what he was up to.

Indecision rooted me to my spot. Which, in hindsight, probably saved my life. Because two seconds later, a second demon burst through one of the doorways of the schoolhouse with a roar. He glared at me, his eyes glowing bright. My sword flamed to life as I turned to face him, angling myself to keep the wall at my back.

The other demon sprinted toward us, stopping when he was a few feet away to smile. "There you are."

CHAPTER 30

I looked between the two of them, not waiting for one of them to make a move. I dodged toward the one on my right. He slipped to the side, but I sliced his arm with my blade as he passed.

He snarled. "That doesn't belong to you. Give it to me."

"Try and take it."

His friend stepped forward. For the first time, I got a really good look at him. He was bigger than any of the others I'd seen. A good few inches taller than seven feet, and his horns were larger. He sneered at me. "That's the plan."

And in that moment, I realized that he was telling the truth. They hadn't been looking for some random stranger. They'd been looking for me.

Or, more accurately, my sword.

An image of the demon from last night flashed through my mind. He'd disappeared as soon as he'd seen the sword. He must have told them I had it. Now they'd come to retrieve it.

The demon lunged at me. I leaped to the side. The other one charged, but I shot out a sidekick that caught him in the ribs. He stumbled back but stayed on his feet. The other one rushed up behind me. I twirled my sword in my hand and plunged it back into him, catching him in the gut. I jerked it out, stepping aside as the demon crashed to his knees. I slammed a roundhouse into his face. He crashed back onto the ground.

The second one snarled. "You'll pay for that." The demon lunged toward me, missing me by a wide margin. Then it danced out of my reach.

The second one stumbled to his feet, holding his large claw to his stomach. Blood oozed over his hand. He backed away, positioning himself so that he was blocking the alleyway between me and the street.

But I had no time to think about him, as the other one started in at me again. This time he swung his sword toward my chest. I dodged back before slicing forward. He yanked his hand out of the way. I missed him by two inches.

He stood across from me, shifting from side to side as if trying to find his way in.

I frowned. Something wasn't right. No demon ever fought like this. They started in on a victim and kept going. There was no retreating, no planning. They rushed in, used their strength to overpower their victim, and then they were gone or they were dead. But it was almost as if these two were drawing the fight out.

To stall me.

My heart jumped into my throat as my eyes focused on the demon across from me. If that other demon had reported back that I had the sword, then yes, they would come looking for me, but they would also check my home.

Which meant I didn't have time for this.

I feinted left and then twirled right, slicing across the demon's midsection before turning and slicing him from his groin to his chin. He didn't even have time to scream.

The other demon stumbled back, but a sword sliced through his chest before I could make a move for him.

From behind him, Tess yanked her sword out and then

impaled him again. The demon's mouth fell open. The life drained from his eyes before he pitched forward.

Laura's gaze was fixed on my blade. "Holy cow. That sword really does catch fire."

I leaped over the demon sprawled in front of me. "They're going to my home!"

I didn't wait to see if they followed. I sprinted down the alley with a speed I didn't know I had. I careened off the skeleton of a long abandoned car but didn't slow. I needed to get home.

Visions of Noel, Micah, and Torr facing off against a group of demons alone took up residence in the forefront of my mind.

Please don't let me be too late.

CHAPTER 31

I had never run so fast in my life. For the first block, I heard Tess and Laura right behind me. But then the blood pounding in my ears blocked them out as I tore down the streets. The demons had been stalling me. They wanted the sword. But this wasn't the only one I had.

Stupid. So stupid to keep that sword. I should've given it to Graham or Marcus. I don't even know why I kept it.

I barreled down the street, the buildings I passed only a blur. The kids were alone in the building. The Sanchezes had gone to stay with Lisa's brother and his family while Manny recuperated. His brother lived one town over. And right now that was probably a good thing. The Sanchezes would only be in the way if the demons went for the sword in my apartment.

I swallowed hard, praying that Torr was still there and at the same time terrified that he would place himself between the demons and Noel and Micah. I didn't know whether I should pray he was there or pray that he wasn't.

He'd never said it directly, but I was pretty sure that a traitor demon was not someone the demons would take pity on.

Up ahead, the apartment building came into view. Candlelight flickered through the apartment windows. I could see movement but couldn't make anything out. And the street was quiet. It was possible it was just—

One of my apartment windows exploded as something flew through it. It took me a moment to realize it was too small to be one of the kids. It hit the ground in front of me. It was one of Noel's books.

I dug down deep and pulled up more speed, crashing through the front door and barreling up the stairs. The door to our apartment was open, the frame shredded. I burst into the room.

Three demons stood with their backs to the door. Noel and Micah were backed up against the counter in the kitchen. Micah had wounds down the left side of his body from his shoulder to his feet. The right side of Noel's face was bright red and already swelling.

And standing in front of them was Torr, holding the other demon sword as the demons advanced on the three of them. Blood soaked the side of Torr's shredded shirt, but he stood his ground as the demons moved toward them.

Noel's eyes were wide as she looked from Torr to the demons.

With shock, I realized she could finally see him. Micah appeared to barely be conscious.

"No!" The room burst with light as I leaped forward. I swung the sword with both hands, putting every ounce of strength I had into the leap.

The demon that turned to face me only had time to widen his eyes before I cut him in two. His body from the waist up slid off his legs and toppled to the ground. The legs stayed upright for a second longer before they fell backward.

The second one charged. I was twisted slightly away from him, so I slammed a sidekick into his ribs and then twisted with a flying round kick to his knee. His legs buckled.

I twirled the sword around and, coming down at an angle, sliced through his shoulder down to his waist.

The final demon watched as the second of his partners crumpled to the floor in two pieces.

Shock splashed across his face as he stared at the pieces of his fallen comrades.

That hesitation spelled his death. I jumped toward him, somehow covering the six feet in one move. I twirled in the air, reaching out with the sword and catching the side of the neck. I pulled it through as I completed the circle, landing on the ground in front of him.

His head rolled from his shoulders. His body went still, standing upright for a second. I kicked it across the room. It crashed through the wall, part of it landing in Micah's room.

My chest heaved, my whole body shaking as I looked at my small little family. The light in the room seemed to dim. "Are you guys all right?"

Torr lowered the sword, his whole body going limp.

Tess and Laura burst into the room behind me.

"Look out!" Tess bolted forward, her eyes locked on Torr.

I darted in front of him, meeting Tess's blade with my own.

"Addie!" Tess's mouth fell open.

I kept the pressure on her blade, forcing her to meet my eyes. "This is Torr. He's a friend."

Tess looked at me, then Torr, then back at Laura, who looked just as confused as Tess.

I met both of their gazes. "I'll explain everything later. But they all need some help."

Tess scanned the three of them again, then gave me a nod and slowly pulled her sword back, placing it in the scabbard.

My shoulders sagged in relief as I did the same. I turned to Torr. His eyes rolled back in his head, and he crumpled. I caught him before he could hit the ground.

CHAPTER 32

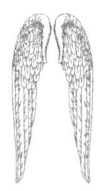

GRAHAM

Stupid, stupid. He'd kept away from Addie for the last week. He hadn't wanted to see that look in her eyes like the last time he spoke with her. Because she was right. The people of Blue Forks hadn't been treated fairly. And he hadn't even thought about it. He'd been just as spoiled and blind as the other residents of Sterling Peak.

He'd taken four shifts in Forks in the last week. The other nights, he'd been out of town with Marcus on a research trip. Every night he was here, he would patrol past Addie's apartment, taking comfort in knowing that she, Noel, and Micah were sleeping quietly up there, safe.

But they hadn't been safe.

He slammed the car to a stop, honking at the dividers on the bridge. Laura had just gotten word to him about the attack. Noel and Micah were hurt.

She said something about a demon being hurt as well. Graham didn't know what that meant, because hopefully all the demons that had attacked them were simply dead. Jade Kwon, who was the Michael family physician for the last thirty years, rode shotgun. Marcus was in the back, and so was Donovan, whom he'd woken up after he'd heard the news. They both carried extra bandages and even had stretchers in the back of the car.

The bridge barricades were quickly removed. The last guard had barely gotten out of the way when Graham pushed the pedal all the way to the floor.

He didn't drive very often. The resources needed to maintain the car were too precious to be used precariously. But tonight he needed to get to Forks as quickly as he could.

The drive itself somehow seemed to take too long and at the same time be instantaneous. He braked to a stop in front of Addie's apartment building and bolted out the door. His breath caught as he sprinted up the stairs, seeing the doorframe completely shattered.

He burst into the room. Addie whirled around, standing in front of her bed while Laura and Tess attended to Micah and Noel on the couch. Micah was incredibly pale. Blood seeped from multiple wounds in his side.

He frowned. Why wasn't Addie over with them? Why would she be across the room? That was when he made out the shape on the bed behind her. The demon was smaller than any of the other ones he'd seen. Growling, he unsheathed his sword.

Addie narrowed her eyes, pulling her own sword. "Don't. You. Touch. Him."

He was shocked by the vehemence in her voice.

Noel struggled to her feet from her position on the ground next to the couch. "He protected us. If he hadn't been here …" Her voice cut off, tears welling in her eyes.

Donovan stepped into the room, catching the tail end of Noel's explanation. His eyes widened at the sight of the small demon, but he didn't say anything, just stepped aside so Jade could enter.

She bustled in and quickly started giving people orders. But Graham kept his gaze on Addie.

When Marcus appeared, she called him over. She conferred with him quietly, and then Marcus went over to Donovan.

Donovan's eyebrows rose up into his forehead before he nodded. He grabbed a stack of bandages from his sack and made his way over to the bed. Graham followed.

Addie stood protectively in front of it. She looked at each of us, the warrior goddess he'd met on the beach back in full effect. "This is Torr. He's my friend. I've known him for nearly two years. He's lived with us all that time. He saved Noel and Micah tonight. He will *not* be harmed."

Even though her voice broke on the last word and tears shone in her eyes, it was clear she was not making a request. She was telling us how it was going to be.

Donovan nodded. "I won't hurt him. Let me help him."

Addie studied him for a long moment. Finally she nodded, stepped aside, and lowered her sword.

Across the room, Jade worked on Micah. Addie watched her with those big eyes of hers. Graham could tell she wanted to be next to Micah, but she didn't trust the rest of them not to harm Torr. How had she met the creature? And why did she think it was her friend?

A shiver ran through her. Goosebumps had broken out on her arms. A cold wind was blowing in through the shattered window.

He slipped his jacket off and draped it around her shoulders. She looked up at him, and the worry in her eyes nearly undid him. He wanted to wrap his arms around her and promise everything would be all right. That he would *make* everything all right.

But he couldn't make that promise. Everyone she cared about was in the room and injured. She was barely holding it together. The only clue to that, though, was in her eyes. But as quickly as she let him see that moment of vulnerability, she dropped the wall over her emotions again. "Thank you."

She returned her attention to her three wards, her gaze continually shifting between Noel, Micah, and Torr.

The doctor finally sat back. "Micah's going to be all right. He needs rest, and he's lost a lot of blood. With rest, food and luck, he should be back to normal in a few weeks."

Addie grabbed on to the back of the chair, her legs weakening. Graham stepped closer to her, not sure if she'd welcome more than his presence. She nodded. "Thank you. Could you look at Torr now?"

Jade shot a glance at Graham. He nodded. "See what you can do."

She grabbed her bags with a shaky hand. With regret, Graham stepped away from Addie and picked up Jade's bag. "I'll take it over for you. We won't let him hurt you."

"It's not that. It's just … I've never been this close to one before."

"He's not like the others," Addie said.

Jade looked up and met her gaze, reading something there. She gave Addie a small smile. "I know," she said softly.

Jade inspected the damage along the side of the little demon's body. Donovan and Marcus had been holding bandages there. They were stained red. Graham was always surprised to see that their blood was red. He didn't know why he expected it to be a different color.

Jade had them pull the bandages back. She tsked, looking at the wound. "This is going to need some stitches. Can you tell him that?"

"He knows." Addie sat down on the bed. She reached down and took the demon's hand, cradling it in her lap. She placed her other hand on his forehead, running her hand over it like you would a child.

Graham couldn't seem to look away from her treating this demon like it was one of her children. Donovan's look of incredulity mirrored his, making Graham feel better. He wasn't the only one struggling with this new Addie revelation.

Tess tapped Graham on the shoulder and nodded toward the stairs. He indicated he'd follow her, but it took him a minute to pull his gaze from Addie. Finally wrenching himself away, he followed Tess outside, flicking a glance at the scorch marks from where the demon bodies had disappeared.

He stopped just outside the door, grabbing ahold of Tess's arm when she started down the stairs. He didn't want to go that far away. He ran a hand through his hair. "Here's good. What happened?"

"In an alley a few blocks from here, Addie was fighting off two demons. But they were toying with her, trying to keep her there. She thought they were going after the other sword. She left it back here in the apartment. We sprinted back here, but she outran us. That woman is *fast*. By the time we got back here, Addie had taken down the three of them. She literally cut them in half." Tess shuddered. "I've never seen anything like it."

"What about the other one. Torr?"

"Noel and Micah were hurt, and that Torr …" Tess shook her head, looking around as if an explanation for what she'd seen would appear. "He *defended* them. He placed himself between the demons and the kids. That was how he got injured. Noel was right: if Torr hadn't been here, I don't think they would have survived."

Graham stared back into the room. He knew Addie was a woman of secrets, but she had a demon for a friend? And how hadn't anyone else seen this guy? Had he been hiding in the apartment this whole time? Was that even possible?

Tess lowered her voice. "Noel said that she's known the demon as long as Addie, but I saw her face. She wasn't telling the truth. I'd bet anything she was just as shocked as anyone when it appeared and defended her. But she's trusting that Addie knows what she's doing."

Graham looked back to the room where Addie sat, still holding the demon's hand, but her gaze continually strayed over to Noel and Micah. Noel might trust what Addie was doing, but Graham wasn't so sure. What the hell had she been up to?

CHAPTER 33

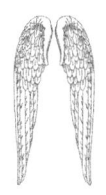

ADDIE

Torr's chest rose and fell. I watched it, worried that at any moment it would stop. I held his hand, but he seemed to have fallen asleep or unconscious.

The doctor worked on him, stitching his side. I winced for him as the needle first went into his skin. "It's okay, Torr. I'm here."

I felt Marcus and Donovan's gaze on me, but I didn't care. They were not my priority. Torr was.

Graham stepped outside with Tess, leaving only Marcus, the doctor, Noel, Micah and me.

I glanced over at Noel and Micah. I'd barely said two words to them since I'd arrived.

The doctor noticed my glance. "It's okay to go to them. This will take another couple of minutes."

I grasped Torr's hand more tightly.

"I will not let any harm come to him. I promise."

I read the commitment in the doctor's eyes. I ran my hand over Torr's head one last time and then stood.

Marcus watched me go but then returned his gaze to Torr, an

unreadable expression on his face. I knew he was cataloguing everything about Torr, filing it away, and I hated it. Torr wasn't a specimen. I wasn't sure what he was—son, brother, friend, but definitely not a specimen.

I crossed the room over to Noel. Crouching down on the ground next to her, I put an arm around her as I took Micah's hand. He slept soundly, just like Torr.

Noel leaned into me, tears rolling down her cheeks. "I was so scared."

"I know. I'm sorry. I should've been here. If I had been—"

Noel shook her head, pushing herself back and wiping at her tears. "No. Forks doesn't have anybody but you. And we had him."

My gaze strayed to where Torr lay.

Noel's voice dropped even lower. "Have you really known him for almost two years? Did you know him before you met us?"

I shook my head. "No. I met Torr about two or three months after I met you. But yes, he's been here since that day. I'm sorry I didn't tell you but ..." I dropped my voice as Marcus glanced over. "But I promise I will explain everything. Just not right at this moment."

Noel nodded. "Did you know about the wings?"

I glanced back at Torr with a frown. "He doesn't have any wings."

This time she was the one who dropped her voice. "No, not him. You."

My mouth fell open. "What you talking about?"

"When you came into the room, wings popped out from behind you. They were on fire. It's how you were able to cross that distance so quickly. You didn't jump, Addie. You flew."

CHAPTER 34

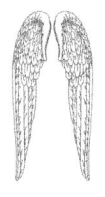

GRAHAM

When Graham returned to the apartment, Addie, who'd been speaking with Noel when Graham walked in, quickly returned to the demon's side. It took everything in Graham not to yank her away.

Jade worked on Torr, but she was worried about his wounds. He'd lost a lot of blood. She wasn't sure it was safe to transfer human blood over to him. But even so, Graham had to admit there was nothing threatening about this particular demon. He was much smaller than any of the others he'd ever come across. He wasn't nearly as muscled. Collectively, it made him seem younger than the other demons.

After working on him for nearly an hour, Jade stood up with a wince, her hand at her lower back. She'd stitched up all his wounds and bandaged them as well. "His wounds will need to be cleaned the same as Micah's, every day. I'll leave supplies so that you'll have enough."

"Thank you, Doctor. I appreciate it," Addie said.

Jade began to remove bandages from her bag. "I'll leave these here for you to use and send someone over with more tomorrow."

Graham stopped her. "That won't be necessary."

Addie glared at him.

Jade's look almost equaled Addie's in ferociousness. Apparently Torr had shifted from frightening demon to a patient in need of protection sometime in the last hour. "I assure you, it *will* be necessary. I did not spend all this time patching these two up to lose them to infection."

"I know, Jade. And I have no intention of letting that happen. It won't be necessary to leave the bandages because they're coming with us. I'll get them settled in at my house where we can keep an eye on them until we can figure out exactly why the demons targeted them."

Addie was already shaking her head before he'd finished speaking. "No, that's not necessary. I can protect them from here. And look after them as well."

"And I can help," Noel said from her spot next to Micah. Both of them looked determined.

Graham had no doubt that they would do just what they said, but he didn't feel comfortable leaving them here. Truth was, he hadn't felt comfortable leaving them here the first time he'd visited, and now that he knew they'd been targeted, he couldn't possibly leave them here.

But Addie had a stubborn set to her jaw.

"It would help my research if you came with us. I'd like to know how you came across your young friend here," Marcus said, nodding toward Torr.

If anything, Addie's face became more mutinous. "Torr is not like the others. I won't have him treated like a prisoner or a guinea pig."

Graham looked to Donovan, expecting some help, but he shook his head, crossing his arms over his chest. "I've no idea what's going on here, but if they say this guy helped protect them, then I don't think he should be treated as a criminal either."

He stared at Donovan in shock. Donovan was more angry at the demons than anyone he'd ever met. If he wasn't rallying for Torr to be locked up … Well, he just never thought he'd see the day.

"I'm not saying we lock him up," said Graham. "But it would be much safer for all of you over in Sterling Peak. You can stay here if you want, but then I'm just going to move into the apartment downstairs to make sure that you're safe."

Marcus sat down on the bed gingerly, trying not to disturb Torr. "I know you want to do what's best for your family, Addie, but for right now I think what's best is accepting Graham's offer. Once you're safely settled at Graham's, you can decide your next steps. Three out of four members of your family need to heal. And I think they will do that better at Graham's home, and I think you could use the help watching them as well."

Graham could tell Addie was wavering. She wanted to do what was right for her family, and she wouldn't let pride get in her way. She took a deep breath. "I won't have him treated badly. You don't understand what it's been like for him. We *are* his family."

"I won't let anyone treat him badly," Graham said, knowing that at that moment, he'd say anything to make sure that they agreed to come over to Sterling Peak. "We'll protect him like we're going to protect Noel and Micah."

He didn't add that it would also be like how he was going to protect her because he had a feeling she wouldn't appreciate that.

But he *was* going to protect her. When he'd received the message from Laura, his heart had leaped into his throat as he imagined the worst. And he realized how stupid he'd been staying away. She'd had every right to say those things about Sterling Peak. It was his pride and embarrassment at not having realized how privileged he was that kept him away.

But he wouldn't make that mistake again.

CHAPTER 35

ADDIE

Graham arranged for another car to come down and pick us all up. Torr would be hidden in the back. His existence wasn't going to be public knowledge until I was sure who we could trust. Tess, Laura, Donovan, Marcus, Jade, and Graham all swore they would not tell anyone about him. Graham promised that if we agreed to go over to Sterling Peak, he would keep Torr safe.

I was torn. I wanted them safe, of course, but I knew how hard it would be for humans to accept Torr. Maybe I had some of the same misgivings that Torr did.

But then Noel, Donovan, and even the doctor had spoken up on his behalf. And I realized that maybe I *could* trust some other people. And the truth was, if I was going to be working during the day, I'd need help looking after them. The demons didn't attack during the day, but we hadn't thought they attacked in groups either. And if I didn't go to work, we would be in much more dire straits. Graham's offer was both extremely generous and a lifeline I couldn't pass up.

After placing Torr on a stretcher, we covered him with a sheet, carried him down the stairs, and put him into the back of the car. I climbed in right behind him. Noel arranged herself on the seat next to me.

Micah was in the car behind us with Donovan and Marcus. I worried about Micah being without us, but there simply wasn't room for his stretcher as well. And the doctor had given him something for the pain, which she promised would make him sleep for the ride at least.

But I couldn't leave Torr on his own. I hoped that Graham was telling the truth about protecting Torr, but I needed to be there to make sure of it.

The ride over to Sterling Peak was blessedly short. The barricades were already removed by the time we reached the bridge. No one could look into the car and see Torr, and for that I was thankful.

As we wound our way up the large hill, I couldn't help but wonder at what had happened. The demons had tracked the swords back to me. I'd killed all those that had come looking for it so far, but there had to be others that knew, which meant that there would be others that were still coming. That didn't mean I was leaving the sword behind. It was a lethal weapon against the demons. I had one strapped to my back even now. I didn't think I'd be going anywhere without it until I knew everyone I loved was safe.

But I'd given the other sword to Marcus. Maybe he could get some answers.

Noel took my hand, her gaze on Torr. I squeezed her hand back, a silent promise to explain everything later.

She looked at me and then away, a tremble in her chin. I knew the fact that I had kept Torr a secret hurt her. And I hoped that once I explained everything, she would understand. She had to understand.

At the same time, the echoes of our previous conversation played on a loop in the back of my mind.

You didn't jump Addie. You flew.

Even as I struggled to accept the possibility, my mind rebelled at the idea. I didn't know what that had been about but there was too much going on right now to even start trying to figure that one out.

Making our way up the hill, Noel's eyes were growing larger the longer we drove and I realized she'd never been this close to one of the mansions. She'd only been to Sterling Peak a handful of times and that had been to visit Sheila who lived closer to the bridge.

"It's massive. How many people live here?" Noel asked as we pulled into Graham's drive.

Behind the wheel, Graham cleared his throat, looking uncomfortable. "Just three, me, Mary and Franklin. There's four on staff during the day, but they don't sleep here."

"And Mary and Franklin? They can be trusted?" I asked.

"Yes. They basically raised me. They're good people." Graham met my gaze in the rearview mirror.

I nodded before turning to look back out the window, butterflies once again in flight. I let out a trembling breath. This was definitely not the time for that.

Graham pulled the car around the back. Donovan pulled in right next to him. Lights were on at the back of the house. The back door opened.

An older woman wrapped in a robe, her hair pulled back in a bun, stood in the doorway, while a balding gray haired man held the door open for us. I placed the sheet lightly over a still sleeping Torr's face before we pulled his stretcher from the car.

"I'll wait with Micah," Noel clambered out of the car and moved over to the other one.

Franklin inspected Graham from head to toe as we approached, relief in his eyes when he didn't spot any new injuries. But his concern shifted to alarm when his gaze took in the stretcher. His eyes widened, and a tremor ran through his body.

Torr's hand had slipped from underneath the sheets.

His green clawed hand.

Damn it. I speared the man with a glare, daring him to make a comment. He looked away.

Graham led us down the hall, through the kitchen, and through another hallway to the right. As we reached the stairwell, Donovan caught up with us. "Let me take that for you, Addie."

I shook him off. "No, I've got it."

Donovan walked next to me, obviously ready to grab the stretcher when the weight of it proved too much for me. But that wasn't going to happen. I could have carried Torr myself up to the room if I needed to, so half his weight wasn't much of a bother at all.

Donovan seemed to realize it halfway up the stairwell. He grinned at me. "You are full of surprises, aren't you?"

He took the stairs two at a time to join Mary, who'd hurried ahead of us. She stopped three doors down and bustled inside. Donovan disappeared into it as well. I followed, not sure what to expect.

But when I reached the doorway, I realized it was just a normal guest room. There was a king-size four-poster bed with white sheets and a navy-blue comforter. A bathroom was off to the right, or at least I assumed it was a bathroom when Mary reappeared out of it.

There were deep-blue drapes on the wall and two chairs positioned in front of the large ornate fireplace across from the bed. It wasn't as ostentatious as the Uriels' guest rooms, which were drowning in gold leaf and cherub statues. Instead, there was a quiet, understated affluence to it.

When Graham said that he would allow Torr to stay here, I'd worried that he meant in some sort of dark, dank dungeon. At best, I thought a storage room. This had not been one of the possibilities I'd considered.

Together we headed to the bed and gently placed the stretcher on it. Donovan walked around the other side of the bed and reached over, carefully grasping the sheet underneath t Torr.

"On the count of three," Graham said. He counted down, and then together we shifted him from the stretcher to the bed.

"Mary, if you can help me get our other guests situated," Graham said, standing up.

"Of course," she said, her gaze locked on Torr's hand still visible from underneath the sheets. I carefully tucked it under the blankets.

Graham stepped toward me. "Micah is going to be right next door. I'll go get him. I assume you want to stay with Torr?"

Once again I was torn, but I nodded. He looked down at me as if he had more to say but then stepped away without another word. He gently placed an arm around Mary and steered her out of the room.

Donovan disappeared with them, leaving me alone with Torr.

I slipped the sheet from around his head, unsurprised to see that his eyes were open. "How are you?"

He grimaced. "I've been better."

"Thank you, Torr. If you hadn't helped them—"

He cut me off. "Are they okay?"

"Micah's hurt, but he'll heal, and Noel has some bruising. You're the one who took the brunt of it."

He nodded, his eyes closing slowly. "That's good." Then he opened his eyes again with a frown as he noticed his surroundings. "Where are we?"

"We're over in Sterling Peak. I needed help taking care of all of you. We're in Graham Michael's home. As soon as you're all better, we'll get out of here." I lowered my voice. "No matter what it takes, we'll get out of here."

Torr met my gaze and spoke slowly. "Am I a prisoner?"

"I really don't know. Graham said you're not, but—"

"But I'm a demon," Torr finished quietly.

I nodded. "Yeah."

"At least I have a gilded cage."

I wasn't sure what to say to that, so I grabbed the medicine that Donovan had placed on the side table. It was the same one that Micah had been given. But I had wanted to wait until we were settled with Torr before he took it. Just in case.

But it seemed that everything was on the up and up. I poured some of the pain meds into a small cup. "You need to take this."

Torr curled his lip.

"Hey, I know. But you need to heal. And the sooner you do that, well, the better for all of us."

I helped him sit up, and he took the glass from me. After staring at its contents for a long moment, he downed it quickly. He grimaced. "That's awful."

"Most medicine is."

Torr lay back down and let out a yawn. Quiet voices came from the hall, followed by the sound of people moving around next door.

I adjusted the blankets over him. "I need to go check on Micah to make sure that he's getting settled in. Will you be all right for a few minutes?"

Torr nodded, his eyes already closing. "I think I'll sleep for a little while."

"I won't be long." I ran a hand over his forehead. It felt warm, but I didn't know how warm he normally ran. I stood up from the bed, and with one last look at Torr, crossed the room quickly, my feet sinking into the deep thick rug. It really was a gilded cage.

I stepped outside the door, nodding at Laura, who stood there on guard. And thought that maybe I had just lied to Torr. Maybe he was a prisoner after all.

CHAPTER 36

A door connected Micah and Torr's room. Mary opened it up and I could easily see the bed from in here. Micah's room was almost identical to Torr's, except it had a deep-green comforter. According to Graham, Laura was situated outside Torr's room, initially to reinforce to the staff that the rooms were off-limits. But Graham promised she'd be gone once he was sure the staff understood the rules.

Noel decided to bunk in with Micah, so an extra bed was brought in for her. I had a bed brought into Torr's room as well. I situated it as close to the door as possible so that I could to see between the two rooms.

I wanted to be with Micah and Noel, but I simply couldn't trust that Torr would be all right if I left him alone. I'd never wanted to split myself in two so badly before.

The doctor came in after everyone was situated and gave both Micah and Torr some more pain meds. She wasn't sure how Torr would react to them, so she started with a lower dose than what she gave Micah. She explained that both of them should be out for the rest of the night. It was only a few minutes later that both of them slipped into a deep sleep.

Noel then went and took a shower.

I wanted to do the same, but I didn't feel comfortable leaving them both unguarded. Noel came out, her hair dripping wet. She told me she would keep an eye on them both and scream if she needed me.

I still hesitated, but I felt grimy, and I knew that now would probably be the best time to grab one. Stepping into the bathroom, I stared longingly at the large tub on the other side of the bathroom. Now, though, was not the time to relax.

Instead, I jumped into the shower, intending to wash up quickly. But when the hot water hit my skin, every cell in my body screamed at me to stay there forever. The heat worked its way into all of my aches and pounded them away.

There was an array of soaps and shampoos, each one smelling better than the last. I settled on a soap and shampoo with an apple scent. Then I closed my eyes, just enjoying the warmth. I really could have stayed there for hours.

Reality, though, soon intruded. I shut off the water. Maybe in a few days I could take a long, leisurely bath. But for now, I dried off with one of the ridiculously fluffy white towels before changing into the clothes that Mary had brought up earlier.

The shirt was obviously a man's, and the leggings were even a little baggy, but my own clothes were probably going to have to be torched, they were so covered in blood.

When I came out, Noel was sitting in one of the leather chairs by the fireplace in Torr's room. I looked at her in surprise. I thought she'd be waiting in Micah's room. She gestured to the fire, which roared brightly. "Tess came in to make a fire, so I came to watch and make sure that Torr was all right."

Sinking into the chair next to her, I stared at the flames as they flickered and waved. It was peaceful. Or maybe I was so tired that my mind had gone completely blank.

I was half asleep when Noel spoke. "He really has been living with us for the last year and a half?"

I nodded slowly. "He has the ability to make himself invisible."

"Why didn't you tell us about him?"

I winced at the hurt in her voice. "I wanted to. But Torr didn't think that you would accept him. So he stayed invisible almost all the time."

"But you could see him."

It wasn't a question. "Yes. I don't know how. Maybe he can choose who gets to see him and who doesn't, but yes, I could see him."

"He's the reason food would show up mysteriously in the kitchen some mornings."

I nodded.

Noel was quiet for a little while. "I heard you talking to him sometimes."

"What?"

"Late at night, sometimes I had trouble sleeping. I would hear you talking in the living room. I didn't really know what to think of it. It sounded like you were having a long conversation. And then I realized if you had an imaginary friend … well, what was so wrong with that?"

"You never said anything."

"Neither did you."

We sat there quietly, the burden of each of our secrets laying between us. I thought that we didn't have secrets.

"I'm sorry. I should've told you. Torr, though, he was all alone. And for him, we're his family. I know it sounds crazy because you guys didn't even know he was there, but he walked you to school every day. He watched over you when I was out on patrols."

"And he saved us from those demons when they attacked."

I nodded, studying her. There were deep shadows under her eyes. "How are you?"

Noel took a deep breath. "When they burst into the apartment, I thought we were dead. I didn't even question it. You've taught us to defend ourselves, but against three ..." Her words dropped away.

I reached out and took her hand, needing to touch her and confirm she was right there, alive.

She took a steadying breath. "I knew there was no way we could fight them off. And then Torr, he just appeared over by your bed. My heart lodged in my throat because then I thought there were four of them. One of them backhanded me. I flew across the room. Another reached for Micah and scraped his nails all along his side. He screamed ... so loud."

I gripped my chair tightly, picturing them terrified.

"And then Torr dove for the couch, pulling the sword out from underneath it. I thought we were well and truly dead then. But then he swung at the largest one. It took my mind a moment to realize he was fighting against them, not with them.

"He yelled at us to get back. They fought, and he kept them at bay even after their swords plunged into his side. But he wouldn't step out of the way." A tear escaped down her cheek, and she wiped it away.

"They told him they had no argument with him. But he wouldn't move. He stood in front of us. He defended us long enough for you to get there."

Tears pressed against my eyes as the scene from the apartment came back to my mind. "Torr thinks of you as his family as well. You didn't know he was there, but he was a part of our lives. We were his only source of comfort in a world where he had no one else. He said he would protect you when I was on patrol. I felt better knowing he was there, knowing that he would keep his word."

"And he did. But he's a *demon*. How's it possible that he's not like the rest of them?"

"I don't know. But I'm so grateful that he isn't. And you have to understand that I will protect him the same way I would protect you and Micah."

Noel's gaze strayed to the bed where Torr slept quietly. "I understand." She met my gaze. "And I'll protect him the same way."

I squeezed her hand. She squeezed it back tightly. And the bond was set. This was our family. And we would protect it by whatever means necessary.

CHAPTER 37

After our conversation, Noel and I sat just staring at the flames for a while, sinking into the peace after all the craziness of the recent events. Noel fell asleep in the chair next to the fire. Her face looked even younger in the firelight.

I nearly dozed off myself. But I knew that Noel would wake up sore from sleeping in that position. And she was recovering too. The side of her face was still swollen, and she was going to have a nasty black eye for a while. I wanted her to sleep in a comfortable bed tonight. So I picked her up and carefully carried her into the other room.

Then I sat with Micah for a little while. He slept soundly. The doctor wasn't too worried about his injuries. The doctor kept repeating that he was young and healthy. He should heal up just fine.

Tess must have been in to make a fire in this room as well. The glow from the fireplace gave the room a warm, cozy feel.

I was just about to leave, when his eyes opened. "Addie?"

"Hey," I said softly. "How you feeling?"

He grimaced. "My side hurts but not as bad as before."

"The doctor said you'll be okay in a few days."

His eyes widened. "Demons were in our apartment."

"I know, but they're gone now."

"There was another demon there. He protected us."

"He's a friend of mine. He's friend of yours. I'll tell you about him tomorrow."

Micah nodded, his eyes started to close before they jolted open again. "You won't leave, will you?"

For a moment he looked so heartbreakingly young. Micah had always been good at putting any childish needs aside. But right now he looked like a scared little boy. I took his hand and held it. "I'm not going anywhere."

Micah nodded, closing his eyes but keeping his hand tightly wound around mine. I positioned myself so I could see through to the next room. Leaning back against the pillows, I closed my eyes, assured that my family was safe, at least for now.

CHAPTER 38

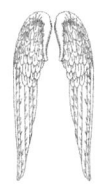

GRAHAM

Mary had tried to talk Graham out of bringing the breakfast trays up, but Graham knew that Addie would want her privacy, and even though he explained about Torr, he could see the skepticism on both Mary and Franklin's faces. So all things considered, he thought it best if he delivered their breakfast personally.

He pushed the cart down the hall and then slowly opened the door to Noel and Micah's room. Noel was curled up in the extra bed. Addie slept sitting up, her hand wrapped in Micah's on the large bed. Her face had lost its fierceness in sleep. She looked soft and vulnerable.

Once again he struggled with the image of her and what he knew she could do. But right now all he could think was that she looked like someone who loved her family very much. By the time he'd pushed the cart to the fireplace, her eyes were open. She leaned down and kissed Micah on the forehead before straightening and stretching out her back. She quietly walked toward him. A sense of masculine protectiveness rolled over him as he noted she was wearing one of his shirts.

Which made no sense. Out of all the woman he'd ever met, none required his protection less than Addie. Even knowing that, he still wanted to keep her safe from the evils of the world.

Noel stirred from the bed, her eyes at half-mast only partly due to exhaustion. Both eyes were rimmed in a dark blue and the left was partly swollen shut. "Do I smell breakfast?"

Graham pulled off the plate covers with a flourish. "Ham, eggs, bacon, and some freshly made croissants."

Noel's eyes opened fully. "That sounds awesome."

Micah stirred from the bed as well. "Did someone say bacon?"

Addie laughed, looking back at the two of them. "Why don't you two go get washed up, and then you can have some breakfast, okay?"

Noel hurried over to the bed to help Micah, who was struggling to get himself out from underneath the blankets.

"How'd you sleep?" Graham asked, looking down at Addie.

"Good, actually. Thank you for all of this."

"It's the least we can do. Um, how is your other friend?"

"I'm about to go check."

"Do you mind if I go with you?"

She hesitated for only a moment before giving him a sharp nod and walking to the adjoining door. Torr was awake. He sat up in the bed, looking around the room with a frown, like he wasn't quite sure what to do with himself.

Graham started at the blueness of his eyes. Torr gave Addie a nervous smile. But Addie's smile was anything but nervous as she hurried across the room. "You're awake. How are you feeling?"

"Better." Torr glanced over at Graham. "Thank you."

Graham started for the second time since walking in the room. A demon thanking him. That was definitely a first. "You're welcome."

The rattle of the cart sounded behind him. Graham whirled

around to see Noel pushing it through the adjoining door. Micah was right behind her, an arm wrapped around his injured side.

"What on earth are you two doing?" Addie asked.

Noel took a breath and then gave Torr a smile. "This family always eats together. And two members of our family are in this room, so I guess we eat in here."

Torr looked stunned, and then a smile crossed his face, a smile full of hope.

"Any chance I could join you guys?" Graham asked.

Micah studied him, his gaze going from Graham's feet to his head. "As long as you promise not to eat all the bacon."

Graham held up his right hand. "I promise not to eat all the bacon."

Micah gave him a solemn nod. "Then you are welcome."

∽

The breakfast was one of the most enjoyable Graham had had in a while. Noel and Micah teased one another and everyone around them throughout the breakfast. Even Torr was pulled into their good natured ribbing. At first appearing shocked, his smile eventually grew and by the end of the breakfast it came easily to his face.

When Tess showed up to spend time with the group, Graham found himself lingering not wanting to leave. But as much as he enjoyed spending time with this strange family, he knew he had duties to attend.

With great reluctance he found himself pushing himself away from the wall where he'd been watching the two teenagers and Torr play charades.

Addie stood by the window watching her gang while also keeping a look outside. She was tense and unsettled. He couldn't blame her.

She looked over as he pushed away from the wall. He walked

towards her stopping when he was just a foot away. He lowered his voice. "I need to go see to some things. Will you be all right?"

She looked up at him with those incredible blue eyes. "Yes. And thank you for everything you've done."

He hesitated, knowing he need to go but finding it incredibly difficult to do so. "About the last time we met and how it ended. I just wanted to say-"

Addie reached out and squeezed his hand. Tingles worked their way up from her grip. "No. It was not my finest moment. And you've done so much."

"I should've done more."

"We all do what we can. And now the people of Blue Forks have people looking out for them. "

"They already had you."

She smiled up at him and he realized he was content to just stand there and stare at her. God, he'd become like a lovesick schoolboy. But he didn't mind. In fact, he embraced it. He'd never felt like this about anyone in his life and certainly not this quickly.

"Morning everybody." Donovan's smile was broad as he walked into the room. He held a tall stack of boardgames in his hands. "Okay. Who wants to play?"

"Me." Noel dashed over with a squeal.

Donovan's arrival broke the spell between him and Addie. She took a hasty step back. "Um well thanks again for everything."

"I guess I'll see you in a little bit." He turned and headed for the door wanted nothing more than to just stay.

With a sigh he straightened his shoulders and strode down the hall. He'd get his work done. And then he'd head right back here. Duties be damned today. He was going to spend some time with Addie and her kids. Decision made, he felt better as he made his way down the hall to his office.

He spent an hour going through paperwork and sending out dispatches. And then he decided he needed a break. He headed back to check on everyone but decided to stop in and see Marcus first.

Addie had given Marcus the other demon blade last night. Graham could picture Marcus pouring over it. No doubt he was up to his elbows in research trying to decipher the Enochian on the blade.

Yet when Graham stepped into the doorway of Marcus's office he was surprised to see demon blade sitting discarded on a side table as Marcus sat at his desk mumbling to himself. He was carefully going through the large tome the two of them had gone looking for last week.

"It's not right. That can't be right." Marcus furiously scribbled in a notepad.

Graham stepped in. "Marcus?"

His head jolted up. He blinked a few times in rapid succession before his eyes seemed to focus on Graham. "Oh Graham. Excellent. I needed to speak with you."

Graham flicked a glance at the demon sword on the side table. "Is this about the sword? What did you find?"

Marcus frowned. "The what?" Then his gaze shot to the sword. "Oh no. No. That's not important."

Graham's eyebrows rose. "That's not important?"

"Well I mean of course it's important. But not as important as what I've found. I kept thinking about how Addie said the demons were stalling her. And why they went after the kids too. That was a coordinated attack."

Graham hadn't thought of it that way, but Marcus was right. And the idea was terrifying. "But the demons went looking for the sword, right? They attacked Addie and the kids because of it."

Marcus shook his head. "I don't think that's what happened."

"What do you mean?"

Marcus took a breath. "I don't think the demons were going after the sword. I think they were after Addie."

CHAPTER 39

ADDIE

After breakfast, Micah and Noel decided to stay in the room with Torr, which made me deliriously happy. Last night was horrendous and not how I envisioned introducing the three of them. Yet that same incident seemed to have created an immediate bond between the three. After Tess stomped Donovan at Parcheesi, Donovan and the kids settled in for a game of poker.

I had a sneaking suspicion that either Graham, Donovan, Tess, or Laura would always be "stopping by" to see how everyone was doing. I suppose I couldn't blame them. They didn't trust Torr yet. And being that every demon they'd come in contact with up to this point had tried to kill them, I suppose it was going to take a little time to establish trust.

From the doorway, I watched the four of them as they sat on the bed and taught Torr how to bluff. He looked completely confused. "Wait, so you lie?"

"It's not lying, it's bluffing," Micah said.

"What's the difference?" Torr asked.

Donovan doled out the cards. "It's just for fun."

Torr frowned. "Isn't that cheating?"

Noel grabbed her stack of cards. "I suppose. But for this game, it's part of the game."

Torr still looked confused. I couldn't help but smile. He was getting a crash course in human complexities.

I didn't want to leave them. I wanted to curl up in the bed and join them, but Marcus had sent a note through Franklin asking to speak with me. His room was just down the hall and hopefully whatever was on his mind wouldn't take too long.

Tearing myself away, I made the short trek down the hall. I paused at Marcus's half-open door and knocked.

"Come in," came Marcus's swift reply. I opened the door, unsurprised to see Graham waiting inside as well.

The room was a former study that Marcus had taken over. The desk was covered with dusty tomes, and there was a pillow and blanket on the couch. I was sure Graham had given Marcus a bedroom, but no doubt the professor had been getting lost in his work. He seemed the type.

Marcus came around the desk and hugged me. "Addie! How are you feeling? How are the others?"

"We're all good. Or at least, as good as can be expected."

"Excellent, excellent." Marcus led me toward the couch. Realizing the blanket and pillow were still on it, he stopped giving me a sheepish smile. He hustled forward showing them to the floor. "Please take a seat."

Graham got up from his seat by Marcus's desk and sat next to me. The butterflies returned at his nearness. and I was at a loss as to what to do about it. He had been so nice, so helpful. So far he'd kept his word and no one else had seen Torr. There were no extra soldiers outside either.

But he was still an Angel Blessed and I wasn't. There was no future in that. Besides, he'd been a perfect gentlemen. I'd caught him staring at me a time or two but he'd just learned I could fight off demons and that I'd had an invisible demon friend for over a year. I'd stare at someone like that too.

So I made a point to not look at him, focusing instead on Marcus. He took a seat across from the two of us after grabbing a heavy book from the desk.

"So what did you want to talk to me about? Torr?" I tensed, waiting for his response. I appreciated what Graham had done for us, but I wouldn't put Torr in any position he wasn't comfortable with.

"What? Oh, no. I mean, I would love to sit down with him and ask him some questions. I'm sure the answers would be fascinating. But, actually, I wanted to speak with you about the attack last night."

"Have you examined the sword?" I asked.

Marcus nodded. "Only to confirm, as Donovan suspected, that the language engraved on the blade is Enochian. I don't think the blade is the important factor, though."

I frowned. "But they were trying to get the blade, weren't they?"

Graham answered. "Marcus doesn't think so. He has another theory as to why you were targeted."

I looked between the two of them. "Okay. Let's hear it."

Marcus placed the book on the table. It was ancient with a peeling leather cover. Whatever the title had been had long worn off. The pages were thicker than normal pages and not uniform, as if they were made from different materials at different times. The book looked like it might have been drenched at one point in its history, the pages getting warped in the drying process.

Marcus carefully opened the book. A few flakes of leather slipped off from the spine nevertheless. Marcus cringed but then simply sighed, accepting, it seemed, that any time he opened the book, he would destroy it a little bit. He turned to a page demarcated with a red silk cord. He turned the book around and pushed it toward me.

Despite the worries of the last twenty-four hours, I had to admit I was curious. I leaned forward. The paper was a dark ivory with wavy stains of a slightly lighter ivory running through it. The entire page was covered in writing, but I couldn't understand a word of it. "I can't read that."

Marcus looked at the page and then frowned. "Oh, sorry. That's the Enochian. Where did I put the translation? Hold on, hold on." He flipped through another few pages and then pulled out a sheet of paper.

The paper was not originally from the book. He slid the book back over, the translation now on top.

This time there were only a few words on the paper. And these words were in English.

The child of flame and the child of darkness will meet.
The world will tremble in their wake.

A shiver went up my spine as my gaze locked on the word flame. Noel had said flaming wings had appeared behind me last night. With everything going on, I'd barely even thought of that conversation.

But now a feeling of dread settled over me.

"I don't understand."

Marcus sat back, crossing his hands over his chest. "I didn't either, at first. This prophecy is very old. It's been around for hundreds of years, long before the Angel War even began. These were the only two lines that had ever been translated. But everyone agrees it refers to the final battle. The battle between the forces of good and the forces of evil."

That sounded horrible but also unrelated to me. Before I could ask a question, though, Marcus continued.

"During the war, the prophecy was well-known, but no events

seemed to fit the words. But then I found this book. It's why I was coming to speak with Graham. The book has the full prophecy."

"I'd never heard of it either," Graham said. "According to Marcus, it hasn't been taught in a long time. It was all the rage right after the first descendants of the angels came of age. But then nothing happened, and it fell away again."

A memory clicked into place. "Wait, that demon who attacked you. He was looking for this book wasn't he?"

Marcus nodded. "Yes."

"Why didn't you just give it to him?" I asked.

Marcus shook his head. "I didn't have it then. I was looking for it too. But even I had it in my possession, I would not have given it to him. The stakes are too high."

"Higher than your life?" I asked.

Marcus nodded. "Yes."

Graham cleared his throat. "We think that the demons you ran into and the ones that went to the apartment were looking for you specifically."

"Me?" I shook my head. "No, you mean the sword."

Marcus's face alighted with excitement. "Your connection to the sword is fascinating. No one but a demon or a Celestial should be able to ignite a demon's sword. Humans are unable to do it. But you can, and you can wield it as well."

"But ... I mean, I'm the only human who's tried. No one else has gotten a demon's sword, right?"

Marcus shook his head. "No. There have been a few demon swords that have been captured over time. Not many mind you. But there have been zero reports of those blades being engulfed in flame, at least when held by humans. People have been able to wield them, but they worked no differently than a normal sword. When *you* wield it, you can cut a demon in half. That means there's something very different about you."

I sat back, flicking a glance at the door. Noel's voice floated through my mind. *You had wings.* My skin felt like it was on fire. I didn't like where this conversation was going.

Marcus continued, seemingly unaware of my discomfort. "Graham told me that you have no memory of your life before two years ago. I think that's because your life was not on this earth. I think you *arrived* here two years ago."

Okay, now we were heading into crazy town. "You think I'm only two years old?"

Marcus gave a little chuckle. "No, no. But I think that prior to that time, you lived your life somewhere else. I think you lived your life with the angels on high."

I stared at him, not sure what to say. Now I wasn't worried about being crazy. Now I was worried that Marcus was crazy. I wasn't angelic. I hadn't spent my childhood and the entirety of my life with angelic beings. That was nuts … wasn't it?

"Look, all we know for sure is that you can wield the demon sword better than anyone else. We also know that they targeted you and your family," Graham said.

"But see, that's why they were going for the sword, not me. Why else go to the apartment?" I asked.

"Because they were trying to capture you," Marcus said. "And if they were able to kidnap Noel and Micah, you would do anything to keep them safe. Even willingly turn yourself over to the demons."

There was truth in his words. But there was a larger problem. "Why not just kill me? I mean, if I'm supposed to be part of this prophecy? And besides, wouldn't I know if I was an angel?"

"We don't think you're an angel but the child of one. I believe you are the child of an archangel, possibly Michael himself," Marcus said.

Shock roared through me. "Michael? The top archangel?"

Marcus nodded. "And as the child of flame, it makes the most sense that he would be your father."

I shook my head. "But that still doesn't answer why they wouldn't just kill me."

"Graham said the same thing. It's possible that due to your ability to fight off the other demons that they were nervous about being able to take you down and were waiting for reinforcements." Marcus paused. "But I think there might be another reason."

I swallowed, not liking the serious look on Marcus's face.

"I don't believe the demons want you dead. Because I believe they *want* the prophecy to come true. They want to usher in an era of chaos. They want the final battle to happen. Because if the child of darkness wins, the doors to Hell open up. And demons will rule the earth."

CHAPTER 40

Marcus went into a long, drawn-out explanation of how he came to his conclusions, but I barely heard him. All I could think about was why couldn't I remember anything from before I woke up on that beach. Was it possible I grew up on some other plane of existence? That seemed crazy.

But then that one flash of memory came back: demons, lots of demons. Had they attacked me? Had I escaped, landing somehow on that beach?

And if it was true, if I was the child of the prophesy, what did that mean for Noel, Micah and Torr? What kind of danger would they be in? What kind of danger would I be in?

Thoughts, fears, and horrible possibilities raced around my head in circles, growing in intensity. How could I possibly keep them safe in the middle of this if Marcus was right?

I stood up, cutting Marcus off in mid-sentence. "I need to get some air."

Without waiting for either of them to say anything, I hurried from the room and down the hall. I glanced in Torr's room. The kids and Donovan were all still there. They were laughing and smiling over some story Donovan told. Even Torr was laughing. I didn't want to darken their happiness, so I hurried past and down the stairs.

I vaguely remembered the way out and ducked down a side hallway, seeing the door leading to the outside with the sun shining through the glass. I picked up my pace and was practically running by the time I hit the door and burst outside.

I took off at a run, sprinting down the manicured lawn and heading into the trees. I ran for a good ten minutes, my mind spiraling in a thousand different directions at once. A child of an archangel. A prophecy of some final battle. The kids looking happy. The demon that I had beheaded. Images flowed through my mind too fast for me to catch, and I was too stunned by Marcus's ideas to even try.

Finally I slowed at the edge of a creek, staring at the water as it rippled over the rocks. Was it true? I wish I could deny it, but the truth was I didn't know anything about my life before I woke up on that beach.

At the same time, it seemed incredible. I was just me. How could I possibly be the child of an archangel? And what? I was supposed to be part of some final battle?

I sank onto a tall rock and stared at the water, as if somehow the answers might reveal themselves. But the water babbled on, providing me with no information.

I'm not sure how long I sat there. It seemed like a long time. My body was stiff when I finally stood.

"There you are."

I turned as Graham stepped from the tree line. "I'd ask how you are, but I think I know the answer to that."

I shook my head, looking away from him, not wanting to meet his gaze. "I don't know how to process any of this. I mean, it just seems too far-fetched."

"As far-fetched as your ability to fight demons with a strength that rivals theirs?"

I struggled to accept it, but he was right. What other explanation was there for my abilities?

"I also wanted to let you know that I told the Uriels you wouldn't be in for a few days."

I stepped back, fear rushing through me. I hadn't even thought about my job. "No. I can't. I'll lose my job."

"It's okay. I told them it was a favor to me to allow it. Now I owe them. They will call on it. But I'm hoping you'll take me up on my offer and become a full-fledged member of the Seraph Force."

I opened my mouth to answer. But he hurried on before I could speak. "Hear me out. You can patrol only over in Forks. Every night if you want. I'd just ask you to help train some of the newer recruits. And some of the not so new. I think they could really learn something from you."

"Graham."

"I'm not asking you to decide now. You have enough on your plate. You have time. Wait until your family is healed and then talk it over with them. That's all I ask."

I stared up at him. It was a more than fair request. And work was the smallest issue I needed to deal with now. With Micah and Torr still healing and the demons after me, the Uriels were just not a priority, not with the demons targeting me.

Oh God. Were they really after me? Had I brought all this pain to my kids? I turned around, emotions clawing up my throat. My words were barely above a whisper. "What does this all mean? What am I supposed to do?"

Graham walked toward me and slipped his arms around me. I hesitated for a moment, worried that I was opening a door that should stay closed. My life was complicated enough as it was. But he felt so warm and it felt so right to be in his arms. I leaned back, letting myself have this one small moment.

"Nothing. You don't have to do anything. I don't know if what

Marcus said is true. Right now all you need to do is help your family heal."

"And how am I supposed to do that? How can I protect them twenty-four seven?"

"You'll stay with me, and we'll figure this out."

"Even Torr?"

I felt Graham stiffen behind me before he relaxed again. "There *is* something very different about him. I will have a member of the Seraph Force in the house at all times, but he's not a prisoner, not exactly."

I knew I couldn't ask for more than that. I'd had nearly two years to get to know Torr. I couldn't expect people who'd only known demons one way to suddenly accept that they could be something entirely different.

"And if I am part of this prophecy? If I am supposed to face the child of darkness?"

Graham gently turned me around, his hands now on my shoulders as he looked directly into my eyes. "You'll face him or her. But you won't face them alone."

I stared into his eyes and read the promise there. I let my arms slip around his waist leaning my head against his chest as he wrapped his arms around me again. And for just this moment, my mind stopped spinning. The full weight of responsibility wasn't on my shoulders alone. I leaned into Graham and just let myself feel safe.

CHAPTER 41

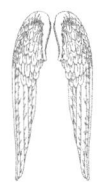

Despite my worry over the prophesy and Marcus's beliefs, after two days in Graham's home, I was going stir crazy, along with everyone else. Our apartment might've been small, but it was ours, so there was a sense of comfort at being stuck inside. Here, everything was new, luxurious, and not ours.

Torr had even gotten so bored he agreed to answer some of Marcus's questions yesterday. Marcus looked like a kid on Christmas morning when he showed up in Torr's room with pen and paper. I hovered nearby as Marcus began to question him. But I had nothing to worry about. Marcus asked him about his own abilities and skills and didn't push when Torr said he didn't want to answer something.

Then in the morning, the skies opened up. Rain slashed against the window, making us all even more desperate to get outside these four walls.

Graham stepped into the room and glanced around. Noel lay on the floor reading a book. Micah lay face down on the end of the bed, hanging half off of it. Torr lay on the bed, throwing a ball up and down, up and down. Tess stood over by the window, looking out. She glanced at Graham and then back out the window.

"Well, you all look bored," he said.

Noel shut the book, sitting up. "Desperately."

I smiled. "We're all getting a little antsy."

Graham's mouth quirked to the side, his eyes narrowing. "You know, I do have a training area. Maybe you'd all like to—"

"Yes, that would be great," I said.

Tess turned from her position at the window with a grin. "I'm game."

Graham's smiled dimmed when he looked at Torr. "I don't know if…"

Torr nodded. "I understand."

But I could tell from the look on Torr's face that he was as desperate to get out as the rest of us were. "I don't have to go. I could just—"

Torr shook his head. "No, Addie. Go. You need to burn off some energy. You can work on that thing we've been talking about." Torr's eyes bored into me.

As a family, we'd discussed my wings. They'd all seen them when the demons had attacked in the apartment. I'd tried on and off to get them to appear, but I honestly had no idea what I was doing. But maybe in some sort of training scenario I might be able to figure it out.

All three of them thought that it was important for me to know how they worked so that I could call on them when I needed to. I agreed, but I really had no idea how to do it and therefore no real chance to work on it.

Micah leaned over and whispered into Torr's ear. Torr shook his head before finally nodding.

"Are you ready now?" Graham said.

Noel jumped to her feet. "Yep."

"Then let's go."

Before we left the room, Micah had stopped at the door,

holding it open to tie his shoe. Torr, cloaked in invisibility, slipped through. And at every doorway that we went through, either Micah or Noel came up with some sort of excuse to pause for a moment longer than necessary to allow Torr to slip through.

I knew that he should be staying back in his room. It wasn't safe for him to be out. But at the same time, I was beyond thrilled that the three of them were working together. They had become a unit, just like Torr had always wanted.

It took us ten minutes to walk to the training facility. It was actually a separate building connected to the main house by an overhang that provided cover from the elements.

Graham threw open the glass doors to the building. I stepped in, my mouth falling open. It was a massive gymnasium. The training "room" could have easily housed thirty of my apartments. The ceiling was three stories high. Mats were laid out in the back half of the room. Weapons lined the wall. There was even an obstacle course laid out on the right-hand side of the area with ropes, high walls, and swinging obstacles that an individual would have to cross to reach the finish line. I smiled, my excitement growing.

Graham glanced over at me. "Good?"

I grinned back at him. "Very good."

∼

Throughout the next week, the kids, Torr, and I spent at least a few hours in the training building each day. Torr and Micah had to take it slowly because they were still healing but Noel and I finished each training session as a sweaty, exhausted, happy mess. During that time, Tess, Laura, Donovan, and Graham all trained with us. And I realized that Graham had unintentionally gotten his way: I was training with the Seraph Force.

I even sparred with Graham a few times. He was amazing. Fast, strong, he knew what he was doing. And each time, I felt a special little thrill at being closer to him. Yesterday he'd offered to show me some takedowns. He stepped behind me and wrapped his arms around me.

"What do you do now?" he asked, his lips right next to my ear.

I shivered, not a single fighting technique coming to mind. Because to be honest, I didn't want to do anything. I wanted to stay right in that moment and not move. Or maybe move, but just not to defend myself.

"No!" Micah broke the spell as he fell from one of the obstacles. I dashed forward, knowing even at my fastest I was too far away.

Torr materialized under him and caught him before any damage could be done.

Donovan, who'd been working with Noel, stopped and stared in shock. "Torr?"

Torr lowered Micah to the floor with a grimace. "Yeah, hi."

"What are you doing here?" Donovan demanded.

Graham spoke up from behind me. "It's okay. I knew he was here. He's been here since the first day."

"What? You guys could have told me," Donovan said.

"My call. Sorry about that," Graham said.

"Man, you think you can trust a guy," Donovan grumbled, turning back to Noel.

I looked back at Graham. "You've known?"

He smiled. "Well, Noel and Micah seem to be incredibly slow at getting through doorways. And ropes seem to magically swing whenever we come in here."

I winced. "Yeah."

"It really is okay. I think it's best if he stays invisible, though, just in case anyone happens by."

I stared up into his eyes. This man, this Angel Blessed, had changed the rules of the Seraph Force so they now patrolled both Sterling Peak and Blue Forks. He'd rushed to my family's side when we'd been hurt and done everything in his power to help us heal and keep us safe. And good Lord, he looked like he'd been carved from granite. But I knew how warm that skin of his was. And now he was only a few inches away. One small step, and I would be pressed up against him.

"Look out!" Donovan yelled.

Graham grabbed me around the waist and pulled me to the floor. A spear flew over my head. I lay sprawled against his chest. I could feel every muscle underneath me, every breath that he took. I licked my lips and stared into his face. It was only an inch away. He reached up and tucked my hair behind my ear.

Noel ran up. "Oh my God, I'm so sorry. Are you two okay?"

Graham stared into my eyes with a smile of regret. I pushed myself off him and onto the floor with a thud, feeling a little lightheaded. "Yup, I'm good. I think we need to work on your aim a little bit."

"I know, I know."

The door to the gym opened. Franklin stepped in. "Graham? The Camiels are waiting for you."

He groaned as he sat up. He reached a hand down for me, pulling me to my feet. "Damn it. I forgot I had a meeting. If you'll excuse me."

I nodded, and he squeezed my hand before he headed toward Franklin.

I watched him walk across the gymnasium, his shirt stretched taut across his shoulders. Man, I was a sucker for his shoulders.

"You're welcome," Noel whispered next to me.

I pulled my gaze from Graham. "What?"

"Oh, come on. How bad a shot do you think I am? You two have been staring at one another for days."

"What? No, he's just helping us out."

"Pretty sure he wants to help you out with lots of things."

My cheeks felt hot. "Um, I'm pretty sure this is not a conversation we should be having."

Noel looped her arm through mine. "Life is short. It's okay to have some fun in it."

She kissed me on the cheek and headed back to Donovan after retrieving her spear. I glanced back at the doorway where Graham had disappeared. Maybe she was right.

CHAPTER 42

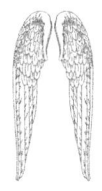

All in all, the days at Graham's turned out to be some of the best ever. We'd all have breakfast in the room and go do some training. At night, board games, and sometimes we would sit out on the balcony and look up at the stars. Graham spent every minute with us when he wasn't patrolling or involved in his Council or Seraph Force duties.

Whenever Graham spent time with us, he made a point of being right next to me. And our hands and arms always seemed to find a reason to touch. I wasn't sure where this was going, but I was looking forward to finding out as soon as we had some time alone together.

And while most of the days followed the same schedule, today things were a little different. Marcus held a briefing with the Seven and a few dozen of the top Seraph Force in the country. Graham invited me to attend. Part of me worried about attending. With that many Seraph Force members in Graham's home, I felt I should stay by Torr, just in case.

But the other part of me was incredibly curious. Marcus had been squirreled away in his office, working for days on end. And if he finally learned something, I really didn't want to wait to hear it.

"Okay, you three promise you will not leave this room?" I asked for the seventh time.

Noel rolled her eyes. "Yet again, we will not leave."

"And, Torr, you'll stay invisible the whole time?"

"Yes, no one will see me," he said not looking up.

Still, I stayed where I was.

Micah rolled the dice. "Addie, go. We'll be fine."

"You want to go, so go," Noel said.

I *did* want to go, and not just because of the information Marcus would impart. I was beginning to think seriously about Graham's offer. Being a member of the Seraph Force wouldn't be so bad, especially if I could patrol over in Blue Forks. Plus the kids would be taken care of. And seeing Graham regularly? I was beginning to think that was going to be a necessity. Even the idea of going back to a time when I barely saw him created an uncomfortable ache in my chest.

The only problem was Torr. He would have to remain invisible almost all the time. But then again, he'd had to do the same over in Blue Forks, so maybe it wasn't that different.

Finally, I nodded. "Okay, I'm going."

The three kids barely glanced at me, completely focused on their Monopoly game. "Uh-huh," Noel mumbled as she landed on Go.

Micah crossed his arms over his chest, his lips arranged in a pout. "Oh, come on. How come no one's landing on Park Place? I have hotels and everything."

Apparently none of them found me leaving as emotionally difficult as I felt it was. "Leaving now," I said again.

They all gave me a wave without looking.

"Hugs?" I asked.

Micah's head jolted up, and he grinned. He bolted up from the floor and over to me, wrapping his arms around me. "Sorry. Have fun. We'll be fine."

Noel hugged me as well. Torr stood awkwardly behind her. I pulled him in for a hug too. He stiffened, and then his arms wrapped around me. "Keep an eye on them. And stay invisible."

He nodded as he pulled away. "I will."

With one last look at them, I headed out, a tingle of excitement running through me. I'd get to see Graham in action as Commander of the Seraph Force and hopefully learn what Marcus had been so focused on.

The meeting was being held in the training facility. As I stepped inside, I stopped short at the crowd. Chairs had been arranged in rows facing a small stage where Marcus was busy flipping through his notes.

Graham stood off the stage to the left, speaking with a group of three older Rangers and Donovan. Graham listened attentively and then replied. The men each had an air of confidence about them. Graham glanced over his shoulder at Marcus and then made another comment to the men, who then took their seats.

"Hey," Tess said as she slipped in the door behind me. "Glad you came."

"I think I am too."

"Come on. We'll sit at the back." Tess moved toward the last row where Laura was already sitting with Mitch. I frowned as I took a seat between Laura and Tess. "Shouldn't you guys be up front as part of the Seven?"

"Graham doesn't believe in all that pomp and circumstance for this kind of thing. The public eats it up, but for meetings, we're all on the same team. All these Rangers are our brothers- and sisters-in-arms. There's no need to lord status over them."

The Rangers in the room had all taken their seats when the back doors flung open. D'Angelo strutted in, a group of three men arranged behind him. One was Hunter Uriel, who was not a member of the Seraph Force. "What's he doing here?" I asked.

"I have no idea," Tess mumbled.

D'Angelo strode down the aisle. His group of three moved off to the side.

"Where does he think he's going? All the seat are taken up front." Laura scowled.

Apparently I wasn't the only one who wasn't a fan of the man.

D'Angelo reached the front of room, and a man stood up from a seat smack dab in the middle of the front row. D'Angelo gave him a warm smile and then took his seat. The man hurried down the aisle and out the door.

"He had a seat saver?" Tess asked, her tone incredulous. "What a tool."

I didn't get a chance to reply because Graham stepped up to the edge of the stage and raised his hands. All the murmurs and restless movement died away.

Graham focused on the three men who'd accompanied D'Angelo. "You three need to leave. Now."

The men cast nervous glances at D'Angelo. D'Angelo waved them away. With a quick bow, the men stepped out of the room.

Tess seethed next to me.

I frowned. "What did I just miss?"

"D'Angelo just made it look like Graham does not have control of his Rangers and his meetings. God, I hate that guy."

But if Graham was bothered by the little interaction, it didn't show. "Good morning. Thank you for joining me this morning. I know many of you traveled far to get here, and I assure you the travel was worth it.

"This is Professor Marcus Jeffries. Most of you have probably heard of him. He has some new information that he believes, and I agree, is important for all of us to hear." Graham stepped back, moving to the edge of the stage, where he stood with his arms behind his back.

Marcus got up from his seat and moved to the lectern at the front. "Good morning. For the last three decades, I have studied the demon threat. During that time, my late wife and I learned about many facets of demonology. We know that they only appear in certain areas, not all areas of the world. We hypothesized that there may be some sort of door or portal that allows them through in those areas.

"Until recently, we believed they needed to return through the same portal. That is something we no longer believe to be true. While they need to access our world from the portal, they can return from anywhere."

A stir rose through the crowd.

"But that is not why you were called here today. Five years ago, I learned about a book, written in Enochian, that allegedly contained many of the demons secrets. I managed to acquire that book just a few weeks ago."

I pictured the ancient tome that Marcus had shown me in his office.

"It is taking time to translate, but I have learned a number of valuable insights. The first involves the missing. There has been a great deal of speculation about why the demon take some and kill others outright. I now believe that they take individuals with the hope and intent of turning them to demons themselves."

"What?" Tess exclaimed next to me. And she wasn't the only one. The crowd had burst into anxious conversations.

Graham stepped forward. "I know this is surprising information. But it tells us two things: one, why they would target stronger individuals when weaker ones would be easier to overcome, and second, it suggests the demons are trying to build their ranks."

"To what end?" one of the Rangers in the front row called out.

Graham looked back to Marcus.

"I believe that we are coming to a time when the prophecy of the fight between the forces of good and evil will be realized. I believe the demon attacks and their increases in frequency have been conducted to test our defenses and to help increase their own ranks. And I believe these attacks will only further increase in frequency in the coming days or weeks until this final battle begins."

More murmuring burst out across the room.

Graham once again took control. "We have trained for this. We are prepared for this. But we will all need to redouble our efforts. We need to shore up the weaknesses in our newer recruits to get them ready in time. But make no mistake, when the final battle comes, we will be victorious!"

The Rangers jumped to their feet. I got to my own feet a little more slowly. I hoped that Marcus was wrong. I hoped the increase in attacks wasn't a precursor to the final battle. But if he was right about this and about who I was, then when the final battle came, that meant I would be leading the charge.

CHAPTER 43

After the meeting, I quickly made my way back to my gang. I needed to see them. Being with them, I could pretend everything was normal and that the looming specter of a battle of good versus evil was something far off in the future.

But when I stepped in, my three had abandoned their Monopoly game. They sat by the cold fireplace, deep in conversation. All three heads jolted up at my arrival.

"What's going on?" I asked.

"Someone stopped by the room," Torr said quietly.

Alarm flashed through me. "What? Who?"

"None of us had seen him before," Noel said. "He was probably in his twenties, with blond hair, brown eyes. He was kind of boring looking."

Immediately I flashed on Hunter Uriel. He'd been here during the meeting. Had D'Angelo sent him to spy? From what I could gather about the man, information tended to be his weapon of choice. Had he heard Graham had hidden us away and just wanted to learn who we were?

"Were you invisible?" I asked Torr.

He nodded. "Yes."

"But we were talking to him. The guy was listening at the door," Micah said.

I took a breath, my worries about the upcoming final battles shoved aside by more immediate concerns.

"He opened the door and peered in at us," Noel said. "I demanded to know who he was. Franklin appeared and escorted him out. But he had this look on his face, Addie., like he'd just won something."

I swallowed, not liking the sound of that. I focused on Torr. "But you were invisible the whole time, right?"

"Yes," he said.

I let out a breath. "Okay, that's good. I'll talk to Graham later. I'm sure it's nothing to worry about." I gave them a smile that I hoped was convincing. Because deep down, I had a feeling that it was only a matter of time before this little paradise we'd created for ourselves was blown apart.

CHAPTER 44

I really wanted to talk to Graham about Hunter Uriel and D'Angelo and get his thoughts, but I didn't see him or any of the Seraph Force for the rest of the day. They were all busy with the visiting Rangers.

Graham didn't stop by the next morning either, for the same reason. So when I stepped into the training room the next day, my need to see him had only increased. I looked, but he was nowhere to be found.

Donovan dropped the weights he was lifting and walked over to us. He read my face and answered the question before I even had a chance to ask it. "Graham was called up to the Academy. There was some sort of problem."

Concern shot through me. "Was it about what Marcus discussed yesterday?"

"No, nothing like that. Just some administrative stuff. He should be back soon. Look, I know what Marcus thinks about who you are, but there's nothing to worry about, not yet."

I considered telling him about Hunter but decided to hold off. I should tell Graham first, and hopefully I'd get a chance to soon.

But still, disappointment wafted through me. And not just

because I needed to unburden myself. Training with Graham had been incredible. It was an excuse to spend time with him, to touch him. And every moment I spent near him I knew that what had maybe started as a little crush had bloomed into something much more. When I was near him, I simply felt more alive, more safe.

And I realized he really wasn't like the other Angel Blessed. To be honest, the members of the Seraph Force I'd met were nothing like the Uriels or the other well-to-do Angel Blessed. Maybe it was because they were soldiers, which grounded them. Since coming to stay with Graham, the barriers in my mind between the Angel Blessed and Demon Cursed had blurred and now disappeared.

Society might still have those hang ups, but I didn't, not when it came to Donovan, Tess, Laura and a few of the others. And definitely not when it came to Graham.

All I knew was, when I was around Graham, I didn't feel like I was in this fight alone. I felt connected to him in a way I've never felt to anyone before.

I felt like I wasn't alone.

And I had the feeling he felt the same way. Of course with him being constantly surrounded by people meant there hadn't been a chance to really do anything about it. But one of these days, I'd make the time.

"You want to do a little sparring? One of the Seraph Force from the south brought some new staffs. I thought we could try them out," Donovan asked.

I grinned. "Sounds good."

~

We'd been practicing for only about twenty minutes when movement outside the window on the lawn caught my eye. I ducked Donovan's swipe with one hand and shoved him back. He stumbled as my head turned toward the doors. I frowned. "What's going on out there?"

Donovan, who'd been getting ready to attack again, straightened, looking past me. "No idea." He'd just stepped toward the doors when they flung open.

D'Angelo strode in, Hunter Uriel with him, and three dozen students from the Academy fanned out behind them. "Students" was a misnomer, suggesting all of them were fresh eyed and straight out of their parents' homes. Most of them were hardened warriors who, after years of training on their own, had been allowed into the Rangers Academy.

I backed up, not sure if this was a threat or if they were simply here to train.

Donovan growled. "What do you think you're doing, D'Angelo?"

Okay, so they weren't here to train.

D'Angelo strode forward, his arrogance leading the way. "We've had some disturbing reports that Commander Graham is harboring a demon."

Tess, who'd arrived only a few minutes earlier and had been working with Micah and Noel, strode across the room to stand at Donovan's side. "You have no standing here, D'Angelo. How dare you break into the home of the Commander of the Seraph Force."

"I will do whatever is necessary to protect Sterling Peak." He raised his voice to make sure that everyone heard him.

I glanced over my shoulder at where Noel and Micah stood. Both looked confused and more than a little scared. Torr was in the back corner of the gymnasium. He'd just finished a round on the obstacle course. I glared at him, trying to say without words that he'd better not move.

D'Angelo stopped ten feet away from us.

Donovan crossed his arms over his chest, staring D'Angelo down. Donovan had a few inches on him and more than a few pounds of muscle. "Do you see any demons here? Get out of here, D'Angelo."

D'Angelo's gaze scanned the room, passing right over the spot where Torr stood. Then his eyes lasered in on Micah and Noel. "What have we here? Who are these two?"

"My wards," I said.

D'Angelo raised an eyebrow at that.

"And they are under Graham's protection," Tess said.

"There are rumors that demons can disguise themselves." D'Angelo flicked his hand toward Noel and Micah. "Seize them."

The soldiers immediately spread out, heading toward the Noel and Micah.

An ache began to build in my chest at the fear on both of their faces. The room seemed to grow brighter. My focus narrowed as I jumped toward them. "You will not touch them!"

The soldiers gasped. The ones closest to me stumbled back. A few dropped to one knee, their heads bowed.

I looked down at them and realized I was hovering four feet from the ground. And holding me up were a pair of wings outlined in flames.

CHAPTER 45

Every time we came down to the gym, I had tried to get my wings to appear. But nothing happed. I had begun to think that Torr, Noel, and Micah had all had some sort of shared delusion the night of the apartment attack.

But now, I hovered above the ground, staring at the soldiers, who quickly backed away.

The wings that had sprung from my back were gorgeous, extending out six feet. Composed of white and pale blue feathers, they were completely engulfed in flames that shifted from white to orange to blue at the very edges. I didn't fear them or worry about getting burned. In fact, the feel of them, the heat of them, filled me with power. They felt right.

D'Angelo's mouth fell open. Then he, too, dropped to one knee. "We didn't know."

Despite my awe at finally seeing my wings, I glared down at D'Angelo. "They are under my protection, and they are not to be harmed."

A tremor ran through D'Angelo's body. I cast my gaze out across all of the soldiers. Some of them looked at me in awe while others did so in fear, but none looked like they wanted to challenge me. "No one will touch these children. Is that understood?"

I scanned the group, waiting for all of them to nod.

Donovan stepped forward. "You need to leave now. Commander Graham will hear of this."

The students in the back began to filter out first. The rest quickly followed. Recognition flashed across D'Angelo's face. He narrowed his eyes. "You're that maid."

"Apparently she's a maid with angel wings," Tess deadpanned.

D'Angelo shot her a glare, the side of his mouth curling in a snarl. The golden boy didn't look so pretty all of a sudden.

My hands clenched into fist to keep me from striking out, I stared down at him. "You need to leave."

He got to his feet, puffing his chest out. "I'm a member of the Seven. You do not give me orders."

My wings flamed higher as I swept them toward him.

He stumbled back.

"You need to leave," I repeated, firmer this time.

He stared up at me, hate and loathing in his eyes, before he turned tail and ran with Hunter right on his heels.

I lowered myself to the ground, completely forgetting about D'Angelo. Because I had something much more important to focus on.

My wings.

I glanced back at them in delight. Now that they were out, I knew how to use them. It was like I just needed them to open to understand. I extinguished the flames and then retracted them.

Torr, Noel and Micah walked over to me, smiles across their faces, D'Angelo's threat seemingly forgotten by them as well.

"That is so cool," Micah said.

Tess grinned from the other side. "So, wings, huh?"

I grinned back at her. "So it seems."

CHAPTER 46

GRAHAM

Annoyance rolled through Graham as he stormed back to his home. He'd been called to the Academy this morning. He had been looking forward to finally being able to spend some time with Addie and her family. Truth be told, he was finally going to see if maybe Addie wouldn't mind spending some time alone with him. They wouldn't leave the grounds because Addie was never willing to be that far from her kids, but he could have a nice private dinner set up in the dining room downstairs.

Marcus's news had made him realize that he needed to stop beating around the bush with Addie. He'd been giving her space because of everything that had been thrown at her. But he felt like they were running out of time.

He'd planned on asking her this morning at breakfast, but then he'd gotten the call and had headed to the Academy. Yet once he arrived, no one knew who had called him. There was no emergency, nothing urgent that needed his attention.

Quickly, he turned around and headed back home, not sure what was going on. But an uneasy feeling settled in his gut. As he approached his gates, students from the Academy streamed out. More than a few of them looked shaken.

Graham grabbed one of them and pulled him up short. "What is the meaning of this? Why are you at my home?"

The man swallowed as he shifted his gaze to his feet. "Major D'Angelo ordered us to accompany him to your home. He said there was a demon that you were giving sanctuary to."

Fear lanced through him, but he kept it in check. "And?"

"And we didn't see a demon, but we did see an angel. I'm sorry, Commander Graham. We were just following orders."

Angel? In his gut he knew whatever had happened involved Addie. That curiosity, though, was out paced by his anger, which boiled to a fever pitch but not at the soldier in front of him. He was telling the truth. He was following orders. In the Seraph Force, you were expected to follow the orders of your higher ranks. Without that authority, it devolved into chaos. In the middle of a battle, you couldn't have people questioning why they were doing what they're doing. They just needed to do it.

But it didn't lessen his annoyance. He released the soldier and stepped back, giving him a nod to indicate he could leave. The man scurried away. Graham scanned the group, looking for the target of his rage.

D'Angelo burst out from around the side of the building. He sprinted across the lawn, Hunter Uriel on his heels, and disappeared out the side gate. Graham frowned, watching them. They looked like death itself was on their tails.

Graham hurried to the gate and around the side of the house. He knew everyone would be at the training facility. He stepped inside, expecting to see a scene of destruction. But there was nothing out of place. Everything looked as it always did, except for one glaring exception: Addie had *wings*.

She flew along the ceiling and then dove down to get targets set up along the ground. She was amazing. Beauty and strength all rolled into one. Graham stared at her, not able to look away, until

Donovan caught sight of him and moved to his side. "D'Angelo was here. He was looking for Torr."

Graham finally pulled his gaze away from Addie. "Did he find him?"

Donovan grinned. "Nope. But he found one pissed-off Addie." Donovan's grin then dimmed. "She made an enemy of today of him today. She'll have to be careful."

Graham knew what damage D'Angelo could do when he put his mind to it. But hopefully Addie would be spared, at least for a little while. From the look on D'Angelo's face, he'd be too scared to do anything any time soon. And hopefully once he figured out what to do, Addie would be too strong for him to do much of anything at all.

"She is the child of flame, isn't she?" Donovan asked softly.

Graham nodded, a knot in his throat. He'd hoped Marcus was wrong. He'd hoped that maybe there was some other explanation for all she could do. He didn't want her anywhere near the fight to come because he knew she would belong to the war effort, to the world.

And selfishly, right now, he wanted her to belong to him.

CHAPTER 47

ADDIE

Two days after D'Angelo came to the gym, my world felt as if it was as it always should have been. I'd shoved my worries about the prophesies to the back of my mind and focused on the new love of my life: flying. Everything about it felt right. At night, when the world was dark, I slipped outside and fly through the air. I had never felt so free in my whole life.

Marcus had been right. I was the child of an archangel, the child of flame. He'd gone through his books and found references to children of archangels who could fly. He'd spent time sitting in the training room with his books, watching me fly. Earlier today, he'd hurried out after only a few minutes without a word, lugging his books. From experience, I now knew that was his eureka look.

I'd expected him to be at dinner to explain what he'd found. I couldn't help but wonder if it had to do with me. I knew he was trying to research which archangel had given me life. He was convinced now that I was the offspring of one of them, or as Donovan put it, the kick-ass result of some rebel angel on a weekend of fun.

But the question still was: which archangel had given me life? Part of me wondered about that too, but honestly, my life, despite the demons possibly targeting me aside, was better than ever. I had my kids safe with me, they were healing, none of us were hungry, something was growing between me and Graham, and I was having one long, serious life-is-good moment.

Plus, I had these incredible abilities. A nonexistent parent wasn't really much of a concern for me at present.

D'Angelo had been quiet ever since he'd come into the training building, but I was worried about what he'd said about Torr. Graham wasn't sure where the leak had come from. It was possible the staff had reported that part of Graham's home was off limits. Maybe someone overheard mention of Torr or caught a glimpse of him when he'd revealed himself in the gym to catch Micah. However the rumor had started, it seemed to have been quelled by a bigger reveal: my wings.

But I knew we would have to find another place to live soon, somewhere a little bit more remote. I tried to shove D'Angelo to the back corner of my mind. Still, after that incident, I'd taken to wearing my sword at all times. Graham hadn't said anything, but I also noticed he'd placed a Seraph Force at the end of our hall after D'Angelo's stunt.

Tonight after dark, Graham had set up dinner on the balcony at the end of the hall. It was a beautiful spot. With the full moon as a backdrop, it offered an incredible view of the bridge and Blue Forks beyond it. Torr even came and joined us at Graham's invitation. Of course, he was invisible, but Noel, Micah, and I could see him.

Micah popped a grape into his mouth. "I finished the obstacle course faster today. I took a full minute off my time. Donovan said I'm a shoo-in for the Seraph Force if I keep training like I am."

Every time I saw him these days, he was eating. But it was

good for him. He needed it. I swear he'd grown a few inches just in the last few days.

"Donovan says you have the makings too," Graham said, looking at Noel.

She pushed the food on her plate around and bit her lip. "Actually, Marcus said that maybe I could go to his old university. I mean, I know it's years away, and I'd have to study a ton, but maybe…"

I smiled, my heart filling. They were both talking about their futures. They'd never done that before. A weight in my chest released. "I think that's great."

Graham watched me from across the table. "And what about you, Addie? What about your future?"

I looked across the table, and the world fell away. "I have some ideas about that."

"Really? Like what?" he asked.

"I—" A strange pull started in my chest. I frowned, turning to stare at the bridge. I got to my feet, scanning the horizon.

"Addie?" Graham asked, concern in his voice.

The tug in my chest grew stronger. "Something's wrong. Something's not right."

I moved away from the table to the edge of the balcony. What was it? The tug was now a throb, but at the same time I knew there was nothing wrong with me. It was a warning. But of what?

Graham came to my side, staring out across the land. "What is it?"

I gripped the metal railing, staring out across Sterling Peak and into Blue Forks. "I don't know. But something's wrong. I just can't figure out what."

Noel and Micah came to the balcony railing as well. Micah pointed. "What's that?"

Beyond Blue Forks, trees would occasionally drop to the ground and disappear from sight. It was as if something was sucking them down into the ground or knocking them over. It was hard to tell from here.

But their path was leading them a clearing. Two minutes later, the phenomenon reached the field, and the cause became clear.

Demons, dozens of them, marched straight for Blue Forks.

CHAPTER 48

Scenarios ran through my head, none of them good. Graham was already issuing orders. "Sound the alarm now!" he ordered Mitch, who'd been standing guard just inside the building. Mitch took off sprinting down the hall.

"What's the plan for this?" I asked.

Graham stared at the advancing horde, his eyes shifting back and forth incredibly fast. No doubt scenarios were running through his mind just as quickly as they were running through mine. "We'll pull up the bridge. That should slow them down long enough give us a chance to get our defenses in place."

"What about the people in Blue Forks?" Noel asked.

Graham shook his head. "There's not enough time to get them out. We'll take in as many as we can, but we won't be able to evacuate all of them before that horde reaches them."

I stared at the wave of violence heading toward an unsuspecting people of Blue Forks. He was right. The Seraph Force would never reach them in time. I looked at Noel, Torr, and Micah. "You stay inside Graham's home. And you look out for one another."

The klaxon of the demon alarm rang out through the night. I'd seen the large speakers at the top of the bridge. I'd known what they were for, but never in my life did I think I would hear them.

Micah started to move forward, but Noel grabbed him, holding him back. "We will."

Torr burst forward and handed me the second demon sword. He'd started carrying it since D'Angelo's move as well. "Be careful, Addie. And be deadly."

I nodded, sliding the scabbard over my shoulder and securing it. I gripped the railing, placing one foot on top.

Graham's eyes were large as he grabbed my arm. "What are you doing?"

"You might not be able to reach them in time, but I can." My wings shot out.

Graham jumped back to avoid getting hit.

I looked at Noel, Micah, and Torr. "I love you." I leaped off the edge of the balcony.

"Addie!" Graham scrambled to the railing.

But I didn't look back, my attention focused on the horde racing toward the edge of Blue Forks. I needed to buy the people of Blue Forks some time to get out.

Because I was quite literally their only hope.

CHAPTER 49

Part of me reeled as I flew down the mountain, not because of the imminent threat or because of the stakes but because I was flying.

Flying.

In the sky.

With wings.

At the same time, it felt completely right and natural. I knew how to do this. And I realized Marcus was right: I was born to do this.

More than one person gasped as they looked up at me. I flew high over the bridge. People scurried across it, some going to the safety on the other side, others setting up barricades. I caught sight of Sheila's dark hair as she ordered her guards to help get as many people through as possible.

Some of the Seraph Force had already made it beyond the bridge. They sprinted forward, rushing into danger. Donovan was at the head of the pack. He looked up. His mouth gaped open, and then he grinned. "Give 'em hell, Addie!"

I tucked my wings closer to my sides, making myself more aerodynamic. I soared through the air, barely able to discern the faces of the people I flew by. They weren't my concern. Those people should make it over the bridge in time.

The others were going to struggle.

I swooped through the air at the edge of Blue Forks, over the buildings, until I landed at the very edge of the boundary. It was chaos. People crammed into the streets, rushing toward the bridge. Their screams, cries, and shouts crowded the air.

A few screams were aimed in my direction. People didn't know what to make of my wings. But I tuned them all out. In front of me, there were no buildings, no homes, just forest. This was the only road leading into Blue Forks.

Taking a breath, I pulled my swords. They immediately ignited. I widened my stance. The flames of my wings arced higher.

The first wave of demons came into view. Tall, green with pockmarked skin, their horns were only slightly larger than Torr's. The first wave raced toward me, letting out a collective ferocious roar, showing off their teeth.

Holding my ground, I gripped the swords tighter, my focus straight ahead. I calmed my breathing. I would take down as many as I could. I would fight until my last breath to make sure as many humans as possible survived.

And maybe, just maybe, I would buy the Seraph Force enough time to save them all.

CHAPTER 50

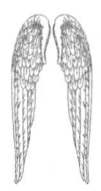

GRAHAM

Graham's heart leaped into his throat as Addie leaped from the balcony. "Addie!"

She didn't even look back as she flew down the mountain. He wasted no time either. He sprinted across the balcony, out the room, and tore down the stairs in record time. Franklin jolted as he burst into the foyer. "Demons coming. Take care of the kids."

He grabbed his bow and arrow from the closet in the front hall and burst out the door. Footsteps sounded behind him. Graham glanced over his shoulder, expecting to see one of the Seraph Force.

Instead, it was Torr. He sprinted down the hill next to Graham, his face serious. And for one moment, Graham forgot what he was running to do. "Are you fighting on our side or theirs?"

Torr speared Graham with a glare. "I'm fighting on Addie's."

Then he outpaced Graham and disappeared from view. Not because he went behind something but because he simply faded into nothing. Graham would've gasped, except it would've slowed him down.

Of course, he knew Torr could make himself invisible. But he'd never seen him shift like that. He supposed it was a good call. With a demon horde racing toward the towns, a demon sprinting along the roads of Sterling Peak was going to cause chaos. And people would not ask questions before they attacked.

A few minutes later, Graham reached the bridge. Sheila hurried over to him. "The citizens of Blue Forks have started making their way across the bridge. I've got all my people helping. But the Council sent word that I should close off the bridge."

Graham's lashed out. "No, we keep it down until the last possible moment."

"The Council won't be happy."

"I'll deal with them," Graham growled.

Sheila paused flicking a glance up at the sky. "Was that Addie who flew by?"

Graham nodded, not taking the time to explain.

"Keep the bridge down as long as you can. Get as many people across it as possible. When the demons have a chance of breaching it, close it. It doesn't matter who's on the other side."

Sheila matched his pace, immediately switching back into command mode. "Does that include you?"

"That most definitely includes me." He started across the bridge.

"Wait!" She tossed him a set of keys. Graham nodded his thanks as he snatched them out of the air and sprinted for her security Jeep.

He leaped into the driver seat, quickly started the car, and pulled away. People scrambled out of his path, but there were too many of them, so he drove along the grass, letting the refugees have the road.

People streamed out of Blue Forks: old, young, male, female, healthy, crippled. All different except for one commonality: the looks of complete and utter terror on their faces.

Graham gripped the steering wheel and swung back onto the road as the largest waves of refugees passed. Now the numbers had trickled down. It was mainly older citizens of Blue Forks and those struggling with some sort of physical ailment or with young children.

Ahead, he saw Tess grab a child from a woman who was struggling to carry two toddlers. Tess looked toward Blue Forks before she sprinted back for the bridge with the child in her arms.

Donovan's form emerged as he cut through the refugees. Graham swerved so that he came around the side of Donovan and slammed to a stop. "Get in."

Donovan glanced over at him in surprise and then quickly jumped into the passenger seat. He took off again before Donovan had fully closed the door.

"I saw Addie land. She's at the edge of town."

Graham nodded. He figured that was where she would've gone. She'd want to head off the horde as soon as she could in case there were any stragglers left behind.

"Did you see her wings? Man, I've never seen them look like that. They left a trail of fire in the sky," Donovan said.

Graham had indeed seen it. The outline of fire he'd seen before was nothing compared to the sight of them fully engulfed in flame. She looked like an avenging angel. And no doubt would fight like one.

"We need to—"

"Look out!" Donovan yelled.

Graham was already swerving the car. A large billboard crashed to the ground in front of them. Two demons appeared in the dust as it settled.

Graham put the car into reverse but then stopped before he hit the gas. There were two right behind them as well.

They were trapped.

CHAPTER 51

ADDIE

From the shortness of their horns, I knew the first wave of demons were new. That was good. The younger ones were always easier to take down. I took a deep breath, focusing my energy as they rushed me.

Then I just let go.
I didn't think.
I didn't plan.
I reacted.

I swirled, dodging out the path of one demon as I sliced another. I didn't stop as I moved from one to the next, slicing down demon after demon without conscious thought.

A large demon swung its meaty fist toward me. I sliced it off. I sensed two rushing behind me. I flared the fire on my wings. They screamed, pulling back their hands, now charred stubs. With one sweep of my swords, I took off one of their heads, and then the other.

That was how it went as the first wave continued. By the time I stopped, over three dozen demons lay in pieces around me.

There was a small break in the onslaught as the next wave stopped, staring at the demons littering the ground, their blood flowing down the street.

I raised my head, twirled my blades in my hands, and smiled. I know I shouldn't be, but I was actually enjoying this.

CHAPTER 52

GRAHAM

The demons blocked their car from the front and the back. "Do you see the horde?" Donovan asked, his gaze moving from side to side.

"No, these must be scouts," Graham replied. He thought about ramming the ones in front, but they were huge, and he wouldn't be able to pick up enough speed to do any damage. "Let's move."

Graham jumped from the car, pulling his bow into his arms. But he was too slow. The demon was on him before he could bring it around. It knocked the bow from his hand. He managed to hold on to an arrow and plunged it into the creature's eye, shoving it as far as it could go. The creature toppled forward.

But a second one was right behind it. It aimed a punch at Graham's face. He ducked to the side, bringing an uppercut into the creature's stomach. It barely moved. He slammed his left elbow into its chin. Its head reared back. And then a knife blade burst through its throat.

Its mouth dropped open. Its tongue lolled to the side. The knife was retracted, and the demon was shoved to the side.

Torr stood there, a bloody knife in his hand.

Graham met his gaze, feeling more than a little guilty at his earlier comment. "Thanks."

Torr just gave him a brief nod. Donovan jogged over to them, slapping Torr on the shoulder. "Thanks, man."

Donovan earned a small smile from Torr. "I set up a barricade at the end of Main Street. It's where Addie is. She needs help."

"What about the people?" Graham asked.

"I got a dozen out before I came across you two. I'm going for another sweep." He nodded down the road where a group of people was running for the bridge.

Before Graham could make a comment, Torr disappeared.

"That is a little freaky," Donovan said.

"Yeah. Come on." They loaded back into the car.

Graham crushed down on the accelerator.

Donovan glanced behind them. "Torr came out of nowhere. He got one of the demons who was about to impale me. I would have been dead."

"Me too."

And Graham didn't know what to think about that. Why was Torr so different? Were there others out there like him? Was it possible that they could find some allies amongst the demons?

But that was a conversation for another time. Right now, they needed to evacuate Blue Forks. And they all, Addie and Torr included, needed to get across the bridge.

"There!" Donovan pointed straight ahead.

But Graham didn't need his directions. He could see her clearly as she fought off a circle of ten demons.

She was a swirl of beautiful death. Every time she moved, a demon was cut in half or lost a body part. She didn't stop. She just moved on to the next.

A small child darted out of a building and down the path. A demon sprinted after it. Addie rose in the air and pulsed toward the small child, her wings leaving of trail of fire in the air.

A demon stepped to the side and released a spear. Addie dove in front of the child, the spear reaching them as Addie covered herself and the child in her wings.

CHAPTER 53

ADDIE

I curled my arms around the trembling child. My wings cocooned around the two of us. I felt the spear as if I had eyes in the back of my head. I fanned the flames of my wings hotter.

The tip of the spear melted to sludge as it reached us before the wooden staff burst into flame. The child in my arms was no more than five. His whole body shook, and tears trailed through the dirt on his face. "Mama," he wailed.

"We'll find her," I promised as I pulled my wings from around us and burst into the sky. The child's mouth fell open.

"It's okay. I've got you."

He grabbed on to my hands before a smile crept along his face. "Angel," he whispered.

With the boy securely wrapped in my arms, I headed for the bridge and safety while scanning the road below me.

A group of ten people was only a few hundred yards from the bridge. With a jolt, I realized I knew half of them. I dropped down to the road in front of them. Lisa Sanchez let out a shriek. Her eyes widened as she took in my face. "Addie?"

"Hi, Lisa."

Lisa already had her hands full with her youngest. Manny had the other young ones by the hand. He stopped still, his mouth gaping as he stared at my wings.

I placed the boy on the ground in front of Cecilia. "I need you to get him to safety."

Cecilia just nodded mutely at me, her eyes also locked on my wings.

I knew they wanted to ask me questions, but there simply wasn't time. I surged into the air, racing back for the front.

The horde had moved on, but a blockade had been erected at the end of the block, made from two overturned cars pushed together. Graham and Donovan were behind them, releasing arrow after arrow. They managed to keep the horde back except for one, who sprinted forward when they were both turned away from him.

I dove down from the air, and with one clean swipe of my sword, removed his head. It fell at the feet of both men.

Donovan didn't slow as he grabbed another arrow and let loose. "Always need to make an entrance, don't you?"

I spared him a small smile. "I'm going to do a quick scan of the buildings to make sure there's no one here."

"We'll hold them off." Graham met my eyes, complete faith and trust in his gaze.

I nodded and took off into the air. I flew through the buildings, calling out and checking them as fast as I could. Six demons sprinted along a side alleyway after an older man and woman who were trying to escape.

I crashed down, landing on one of the demons and driving it into the ground. With a yell of rage, I split the other two in half with two swipes of my sword before the other three bolted away. The man and woman looked at me, shock splashed across their faces.

I nodded at them over my shoulder. "You need to hurry."

The man shook his head, indicating his wife. She reached out for the wall, her face pale. A line of blood stained her pants leg. "She's hurt. She can't move fast."

I walked over and picked the woman up. "Stay with me."

The man moved quickly, staying on my heels as I darted down the alleyway. I was beyond Donovan and Graham. I debated how to get these two to the bridge when a van screeched into view, coming to a bone-jarring halt in front of me.

Tess was behind the wheel. Laura jumped from the passenger seat. I lowered the woman to the ground. "Can you get them to the bridge?"

Tess nodded as Laura swept open the back of the van. There were seven more people in the back. Two of them hurried out to help the couple inside.

"Any more stragglers?" Laura asked.

"I don't know. Those were the only two I could find. The demons are getting close. You need to get to the bridge now."

"What about Donovan and Graham?"

"I'll get them. Go."

Tess nodded and leaped back into the driver seat. Laura looked toward where the demons were.

I knew she wanted to jump into the fight, but the demons were massing. We needed everyone over the bridge so we could make our stand there. It was the more strategic location. "Head for the bridge. You can do more good there if they get past us."

With one last glance at me, Laura reluctantly climbed into the passenger seat of the van. Tess wasted no time pulling a U-turn and racing back toward the bridge.

I took off into the air and flew straight back to where I'd last seen Donovan and Graham.

They'd had to retreat. Demons streamed toward them. They were backed into an alley with a fence at their backs. I dove down and slammed my two feet into the top of the fence. It crashed backward. Donovan and Graham scrambled over it.

I landed in front of them and expanded my wings as the demons closed in. Pressure built in my chest as the flames grew higher.

Donovan backed away, his mouth hanging open. But Graham stood close, wanting to help. I shook my head. "You need to run now."

Then the fire grew hotter and hotter. The flames flared out ten feet high. The demons paused, not seeming to know what to do.

The pressure in my chest continued to build, becoming almost painful. I couldn't hold it back much longer.

Donovan and Graham had disappeared. I glanced over my shoulder at the demons crowding closer. The feeling in my chest began to spiral outward, calling for release.

Closing my eyes, I let go. Fire blasted out from me twenty feet in all directions, incinerating any demon that came close. Screams and cries met my ears, and when I opened my eyes, the entire alleyway was on fire. The corpses of demons burned where they'd fallen before being reduced to ash.

I burst back into the air, seeing Graham and Donovan heading for the bridge. Donovan limped while Graham covered his retreat. I could see Donovan yelling at him, no doubt telling him to go on without him. But I knew Graham would never do that.

I bolted toward them and landed next to Graham, but my eyes were on Donovan. "What happened?"

Donovan's face was tight with pain. "It's nothing. It's a sprain. Demon horde, people, focus on the priorities."

"He can't run. You need to get him out of here," Graham said.

I looked toward the advancing horde and then back to Graham.

He nodded. "I know what I'm saying. Get him out of here."

Swallowing hard, I stared at him, and then grabbed him by the front of his shirt and pulled him close, pressing my lips against his. I'd wanted to do that for the last few weeks. Truth be told, I'd wanted to do that ever since he'd caught me at the Uriels' home.

But there never seemed to be the right time. But right now it looked like we were out of time.

And for a few blissful moments, everything disappeared: the fear, the demons, the worry, even Donovan. For one moment, it felt like no one existed but me and Graham.

I might have started the kiss, but he quickly claimed it, wrapping his around me and pulling me tight against him. My whole body shook, and a whimper emitted from my throat.

A crash of glass cut through the haze. My chest heaved. My heart raced as I released him and stared into his eyes. "Don't die. I'm coming back for you."

He smiled and ran a hand down the side of my face. "Yes, ma'am."

Without another word, I grabbed Donovan under the shoulders and yanked him up into the air.

He let out a yelp and grabbed at my hands. "Holy crap. I'm flying."

"Technically, I'm flying. You're dangling," I said, still feeling like I'd had an out-of-body experience. A demon horde was rushing at us. I was flying Donovan to safety, and yet I couldn't get Graham's lips out of my mind. It was like I was on two tracks, one in this moment and the other still wrapped in Graham's arms.

"Hey, if anybody asks, I am totally saying I was flying. And I'm not mentioning that you were part of the equation at all."

I smiled. "Don't worry, I won't infringe on the stories of your masculine adventure. Of course, if I were to land in Sterling Peak cradling you like a baby, your story might be hard to sell."

His whole body stiffened. "Don't you dare. I swear I will fling myself to my death if you even try."

I laughed in spite of the fear crawling through me.

Up ahead, the bridge was bathed in light. I put on a bolt of speed. Donovan grasped my hands tighter. But I didn't have time to make this a nice peaceful flight. Graham was still back there, and I needed to get Donovan to safety and get back to him.

The front of the bridge was still down. I lowered the two of us to the bridge. Sheila waited at its entrance. She hurried over. "Who's left?"

I dropped Donovan gently on the ground. He grimaced as he put weight on his bad ankle. "Graham's still back there," I said. "And Tess and Laura are coming with a van full of refugees. They should be last. When they're over, close it up."

"What about you and Graham?" Sheila asked.

"I'll take care of it." I went airborne. As I flew back toward Blue Forks, I saw the security van driven by Tess. They'd make it. Now I just needed to make sure that Graham and I did.

CHAPTER 54

GRAHAM

The demons kept coming. Graham would take one down and another one or two would take its place. He didn't know how Addie managed to take down so many. He and Donovan had taken down one after the next, but it seemed like they'd barely made a dent.

Graham sprinted toward an abandoned car flipped on its side. He needed some sort of cover. It wasn't long though before the demons reached him. He took out five with arrows as three more sprinted toward him. One came around the side of the car. Graham slammed his boot into its chest. It stumbled back far enough to give him room to free one of his arrows.

The second one grabbed him from behind, both its arms wrapping around his. Graham dropped his body weight, slipping to the side, his left leg stepping behind the demon as he slammed his elbow into its gut. It tripped over his leg and landed on the ground. But before he could finish the job, a third grabbed him, again from behind. This one swung him around and then with one hand, lifted him up.

It sniffed as it leaned down. "This one has her mark on it. Perhaps we'll play with it for a little bit before we take its head."

Graham pulled his knife from its sheath and rammed it into the creature's gut, dragging the blade up toward its sternum. The demon squeezed Graham's neck for a moment before flinging him away with a roar. Graham hit the ground hard, rolling to lessen the impact, but his shoulder still felt like it was on fire.

He got to his feet, pain in his shoulder causing spots to dance before his eyes. His left arm hung uselessly at his side. He'd dislocated it in the fall. *Oh, that's not good.*

He held on to it as he ran. Each step was painful, but not running was deadly.

The demons gave chase. They were getting closer. Graham knew that this was the end. He wasn't going to make it.

A demon sprinted ahead of the pack, and just before it reached him, Addie soared in, feet first. Her boots crashed into the demon's chest. It flew back twenty feet, rolling a few times before it stopped.

She looked at his arm. "What happened?"

"Big demon."

She smiled. "Want a ride?"

He grinned back. "With you? Anywhere."

CHAPTER 55

ADDIE

The front of the bridge was already up as I raced Graham toward it. I worried that I was injuring his shoulder as we flew, but there was no helping it. I flew over the bridge and landed on the other side. I touched down as gently as I could, but I still saw the grimace on his face.

"What happened?" Donovan asked as he limped over.

"He said big demon."

Pain lined Graham's pale face, and I could tell he was struggling to stay conscious. He gripped my shoulder. "Torr."

"What about him?" I asked.

"Is he here? Is he safe?" Graham asked, his face pale.

I frowned. "What are you talking about?"

"He was on the other side of the bridge," Donovan said. "We lost him in the fighting. One second he was there, and then he was gone."

"Can you see him?" Graham asked.

I looked around but saw no sign of Torr. I knew if he were

here, he'd reveal himself to me. My stomach clenched. "I don't see him. I need to go find him."

Graham grabbed me and looked deep into my eyes. "Be careful." This time it was Graham who pulled me close.

Donovan let out a chuckle when Graham finally released me. "About damn time you two figured that out."

But I didn't stop to answer him. I was already throwing myself into the sky and once again hoping that I wasn't too late.

CHAPTER 56

I wasn't sure where to look for Torr. He wouldn't take on the whole horde directly. That would be crazy. At the same time, I knew that he would undeniably try and protect as many humans as he could. He would most likely hold up somewhere once he realized the humans were safe—if he couldn't make it to the bridge.

The question was, where would that be? Where should I even begin to look? I raced back the way I came, scouring the area for Torr. But I didn't see him.

Or anyone else.

Main Street had gone quiet. What had happened to all the demons? There were scorch marks from where they had burst into flame, but there were no living demons.

They were gone.

A flicker of movement caught my attention. I doused the flames on my wings, pleasantly surprised when they went dark. I flew cautiously, scanning all around me even as I headed toward the movement in the distance.

In only another few short feet, I recognized what it was: the demons. Dozens of them marched toward the beach.

A sick feeling began to develop in my stomach. I prayed I was wrong. I flew well above the reach of any of them, heading in the same direction they were going. None of them glanced up at me or seemed to even realize I was there. The roar of a crowd grew the closer to the beach I got.

And that's when I saw Torr.

He stood on the roof of the old boardwalk arcade. Torches had been lit at each corner of the roof, giving me a clear view. Seven demons stood next to him while dozens of them stood on the ground, looking up and yelling. One demon stood in front of Torr, holding him by the back of the neck, a giant sword in his hand reared back, ready to strike.

CHAPTER 57

Everything went dim except for the sight of that sword heading toward Torr's neck. Pressure quickly built inside me as I desperately scrounged for a way to save him.

A glowing ball of fire appeared in my hand. I didn't question it. I didn't marvel at it. Without hesitation, I flung it toward the demon. It caught him in the back. He flailed forward before bursting into ash.

Torr darted to the side. One of the other demons grabbed him, holding him tight, his sword now at Torr's throat. The demons on either side of him stirred, and then as one, they turned toward me.

Torr lifted his chin to avoid being cut. I ignited my wings. They knew I was here. There was no point in hiding. And maybe the wings would intimidate them a little bit. I flew closer, my mind scrambling to come up with a plan.

Nothing came to me.

Maybe I could create another dozen fireballs, but I didn't know how I'd made the first one. I tried to think of the first fireball, but that pressure that had built inside me was absent. It looked like this time, I was on my own.

Torr watched me with terror in his eyes. But I knew that

terror was for me not him. If he could yell, he'd be screaming at me to save myself.

But I wasn't leaving him behind. I flew closer, staying well above the heads of the other demons. I reached the edge of the roof and floated six feet above it, knowing I could soar straight up out of their reach if I needed to.

The large demon that held Torr laughed as he watched me, an actual smile crossing his face. "So you finally figured it out."

"Figured what out?" I asked.

"What you're capable of." He tilted his head, studying me. "You still don't remember everything, though, do you?"

A finger of dread traced up my spine. I didn't sense any subterfuge in his words. He seemed so confident, so comfortable in my presence.

And so familiar. Unlike all the other demons I had seen, this one wasn't gray or green. No, he was red, a bright, bold red. A color that screamed authority. A flash of memory whipped through my mind. This red demon laughing in a dark cave.

The demon smiled more broadly. "Now you're getting it. You and I go way back."

I stared at him in shock, my mind struggling to deny what he was suggesting, even while somewhere down deep, his words rang true.

I knew him.

For two years, not a single living soul I had met seemed even slightly familiar. And yet something about this evil creature stirred some memory from the deep recesses of my brain.

I didn't know how, and I didn't know when, but somewhere in my life before Blue Forks, I had met him.

"Abbadon." The name escaped my lips before I could pull it back.

He smiled broadly. "You *do* remember."

I ignored the chill of familiarity his voice brought. "I don't remember anything. I don't know how I know your name."

"Well, now, that's a pity. I was so hoping this would be a better reunion than that. Perhaps this will jog your memory." He raised his knife.

Power welled up inside of me. "Do not harm him." My words blasted across the air. Waves of power shot out from me toward all of the demons. A few even stumbled in response.

Abbadon took a step back, his yellow eyes narrowing to slits. With a growl, he slid his knife back into his sheath. "You'll pay for that one. But I suppose this is for the best. I wouldn't want to spoil all the fun. But soon you and I will meet, and only one of us will live." He inclined his head. "Until then."

With a flash of light, he disappeared. In quick succession, each of the remaining demons disappeared as well until it was only Torr and me.

I didn't relax, waiting for the trick. But nothing moved except for the wind and the waves crashing onto the beach.

I landed softly on the roof next to Torr.

"What just happened?" Torr asked.

"I don't know. Are you all right?"

His gaze focused on me, he nodded . "Addie, I think you *made* them go."

I shook my head, though part of me thought his words were true. How had I done it? *Why* had they listened?

It didn't matter. They were gone. That was the important part. "Are you okay to walk?"

Torr nodded with a grimace. "Yeah, a little bruised, but nothing too bad. How about you?"

"Not a scratch."

Torr raised an eyebrow. "You did actually fight some demons, right?"

"Actually, I fought dozens."

"So how come you don't have a scratch?"

I opened my mouth to answer and then shut it. He was right. I should, at the very least, have a scratch on me.

But I had nothing. I had avoided every single strike. I was a good fighter. I knew that, but I couldn't be *that* good. Some hits should've landed. Some of the demons had snuck up behind me. They should have managed to reach me. But I could sense where they were, so none of them could get the drop on me. "I don't know. Maybe it's one of the perks of being the child of an angel. Let's get back to everyone, and then we'll figure it out."

Torr walked to the edge of the roof and lowered himself down with a quick jump. "I'm going to go to the apartment. I think everyone's a little jumpy right now, and having a demon in their midst might not exactly ease their minds."

I wanted to argue, but I knew he was right. "I'll come by after I've checked on everyone. Okay?"

Torr nodded. "And thanks, Addie, for coming for me."

"Always."

CHAPTER 58

After escorting Torr back to the apartment by foot—he refused let me fly him—I made my way to the bridge. The entire time, I went over the confrontation with the demons. How was it possible that I was able to get myself out of that without a single scratch? And the scene at the beach should have ended so much worse than it did. The demons had us overwhelmed. Why didn't they kill us? Or at least Torr? Why had Abbadon listened when I told him to stop?

And why did they all group on the beach with Torr? Why not finish their march toward Sterling Peak? The retracted bridge couldn't be much of a deterrent.

Ahead, the Seraph Force was lined along the bridge, which had already been pulled up. Beyond them were Sheila's security forces. All of them were armed.

I flew over the crystal waters. The Seraph Force murmured their gazes following my flight, but they kept their attention on the road to the bridge. I scanned the line of individuals for Graham. I didn't see him. But I spotted Donovan and Laura. I dropped lightly down to the ground next to them.

Donovan crossed his arms over his chest. "You look way too relaxed for someone being chased by dozens of demons."

"That's because I'm not. They're gone."

"Gone? Gone how? Did you kill all of them?" Laura asked.

"If only. No, they just left. One minute they were there, and then poof, they were gone."

"Not that I'm complaining, but why did they leave?" Donovan asked.

I kept my tone light, my expression hopefully confused. "I don't know. They just did."

Torr and I had decided that until we understood exactly what had happened, we were not going to share the details with just anyone. And right now, there were way too many ears around to share with Donovan and Laura what had happened. But I would tell Graham and Marcus later, and then hopefully together we could figure out what was going on.

"Where's Graham?" I asked.

Donovan nodded his chin toward the hill. "We insisted that Graham have the doctor set that shoulder. Graham, of course, fought us, but he eventually conceded, knowing he's useless in a fight until his shoulder is popped back into place."

I hovered a few inches off the ground, anxious to see him. "What about the citizens of Blue Forks? Are they all right?"

"They're staying in the hotel ballroom for now," Donovan replied. "People have been bringing over supplies, and the doctors are working there. Cots have been set up for people to sleep. We had more than a few injuries, none of them life-threatening."

"We'll get a head count and see who's okay to head home and take care of the ones that can't," Laura said.

"What about the Council?" I asked.

"They're making noises about the 'riff raff' being over here. But Graham ordered that no one is allowed back in Blue Forks until it's been swept. That will have to wait until morning. No sense endangering anyone now," Donovan said.

I pictured the destruction done to some of the buildings. "And if people's homes are unlivable?"

"Then we'll set something up here until we can help them rebuild," Laura said.

I smiled. That was good. Hopefully this was a new day, opening up better lines of communication between the citizens of Blue Forks and those of Sterling Peak.

I flew upward, scanning the ground below me as I did. More than a few people pointed and waved, although a few looked fearful at the sight of me. I suppose I couldn't blame them. Flying humans was not a normal sight. A woman flying with flaming wings was definitely not a normal sight. I touched down lightly inside the gate of Graham's estate. I extinguished my wings and retracted them.

The front door burst open. Noel and Micah raced out.

I smiled, opening my arms. They tackled me, nearly knocking me over. I held on to them tight, and they hugged me back just as hard.

Noel pulled back first while Micah stayed clutched to my side. She scanned me from head to toe. "You're not injured?"

"No, not at all."

"Where's Torr?" Micah asked.

"He's back at the apartment. He thought he might stay there tonight. Are you two okay?"

She scoffed. "Us? We've just been sitting here. Our greatest danger was being overfed by Mary."

Micah looked up, his face serious. "Is it over?"

I struggled with how to answer that question. Because I had a feeling whatever was going on had just started, so I decided to sidestep his question a little bit. "The demons have gone. Where's Graham?"

"He's in the kitchen with Mary, Franklin, and the doctor. They're arguing. He's been trying to get back to the bridge."

I smiled, picturing the scene. "Well, let's go tell him he doesn't have to hurry."

Halfway down the path, a loud boom sounded from overhead. All three of us jerked our heads up.

A large ball of light descended quickly toward the back of Graham's house. It was so bright it made the night appear as day.

I watched it, my dread growing. "You two get down to the bridge now."

"Addie—" Micah began.

"No arguments. Find Donovan and stay with him." I pushed the two of them toward the gate. Noel's gaze met mine, expressing a million different emotions. I nodded, a lump forming in in my throat. She grabbed Micah's hand and tugged him through the gate.

I turned, my whole body tensing. The ball began to dim and landed lightly at the back of the house. There was no explosion. There were no shouts of pain.

Carefully, I made my way around the side of the house.

I reached the side porch and did a quick jump over the wall. I wended my way across the large patio's tables, chairs, and sitting area. I moved against the wall of the house, keeping myself hidden from anyone in the backyard. I reached the edge of the house and paused.

Then I peeked around.

Standing on the balcony, wrapped in what could only be considered a holy glow, was the archangel Michael.

CHAPTER 59

Everything about the man, or Archangel, screamed power. And yet there wasn't an aggression to his power. He looked just like the paintings. Tall and muscular with dark hair and a dark complexion, he was handsome. And why wouldn't he be? He wore some sort of gray tunic over white leggings. Two swords were strapped to his back. I stared in absolute awe at the sight.

Graham stood in front of him. Michael reached out, placing a hand on Graham's injured shoulder. Light flared for a moment, so bright I had to look away. When I looked back, Graham had removed the sling on his arm and was flexing his arm and rolling his shoulder.

My mouth dropped open. He'd healed him. In only a few seconds, Michael had healed him. My awe only grew. I took a step forward. More than anything, I wanted to join the two of them.

A hand landed on my shoulder and yanked me back. "Addie, it's not safe."

I stumbled back, unprepared for the pull, and turned, ready to strike.

Marcus held me firmly in his grip.

"Marcus, what are you doing?"

"Addie, you need to come with me. He can't see you."

I stared at Marcus. His whole body was shaking, his face pale. What was wrong with him? Concerned, I let him pull me away from the edge of the balcony. He stopped just before the door and wiped his forehead with a shaky hand.

"Okay, what's going on?" I asked.

Marcus let out a breath, his gaze darting around before settling back on me. "You cannot go out there. The archangel cannot see you. We're lucky that he hasn't been able to sense you."

"What are you talking about? He might be my father or at least know who my father is."

Marcus shook his head even more frantically. "No, no. You don't understand. I finally figured out the full translation."

"The one about the fight between the child of flame and the child of darkness?"

Marcus nodded. "Yes." He pulled the cloak he was wearing off and threw it around my shoulders. He pulled the hood over my hair.

I stared back at him in shock. "What are you doing?"

"You need to run, Addie. You need to get as far away from here as you can."

Now I was really worried about him. "Marcus, are you okay? Maybe I should call the doctor."

His eyes grew even more wild. "No, no. I'm fine, but you won't be if you stay here. You need to go, and quickly. Don't let anyone know where you're going. And don't let anyone see you go."

"Marcus, I'm not going anywhere."

I tried to step around him, but he gripped my forearms with surprising strength. "Addie, you are not the child of flame."

I paused for only a moment before shaking my head. "Of course I am. I can fly. I have wings. They literally flame up."

Marcus ran a hand over his mouth, glancing toward the back

of the house. He pulled me another step away. "No, no, that was my fault. The lines were mistranslated. It was the accepted translation, so I didn't look at the original too closely. When I did, I realized the original translators had made a mistake. They said it was the child of flame versus the child of darkness. But that's not what it said. That's not it at all."

I backed away from him, not sure why his words were scaring me. "This is crazy. You need to get some sleep. Let's get you inside. Graham will—"

Marcus's voice shook, filled with dread. "Graham won't be able to help you. And he won't be Graham for much longer." He took a deep breath and then took my hand, gently this time, pulling me toward the edge of the balcony. "Watch, but don't let them see you."

Graham now stood face-to-face with the archangel.

A ball of fear took root in my chest. Something was off. Something about the posture of the archangel made me hold my tongue. His face was incredibly serious as he stared down at Graham. Graham stood perfectly still as well. And I mean perfectly still. He didn't shift his weight. He didn't twitch or even move a finger. It was as if he was paralyzed standing upright.

"What's going on?"

Marcus squeezed my hand. "Just watch. You need to see to understand."

The angel placed his hand on top of Graham's head. Once again, it began to glow. Waves of light shot down and around Graham's body, completely encapsulating him. The glow surrounded him for what felt like forever, but it was probably only about a minute. The glow took the shape of an oval, reminding me of a cocoon.

With Graham being the caterpillar about to be transformed.

As the glow began to dissipate, Michael stepped back. He nodded, his lips moving, but we were too far away to hear. Once the glow was gone, Michael's lips stopped moving. A smile, one that was not kind, crossed his face.

Graham turned, scanning the area, his entire body stiff. His eyes were somehow Graham's and not Graham's. His head turned in our direction. Marcus pulled me back.

I was shaking. Graham's face had been cold, devoid of the expressions that made him who he was. "What just happened?"

"Humans are given free will, but angels are not. Graham's free will was just removed. He will now act on the archangel's orders."

My jaw gaped at Marcus's words. But I couldn't deny that the Graham I just saw was missing the spark that made him Graham. "Why would the angel do that?"

"Because it is time for the prophecy to be fulfilled. Graham is the child of light."

"The child of light? You mean the angel the child of flame? That's me."

"No," Marcus said softly, "that's what I've been trying to tell you. The text was mistranslated. It doesn't say the child of flame versus the child of darkness. It's the child of light versus the child of fire." Marcus swallowed noticeably, as if the next words were horrible to taste. "The text goes on to explain that the child of fire will be identified by their burning wings."

My whole world seemed to stop and crash in on me in one blink.

"That means …"

Marcus nodded slowly, his voice filled with pain. "Graham is the child of light. You are the child of fire. You two are destined to fight to the death for the fate of humanity."

I stared at him, hearing his words but feeling as if he must be talking about someone else.

"So I'm not the child of Michael."

Marcus shook his head, not meeting my gaze. "No."

I stared at him, but he refused to look at me. "You know whose child I am."

Tears swam in Marcus's eyes as he finally looked up. "Yes."

And in that moment, I knew the truth. But I needed to hear Marcus say it. When I spoke, my voice was barely louder than a breath. "Who Marcus? Whose child am I?"

"You are the daughter of Lucifer."

CHAPTER 60

L ucifer? I was the child of Lucifer? The devil himself? "That can't be right."

Marcus looked as if he wanted to be anywhere but standing in front of me telling me this. "I'm sorry Addie. I know you don't want to hear this. I didn't want it to be true either. It was when I saw you flying, and the flames on your wings, it clicked something on in my mind. I scoured the books and re-translated the original, myself this time. You are the daughter of Lucifer. There is no doubt about it. And I'm afraid there's more."

"More? As in worse?"

"Yes. You are destined to fight the child of light. And the whole world will be changed because of it."

My gaze flew to the backyard, my mouth dropping open. I couldn't see Graham from here, but I could picture him. I could feel his touch. I could see those incredible eyes that seemed to look right into my very soul. "Graham. You think I'm destined to fight Graham."

"I don't think. I know it. The prophesy will come true. You are proof of that."

I stared at Marcus wanting to see some glimmer of doubt in his face. Some hint that he didn't believe the words he was saying. But there was nothing but deep resignation. "I won't fight him."

"You won't fight him because you can choose. Graham cannot. He will have no choice but to fight you. And he *will* kill you."

"No, Graham wouldn't."

"You're right. If he could choose, he would never make that choice. I've seen how he comes alive around you. But that choice is gone from him now. He is the agent of the angels. And he will come for you. And when he does, he *will* kill you."

"I can't … I just …" My mind spiraled out, along with all of my hopes for my future. It was all too much. I couldn't seem to form a thought.

Marcus grabbed me by the shoulders, staring into my eyes. "You need to run, Addie. Run far. And don't look back."

"But Noel, Micah …"

"I will look after them. If they go with you, they will be killed. Anyone who gets in the angel's way will be killed. Anyone who tries to defend you will die."

"But, but he's Michael."

"Angels are not what we've imagined them to be. They are ruthless warriors. We overlook that because in our history they have been on our side. For them, there is nothing but the mission. Now that is true for Graham as well. And his mission is to kill you. And he will go through anyone to accomplish that task."

It felt like the oxygen had been sucked from my lungs. This couldn't be happening. It wasn't possible.

"Addie, look at me."

I focused on Marcus's dark eyes.

"I will take care of Noel and Micah. I will make sure they are safe. But you need to run. If you are going to live, if *they* are going to live, you need to run, Addie, *run*." He pushed me forward.

I stumbled, nearly losing my balance. I pictured Graham's face, or the face of the man who used to be Graham. I moved back to the edge of the patio. I needed to see him again. I needed to know. Staying flat against the side, I peeked carefully around.

Graham and the archangel strode for the house. Franklin moved toward Graham but Graham brushed past him, barking something at him, I couldn't make out what from this distance. But I could see the look of shock on Franklin's face, his hand which had been held out, falling limply to his side.

I leaned back, my breath catching. Graham would never treat Franklin like that. Something had happened to Graham. The archangel had done something, had changed him. I moved away from the edge of the patio back toward Marcus.

"I can't fight him. I won't."

"What will you do then? Will you let your friends and those that care about you die trying to protect you from Graham? He has the power of heaven on his side. He will destroy everything in his path trying to get to you. You may not be able to bring yourself to kill him but I assure you, he will have no such reservations when it comes to killing you. He *will* kill you."

There was a finality in Marcus's tone. He truly believed Graham would kill me and anyone who stood in his way.

And now I had people who would stand in his way. Tess and Laura wouldn't let that happen, neither would Sheila. Marcus would throw himself in the way, trying to stop Graham. And Donovan, Noel, Torr, and Micah: they would all try to reason with him, try to stop him.

But I'd seen that look on Graham's face. He was no longer in control. In my gut, I knew Marcus was right. I'd heard the tales of the power of the archangels, of their ruthlessness. And if Graham was like them now, then he would kill those I cared about to get to me.

Which meant I had no choice. I leaned up and kissed Marcus on the cheek. "Take care of them for me."

He nodded back at me, tears in his eyes. "I will. Now go Addie, quickly before he sees you."

My heart breaking, I did.

I ran.

Continue Reading for a Peek at the second book in *The Demon Cursed* Series

CHAPTER 1

ADDIE

"Look!"

I didn't know who had called out. But all eyes around me turned up. The same bright light that had appeared just minutes ago was now disappearing into the sky. Did that mean the threat was over?

The residents of Sterling Peak didn't seem to think so. More and more of them streamed out of their homes. Those racing up the hill tended to be younger, stronger. Most of them were Rangers of the Seraph Force, the security force that protected the people of Sterling Peak from demon attacks. They had only recently extended that protection to the people across the bridge in Blue Forks.

I knew they had no idea what they were racing toward. From down the hill, all they would have been able to see was a rapidly descending ball of light. They had no way of knowing that it was the arrival, and now the departure, of the archangel Michael.

But I knew.

I kept the hood of my cloak up, my long dark hair tucked

underneath. I dropped my chin whenever I spied a Ranger, praying none of them recognized me.

I slipped behind a group of six people, all staff from one of the higher houses.

"What do you think that was?" a woman with bright-red hair cut short asked.

A man with gray hair glanced over his shoulder, his brown eyes worried. "It has to be some sort of new demon attack."

It was not a surprising guess. The archangel's appearance right on the heels of a ferocious demon attack was not something anyone would guess. After all, no one had seen an angel in over a hundred years.

When I had first seen the ball of light, I'd been terrified. But fear had turned into awe as the archangel Michael stepped from the glowing light.

But that fear shifted once again to terror as the archangel Michael reached out for Graham and removed his free will, making him the archangel's tool.

The group in front of me slipped down a separate road, heading toward the theater. I continued on toward Celestial Bridge, even though everything in me rebelled and wanted to head back up the hill, back to Graham.

For the first time in the two years since I'd woken up on that beach, I had felt safe, which was crazy because I had just fought off a demon attack.

But it wasn't the physical harm that had ever been a problem. I had been fighting demons every night since. The difference was now, I felt like the kids and I weren't alone. We had people in our lives looking out for us, who cared about us. And walking away from that was just so incredibly hard. But to keep them safe, I needed to keep them away from me. I needed to go.

Because if Marcus was right, Graham would be looking for me.

To kill me.

I still struggled with that idea. I'd thought Marcus was crazy when he'd first relayed it. But there had been something about Graham, a coldness in him after the archangel had encapsulated him in light.

A man bumped into me. "Sorry, sorry," he panted.

I didn't even have time to respond before he slipped through the crowd. Everyone was terrified. And so was I.

Not just because of the prophecy that Marcus had told me about. But because Marcus had finally figured out who my father was. And that revelation drove terror straight through my heart.

Because I was the daughter of an archangel, all right, but that archangel was Lucifer.

My skin crawled at the idea. Since I'd woken up on the beach two years earlier, I'd been trying to figure out who I was. I had no memory of my time before the beach.

But in my wildest dreams or nightmares, I never imagined this. Just a few hours ago, I thought my life was on a trajectory that would bring me everything I had ever wanted: a safe home for myself, Noel, and Micah; new friends like Donovan, Tess, Marcus, and Laura; and a new job, if I wanted it, with the Seraph Force that would actually provide me with a livable wage.

And I had Graham.

For the first time in my life, I felt powerful. I'd just discovered that I actually had wings that I could call upon at will. And the wings became enflamed when I needed them to. It was the best discovery of my life.

When the demon horde had reached Blue Forks, I'd been able to fight them off. And I had been exhilarated about it. I knew that was what I was born to do. I'd protected the people of Blue Forks and the people of Sterling Peak. I'd returned to Graham's home content, despite the horror of what I'd been through. I knew my purpose in life: to protect people.

And I knew that I wanted Graham to be part of that future.

In one fell swoop, Marcus's revelations had ripped all of that away. According to the prophecy, I was destined to fight Graham. With Graham's free will removed, he would fight me to the death. But I can't say the same. I know I would never be able to look into his eyes and watch the life drain from them. There was no way I would be able to kill him.

So instead I ran. Now, I just needed to figure out where I was running to.

CHAPTER 2

NOEL

Fourteen-year-old Noel Rikbiel hurried down the hill toward the bridge. Next to her, Micah Rikbiel cast a glance over his shoulder.

"Don't look," Noel said.

Micah turned his gaze back to her.

She forced a smile to her face. "Addie will be okay."

"What do you think that was?" he asked.

Noel shook her head, clasping his hand more securely. She had no answer beyond the obvious: trouble.

She'd seen the light in the sky. At first she'd thought it was a meteor. But then it had slowed. She'd wanted to argue with Addie when she told them to find Lieutenant Commander Donovan Gabriel, second-in-command of the Seraph Force, but something deep and primal inside of her told her to get Micah away from that light.

It was an old reflex, one Noel had felt deep inside her ever since they'd first met in that horrible orphanage six years ago. He'd been so small, smaller than the other kids his age. She, at least, had been hardened, even at that young an age. But Micah, at age six, could still be shocked by the cruelty in the world. And therefore he was completely unprepared for it.

Protecting him had been her job ever since. Then two years ago, Addie had shown up, and she looked out for both of them. Rarely did Addie need looking after. But Noel worried that right now she might be up against something stronger than even her.

Noel had grabbed Micah's hand to run, expecting a massive explosion. But there'd been nothing. She didn't know what that meant. She didn't know if she should allow herself the luxury of thinking everything was all right.

Micah's dark-brown eyes looked up at her with complete trust. "We should be with Addie."

Noel shook her head. Everything in her told her to run a little faster. "No. Whatever she's handling, we'd just be in the way."

"We're not in the way."

Noel winced, realizing how harsh her words had come out. "Not like that. Addie will always be on our side. But if she has to fight or help people, you know she would be looking out for us first instead of herself. And then she could end up getting hurt. Let's just find Donovan, okay?"

"There he is." Micah pointed toward the bridge.

The Celestial Bridge connected Sterling Peak to Blue Forks. Built at the end of the Angel War, it had been created from stone and steel. Standing on its highest point, looking out over Blue Forks, were statues of the archangels Michael and Gabriel, as if keeping an eye on them. But the bridge's most prominent feature belied that suggestion: the bridge could be retracted to protect the residents of Sterling Peak from a demon attack. The fact that such an action left the residents of Blue Forks at the mercy of the demons hadn't been much of a consideration to the residents of Sterling Peak.

At least until recently, until Graham had started to change things.

Noel still didn't know what to think of Graham. She liked him, and he seemed to be trying to do the right thing, but Noel's trust was hard won, and she wasn't ready to give it, not quite yet.

But she was still worried about him. She hoped both he and Addie would be okay. Because Graham was a lot like Addie: he would put other people's safety well before his own.

Although the bridge was crowded with anxious people, it was easy to pick out Donovan. He stood head and shoulders above all the other people there. His dark hair had come loose from his ponytail, and his face looked unusually serious. Noel had never really seen Donovan look serious. She knew he was the lieutenant commander of the Seraph Force, but whenever she or Micah saw him, he was smiling and telling them some ridiculous story. But right now, there was nothing ridiculous about his mood.

And that made Noel feel better.

He walked with Sheila Castiel, the head of bridge security. Noel frowned when she noticed the limp.

"He's hurt." Micah pulled his hand from hers and darted ahead, slipping more easily through the crowds due to his smaller size.

"Micah!" Noel picked up her pace, trying to keep up with him. He'd just reached the edge of the bridge when she caught him.

"Donovan," Micah called.

Donovan turned around. Looks of surprise splashed across both his and Sheila's faces. "What are you two doing here?" Donovan asked as he waved them forward. The guards at the gates stepped back, allowing them entrance.

Donovan looked back toward the hill. "Were you at Graham's house?"

Noel nodded. Donovan pulled Noel and Micah a short distance away from the crowd, lowering his voice. "Does Addie know where you are? She was heading to Graham's house."

"We saw her. She told us to run as soon as she saw that light," Noel said.

"What is it?" Micah asked.

Donovan narrowed his eyes, his gaze going to the top of the hill. "I don't know. Tess and a bunch of the others went to go check it out."

"How come you didn't go with them?" Micah asked.

Donovan blew out a breath, running a hand through his hair. "Two reasons. One, right now I am in charge while Graham's healing, and two, this stupid ankle makes me slow. I sent half of the Seraph Force up to see what was going on. But I need to keep the other half down here to keep on guard for the demons."

"But Addie said they were gone," Noel said.

"And I hope she's right. But we need to keep watch, just in case."

Noel looked back toward the hill, not happy at how quiet it was. "Addie told us to come stay with you. She didn't want us to be anywhere near that light."

Donovan stared off in the distance again. Then he met Noel's gaze. And for a split second, she saw his concern. Then he seemed to shake himself from his musing. He looked at Micah and grinned. "We can always use an extra pair of eyes on the bridge."

He glanced at Noel. "Or two."

Noel felt her cheeks flush. Donovan always had that effect on her. She knew her crush was crazy. He was way out of her league. Her body, though, didn't seem to want to listen to that.

"Come on. I'll put you two to work."

CHAPTER 3

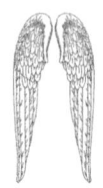

ADDIE

Up ahead, I could see the bridge. The crowd parted as a group of Seraph Force soldiers appeared. I ducked my head as they sprinted past me. But I caught sight of Major Tess Uriel, one of the Seven, at the head of the group. I clamped my mouth shut to keep myself from calling out to her. She was a friend. She would help if I asked her to.

But I couldn't put her in the middle of this. If Marcus was right, Graham would kill anyone who got in between us.

Once the group had passed, I continued onward, careful to keep my eyes searching the crowd for anyone I knew. I couldn't be recognized. Luckily, the darkness helped with that. Although every light in Sterling Peak seemed to be on. Ahead, I saw a familiar snatch of dark hair in the bright lights of the bridge. Donovan stood speaking with someone. The crowd shifted, and I saw Noel. My heart lurched.

I searched the crowd and saw Micah just a few feet away. My steps slowed at the sight of the two of them. How could I leave them? They were my family. Maybe I didn't have to. Maybe I could bring them with me. Maybe—

The screech of a horn cut off my thoughts. A man next to me pulled me out of the road as a car sped by. I stumbled over my feet, nearly face-planting onto the sidewalk.

"Watch out." The man held on to me, making sure I was secure before he released me.

I nodded my thanks, keeping my face turned away. "Thanks."

"Be careful out there," he said by way of farewell.

I barely heard him, my gaze focused on the car that sped down the road. Cars were rarely used in Sterling Peak. They were rarely used at all in this new world.

But I knew that car. It was Graham's.

The car slammed to a stop at the edge of the bridge's barriers. Graham stepped out, casting a look around. I hunched my shoulders and moved with the slower pace of an older person, careful to keep my head down, while watching him from the corner of my eyes. His gaze slipped right over me. Then he abruptly turned and marched toward Donovan.

I made my way closer to the bridge, keeping an eye on the two of them. Donovan's face shifted from a look of concern to one of confusion as they talked. Donovan crossed his arms over his chest, shaking his head as he glared at Graham.

Graham went to step around Donovan, but Donovan held out his arm, keeping him back. Graham pushed Donovan's arm away and slammed his fist into the side of Donovan's face.

My jaw dropped.

Donovan's face reflected my own shock. I couldn't believe what I was witnessing. Donovan was the closest person on this planet to Graham. An hour ago, the idea of him hitting Donovan was completely unbelievable, especially for something so small.

Yet a lot had changed in a very short time.

That action brought home the truth. Graham was no longer Graham. Marcus was right.

Which meant I needed to get as far away from here as possible before anyone else got hurt.

CHAPTER 4

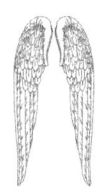

NOEL

Noel's nerves were stretched tight. She kept looking back toward the top of the hill. The glow that had been there had long since disappeared. But she couldn't stop the feeling that something horrible had just happened.

Yet no noise came from up the hill. There were no screams, no cries. Everything was silent.

More and more residents of Sterling Peak streamed down the hill toward the bridge. Obviously they had seen the light and wanted to get as far from it as possible. The problem was that the only place to go *was* the bridge. Yet no one wanted to cross it because they hadn't checked Blue Forks yet to make sure that the demons were completely gone. They were waiting until morning. Which meant that the area around the bridge was completely packed with people.

"Tell Mrs. Uriel that I am not going to clear a section for the Angel Blessed," Donovan growled. "She wants her own space, tell her to go back to her damn house."

Major Laura Raguel stood next to him, an eyebrow raised. "I'm guessing you want me to put that in my own words."

"Your words, my words, I don't give a damn." He took a breath, running a hand through his hair before he closed his eyes and pinched the bridge of his nose. "Okay, on second thought, use your words."

Laura smiled and then slapped him on the back. "Don't worry. Graham will be down here soon, and all of this misery will be just a memory."

"God, I hope so," Donovan mumbled. Then he caught Noel watching him. He gave her a shrug. "I'm not great at being political. Graham is much better at it than me."

Noel grinned. "Yeah, I kind of noticed. You're more of a hammer."

Donovan's face lit up. "That's the nicest thing anybody's ever said to me."

Noel laughed out loud despite her nerves.

Her laugh elicited a wider smile from Donovan. Then his smile dimmed. He glanced back up the hill. It had been fifteen minutes since the light appeared and then disappeared again. A group of Seraph Force had gone up to see what was going on, but none of them had returned yet.

"No word?" Noel asked.

Donovan shook his head. "You know what they say, no news is good news."

Noel nodded, but she actually did it more to make Donovan feel better than because she believed him. Besides, she had the distinct impression he didn't believe his words either.

Movement from the corner of her eye caught her attention. She turned her head, looking through the crowd. A face turned away, their head covered in a cloak. Noel watched them go with a frown. Strange.

"Finally," Donovan growled.

He started toward the main entrance of the bridge.

Noel glanced over at where Micah was standing with Sheila's sister, Marjorie. He'd be good for a few minutes. She hurried after Donovan.

As soon as she broke free of some of the crowd, she realized what had caught Donovan's eyes. Graham strode out from a car, twelve Seraph Force Rangers spread out behind him.

Noel smiled, relief filling her at the sight of him. Graham was in one piece. That was a good—

But Noel's steps faltered as she took in his face. Something was different. He looked so serious. And where was Addie?

She picked up her pace again, but not right next to Donovan, not sure if she would be ushered away, being this was probably Seraph Force business. But she knew how to be around and not be noticed. She slipped in next to one of Rangers so that she couldn't be seen by Graham or Donovan.

Graham marched up to Donovan and then stopped. "Have you seen Addison?"

Addison? No one called her Addison.

Donovan frowned. "No. I thought she was up at your house."

"I need everyone here searched. I need Addison found and brought to me." Graham's tone was harsh. Noel peeked around the Seraph Force in front of her to get a look at Graham's face. His eyes were narrowed, his jaw set. He looked angry. What the heck was going on?

Donovan's eyes narrowed as well as he looked at the Seraph Force surrounding them and then back at Graham. "Can I talk to you privately for a moment?"

Graham shook his head and started to walk past him. "No. Find Addison."

Donovan put out his arm, blocking his way. "What's going on, Graham? Why are you looking for—"

Graham's fist came up and slammed into the side of Donovan's face. Donovan turned his head at the last moment, escaping the full force of the hit. "What the hell, man?"

"You've been given an order. Find Addison Baker. You're the second-in-command. That means you *follow* my orders. If you can't do that, then you will be removed from your position."

Noel's mouth fell open as she stared at the two of them. What had gotten into Graham? Hitting Donovan? Threatening his removal?

Something was seriously wrong.

CHAPTER 5

ADDIE

My heart pounded. Everything in me told me to go back, to get Noel and Micah. But would I be able to protect them from Graham? If he came for me, would they just get caught in between?

He had hit Donovan.

Donovan.

Marcus was right. No one would be off-limits when Graham came for me. Which meant Noel and Micah needed to be as far from me as humanly possible.

I turned, my whole body shaking as I moved along the edge of the bridge's foundation. No one paid any attention to me as I slipped along the path that edged along the river.

The water churned and rolled below me. I had always loved looking at the water, but right now, it seemed angry. The whole world seemed angry.

I forced my gaze away from it. I kept my shoulders hunched as I moved quickly away from the bridge and prying eyes. The lights along the path ended about a hundred yards from the bridge. I continued in the dark another two hundred yards, not wanting to take any chances. The river curved. I could only make out the top of the bridge, so I was sure no one would be able to see me.

I perched on the edge of the cliff, staring down. Was I really going to do this? Was I really going to leave everything I knew behind?

The cold look in Graham's eyes drifted through my mind. I straightened my shoulders, dropping the cloak. Whatever the archangel had done to him had removed the Graham I knew. And I needed to leave to keep those I cared about safe.

My wings burst out from my back without my flames. Taking a deep breath, I plunged off the cliff, skimming near the water as I made my way to the other side, praying that one day I would be able to make my way back.

CHAPTER 6

NOEL

Noel slipped away from the Seraph Force. She didn't know what exactly was going on, but the idea that Graham was looking for "Addison" did not sit well with her.

And if he was looking for Addie, it wouldn't be too long until he started to look for her and Micah.

Noel scanned the crowd. She moved to the spot where she had last seen Micah, but he was no longer there. She turned around, frantically looking for him. Then she heard Marjorie's laugh. She turned to the right and saw that the group had moved a little farther down the bank. They'd been partially hidden by some trees. She hurried down the path toward them. The group knelt down at the edge of the cliff, chucking rocks into the water.

Micah bent down to grab another rock, but Noel grabbed his arm and hauled him up. "Micah. Come on."

He frowned as he straightened. "What's going on?"

"We need to go."

He opened his mouth to reply, but then took in her face. He immediately dropped his rock. "Okay."

They dashed up the path, but when they reached the top, Noel put out her hand to slow him. They couldn't draw attention to themselves.

"What's going on?" Micah whispered.

"We need to get to the other side of the bridge. Something's going on with Addie. I don't know what. But I don't think it's good."

Micah looked up at her. "Donovan—"

"Can't help us. It's Graham who's looking for Addie. And something's wrong with him. We need to go now."

Micah opened his mouth to ask more questions but then shut it again, looking around uneasily as well.

Noel scanned the area, looking to see where Donavan and Graham were. She couldn't see either of them.

But there was a line of Seraph Force guarding the bridge. They were going to have to somehow figure out a way to slip by them. "Look, we need to find a way past the guards. Damn, I wish Torr were here."

"So do I." Graham stepped from behind the crowd and in front of them. Noel's mouth dropped open and she turned to run but two Rangers appeared from behind them. They grabbed their arms.

Graham smiled, a smile that held no warmth. "I need to ask you two some questions."

Buy Demon Revealed on Amazon!

ALSO BY SADIE HOBBES

The Demon Cursed Series

Demon Cursed

Demon Revealed

Demon Heir

The Four Kingdoms Series

Order of the Goddess

ABOUT THE AUTHOR

Sadie Hobbes is a dog lover, martial artist, avid runner, mother, wife, and Amazon best selling thriller writer under the name RD Brady. She can often be found before dawn wandering her yard with her dogs, dictating her latest novel. If anyone were to see her, they would seriously question her sanity as well as her fashion choices. (Think rain boots over pajamas plus a bulky cardigan). But it works for her!

If you'd like to hear about her upcoming releases, sign up for her newsletter through her facebook page.

She can be reached at sadiehobbesauthor@gmail.com or on her Facebook page.

Copyright © 2020 by Sadie Hobbes

Demon Cursed

Published by Scottish Seoul Publishing, LLC, Dewitt, NY

All Rights Reserved. No part of this book may be reproduced or transmitted in any form or by any means, electronic or mechanical, including photocopying, recording, or by any information storage and retrieval system without the written permission of the author, except where permitted by law.

Printed in the United States of America.

Printed in Great Britain
by Amazon